SKIES OF GOLD

By Zoë Archer

Skies of Gold
Skies of Steel
Skies of Fire

By Nico Rosso
Nights of Steel
Night of Fire

SKIES OF GOLD

The Ether Chronicles

ZOË ARCHER

AVONIMPULSE
An Imprint of HarperCollinsPublishers

SKIES OF GOLD. Copyright © 2013 by Zoë Archer. All rights reserved under International and Pan-American Copyright Conventions. By payment of the required fees, you have been granted the nonexclusive, nontransferable right to access and read the text of this e-book on screen. No part of this text may be reproduced, transmitted, decompiled, reverse-engineered, or stored in or introduced into any information storage and retrieval system, in any form or by any means, whether electronic or mechanical, now known or hereinafter invented, without the express written permission of HarperCollins e-books.

EPub Edition AUGUST 2013 ISBN: 9780062109163

Print Edition ISBN: 9780062241443

JV 10 9 8 7 6 5 4 3 2 1

To Zack, for all the battles we fight together

ACKNOWLEDGMENTS

Special thanks to Suleikha Snyder for her language assistance, and Glossaria for her help with ship terminology. Any inaccuracies in this book are entirely my own, and shouldn't reflect on these awesome women.

And thank you so much to Amanda Bergeron, for believing in the world of the Ether Chronicles.

CHAPTER ONE

The Outer Hebrides.

A dark serrated shape pushed up from the gray horizon. Were she a more fanciful sort of person, Kalindi MacNeil might have imagined the shape to be an ancient beast, the sort that legend told lurked in the cold waters off the western coast of Scotland, eager to drag ships down into the sunless sea. Standing in the prow of the small steam ferry, she shivered, drawing her cloak more tightly around her.

Don't be a grease brain. It's only an isolated island. Exactly where you want to be.

The boat chugged closer, spewing peat smoke into the air. Tetrol fuel didn't make its way into isolated places like the Outer Hebrides, and coal was just as rare. She might be able to tinker with the ferry's engines, design a way for it to process its fuel more efficiently and without churning black smoke into the atmosphere. Before she'd left Liverpool, she'd been in the process of analyzing new engine designs for sea-faring vessels so they could compete with airships in terms of speed and productivity. Airships were strictly in service to the military at the present, but some day in the future, they'd certainly be used for commercial purposes, and Kali had been planning for that time ahead.

But then the world had turned to flame, and all thoughts of tomorrow burned with it.

She pushed the thoughts from her mind. All that mattered for the foreseeable future was the island ahead of her.

The ferry passed a few miniscule outcroppings of rock jutting out of the sea. Some were furred with long grasses, and one even had a tree of some sort growing out of it in a display of brave defiance. But aside from half a dozen seabirds perched on the tiny islets, she'd have no neighbors. None within a dozen miles over choppy waters, anyway. And she didn't have a boat of her own.

"Certain of this, lass?" The ferry's captain—and sole crewman—called from the wheel. She didn't want to stand beside him. Captain Campbell smelled of peat smoke and brine and a woolen jumper seldom cleaned. "Ain't nobody lived on Eilean Comhachag in near fifty years."

"Thirty," Kali corrected him. "The last member of my family left the island almost three decades ago. Sought their fortune in Skye and never went back."

"Can't say as I blame them. Nothing out here but wind and solitude."

Kali smiled. "Perfect."

She glanced over her shoulder to see Campbell eyeing her warily. Was it because of her odd answer, or was it because he'd likely never seen a woman of half white, half Indian blood before? It didn't matter. All she cared about was reaching Eilean Comhachag and being blessedly alone.

The captain fell silent as he steered the boat closer to the island. As they neared, details emerged. A rocky beach faced an eastern bay, one of the only places a vessel could approach safely. The beach sloped up, disappearing into thick gorse. Sharp hills jutted in a line from north to south, forming the island's spine. Rowan trees gathered in clusters along the base of the hills. As they had approached, she had noticed the high, jagged cliffs plunging into the sea on the island's western shore. Eilean Comhachag was longer than it was wide, somewhat kidney-shaped. But most of it remained a mystery, including its size.

Sailing closer, she studied the vague map her father had drawn for her. The map itself was over fifteen years old, and shaped by her father's hazy memories. Alan MacNeil had only been to Eilean Comhachag once, as a very small boy.

"Dismal place," he'd said to her when she'd asked him about it. "Only rocks and bogs and trees that moaned with the wind. Cold as the Devil's arse." Then he'd grinned beneath his gingery beard. "Not like our comfortable home here in Nagpur."

Her father had been one of the few British soldiers who'd loved the heat of India. Kali missed its warmth, too, but she wouldn't go back. Not to Nagpur, not to her mother and father. How could she . . . now? If she returned to Nagpur, it would be too easy to become simply her parents' daughter. But she needed to know who she was now, and she couldn't do that if held too close in the sheltering embrace of home.

The faded map she held revealed few clues about her future home, so she stuffed it into the pocket of her cloak. She'd just have to explore it, once she'd gotten set up. Hopefully, the terrain wasn't too rocky. That'd prove a challenge.

Campbell guided the boat into the bay, slowing and then stopping the engine before the vessel's hull hit the beach. As expected, the only occupants of the shore were a small number of wading birds, who took to the sky as soon as the boat stopped.

"Where are the owls?" Kali asked. "It wouldn't make sense to name this place Owl Island otherwise."

Dropping anchor, the captain said, "Night creatures, they are. I expect you'll hear 'em after the sun goes down." He glanced back and forth between the pile of Kali's belongings lashed to the deck and the beach. Some twenty feet of shallow water separated them. "I don't have a dinghy, lass, and, begging your pardon, you don't seem strong enough to help me carry that lot onto the shore."

"I'm not," she answered. Between her trunk and numerous mechanical devices, only the burliest of stevedores could transport her things. A Man O' War could do it without any problem, but one seldom found the technology-enhanced men on tiny Scottish islands. Either they were in the skies serving their countries, or they'd gone rogue and used their strength and airships in the service of their own desires, turning mercenary. Fortunately, no rogue Man O' War would ever bother with a dot on the map like Eilean Comhachag. Neither would a Man O' War in military service. She was safe. But she still had twenty feet of shallow waters to negotiate before she'd be truly secure.

Back on South Uist, it'd taken four brawny shoremen to load up the ferry with her belongings. "I've got a way to get everything safely, and drily, to shore."

The captain watched her with bald curiosity as she bustled around her belongings. Everything was fastened together with lengths of steel-enforced cords onto a large wooden pallet, ensuring that none of the ropes would snap from the weight of her possessions. Though everything was well secured, she was able to open one of her traveling cases, and the captain cursed softly when she produced four tiny brass-encased ether tanks.

"How'd you get those?"

A corner of her mouth curled up. "Connections."

She secured each of the tanks to the corners of the pallet using leather straps. A small metal box was mounted to one of the tanks, with a long insulated wire tethered from the box to a handheld device. Mounted in the center of the handheld device was a dial, with a brass pin sticking out of the side. She pulled on the brass pin, and the box she held suddenly hummed to life.

Campbell swore again when the ether tanks began to glow. They seemed to struggle for a moment, and then the wooden pallet rose up, lifted by the tanks. Setting the box aside, she crossed to the small tetrol engine affixed to the pallet and pulled on its starter cord. The engine growled to life, and the pallet moved over and beyond the rail of the boat. Picking up the control box, she used its dial to guide the pallet over the shallows leading up to the beach. Louvered fans were attached to the back of the pallet, pushing the whole thing toward the shore. She frowned in concentration, hoping none of the ether tanks suddenly lost buoyancy and sent her belongings plunging into the water.

Slowly, the pallet drifted closer to the beach. The cord attached between the device on the tank and the control box stretched tight. Kali sighed with relief when it finally reached the shore, and she set it down onto the rocks. But the length of the cord wasn't quite long enough, and it tugged from her hands. At least the cord and the box were both waterproof.

"The name of God was that?" Campbell asked, awed.

"Something we'd been working on in Liverpool," she answered. "To help loading and offloading cargo ships." But she and her colleagues hadn't gotten too far before their work had been interrupted. Destroyed. A half dozen tanks and a handful of the control boxes had survived. Given the state of Liverpool now, it'd be a long time before the docks would need anything like the loading devices. Guilt had gnawed at her as she'd taken a few for her own use—but it'd been more important to get out of the city and as far away as possible, so she'd grabbed what she could and fled.

"Saali kutti," she cursed now. She'd safely transported her possessions to the shore, but hadn't thought about how to get herself from the boat to the beach. The water was only a few feet deep, but she couldn't risk it.

She turned to Campbell. "Captain, I'm afraid I'm going to have to ask a very great service of you."

He grinned knowingly. "'Course. Fine ladies don't much like water."

I'm not a fine lady and I don't give a damn about water, she thought. Her father had taught her to swim in Shukrawari Lake. Now, however, she wasn't certain she'd be able to make the trip to the beach. Anger rose up, red-tinged. What had once been so easy, even pleasurable, was fraught with possible danger.

"There's an extra sovereign in it for you," she answered.

At least he looked offended by her offer. "As if I'd take money for doing the honorable thing."

Easily, he swung over the rail of the boat and landed in the water with a small splash. Standing in the shallows, he opened his arms to her.

Kali gingerly lowered herself into his embrace. This was the first time a man other than a doctor had held her in over three months.

Campbell mistook the stiffness in her body for fear. "Never fash yourself, lass. I'll have you safe and dry in just a minute."

He slogged through the water, and though the hem of her skirts dragged a little in the surf, the captain held to his promise and kept her dry.

He set her down awkwardly on the rocky beach, and she fought to keep from stumbling. When he reached out to steady her, she held him off with an outstretched hand. "Only getting my land legs," she said briskly.

Which must have been a common complaint, because he didn't press for more details.

She shook out her skirts and readjusted her cloak. She tugged the tethering cord through the waves, pulling the control box out of the water. "Many thanks, Captain. I can manage from here."

He stared at her, appalled. "Just leave you here? In this blighted place? Alone?"

"I made myself perfectly clear when I hired you. You were to ferry me to Eilean Comhachag and then return in a month's time to resupply me."

"But . . . but . . ." He turned in a circle, taking in the beach, the slope leading away from the shore. The utter isolation. "You'll need shelter."

"And I have it." At the captain's skeptical look, she sighed inwardly. Normally, she'd have been charmed by Campbell's consideration. Yet things hadn't been normal for her in months. "Here—I'll show you." It'd be the only way of getting rid of him. Damn these islanders and their thoughtfulness.

Leaving her belongings on the beach, she climbed the slope leading away from the shore. Tall grasses shivered in the breeze. Campbell's heavier footsteps sounded behind her, and he snorted with effort. He was like a turtle—far more fleet in the water than on land.

Away from the beach, they headed inland, crossing a small, rock-strewn field. More windblown trees stood like lost souls hovering around the gates of Paradise, denied entrance but unable to move forward or back.

"There." She pointed to the far edge of the field. "My shelter."

"It's naught but a pile of rocks," Campbell protested.

"But it's my pile of rocks."

The cottage had been built some hundred years ago by an enterprising MacNeil, presumably thinking that because the island wasn't inhabited, it would make for perfect fishing. Alas, the catch hadn't been enough to warrant the relentless loneliness, and the cottage had been abandoned. But every few decades, another MacNeil thought to try their luck again. And every few decades, the cottage was deserted again.

Now it had a new MacNeil taking up residence. Though she had no intention of fishing. And the very thing that had driven her ancestors away was precisely what drew her.

She approached the cottage, with Campbell slowly following. For all the wonders of this modern age, none of those advancements had touched this place. The cottage was nothing more than four stone walls with a slate shingled roof. Two narrow windows—the glass cracked—flanked a single door, barely holding onto its hinges. A heavily rusted pump stood close by. Likely the only source of water.

Pushing open the protesting door, Kali peered inside. The movement startled some creatures living within. Birds darted past her, chittering as they wheeled up into the sky, and furred little beasts scuttled into the walls. She smiled to herself as Campbell yelped in alarm.

The interior of the cottage held a table, a single chair, and something that at one time had been a rope-strung cot and horsehair mattress, but was now likely the furry little beasts' nest. A cupboard had been mounted to one of the walls, its sole occupant a chipped clay mug and plate. Smoke from the hearth had stained the ceiling. The hearth itself contained just a spit and a grate for burning peat. It had been so long since anyone had lived here, there weren't even ashes in the grate. A rusty basin on a narrow stand must have served as the sink. There were no taps. No running water. No water closet.

For the first time in her life, she actually hoped for an out-house.

Dust and cobwebs filmed every surface, giving the inside of the cottage a hazy look, as if it was a half-remembered dream that the dreamer would gladly forget upon waking.

"I have ample shelter," she said.

"Here?" Campbell's eyes were round. "You can't mean—"

"But I do."

"It's not fit for the veriest bedlamite."

She walked farther into the cottage. Cleaning wasn't one of her favorite activities, but she'd have a full agenda for the next few days. Or weeks. At least she came prepared. "Perhaps I am a bedlamite, Captain. And this is my asylum."

He chuckled at that, then his laugh turned uncertain when she simply looked at him.

"Lass—Miss MacNeil, it's not safe here."

"On the contrary. No place could be safer."

"What if the Hapsburgs or Russians find you?"

Burning ice spread along her back, and ached in her leg. "The Russians and Hapsburgs were chased from Liverpool three months ago. They won't be returning to Britain for a long while. And they wouldn't bother with this place. No one cares about Eilean Comhachag." Exactly why she'd come here.

The captain exhaled loudly. "I don't like it."

"Fortunately," she answered, "you don't have to." Her conscience pricked at her rudeness, but now that she'd finally set foot on the island, all she wanted was its promise of solitude.

"What if I came back in two weeks instead of a month?" he offered. "Just to be certain you're well."

"A month will suit me perfectly. And I want you to let your fellow watermen know that I don't desire any visitors. Only you, once a month."

"For how long?"

She hadn't considered that. How long did she need this self-imposed exile? How long before she'd want to join the world again? "As long as it takes," she finally answered.

Campbell tugged on his beard, his gaze fixed upon

the floor. "Lass," he said haltingly, "is there . . . are you in hiding?"

More cold fire fanned through her. She could barely move her lips to say, "Don't be ridiculous."

"There's no shame in it." The captain spoke quickly. "My own grandda was a smuggler—whisky, silk, clockworks— and he'd have to go underground sometimes when the tariff men came sniffing around. If maybe you took something, and needed to keep low for a while, well, I'd not think less of you."

Kali almost laughed. "I assure you, Captain, that I'm no thief." Aside from the ether tanks and control box, everything in her possession truly belonged to her. If anyone had been stolen from, it was her.

"Time for you to go," she said.

Despite her poor manners, Campbell still looked reluctant to leave her. She pulled a half crown from her pocket. "This is yours, if you leave now."

He eyed the coin warily, clearly torn. Finally, he took it from her. "What about your things on the beach? You'll need to get them up here."

"Same way I got them off the ship."

"And setting everything up?"

"I'm stronger than I look."

At last, he seemed to run out of excuses to stay. Grumbling, he walked out of the cottage. Kali followed him down to the beach. His little boat bobbed in the surf, looking almost eager to leave the island.

Summoning the last of her civility, she stuck out her hand. "Thank you, Captain."

He shook her hand, though he also shook his head. "It's

an ill world when a pretty lass like yourself strands herself on a cursed piece of rock."

"It's an ill world, indeed," she answered, pulling her hand from his grip. "Goodbye."

With that dismissal, Campbell waded back into the surf. He pulled himself over the rail of his boat and hoisted the anchor. Taking the wheel, he backed the vessel out of the small bay. For as much as he protested leaving her there, a look of profound relief crossed his face the farther he got from the island. His hand went up in a final wave, and she returned the gesture. The boat chugged as it sailed away, growing smaller and smaller. She watched until it wasn't more than a speck, then it disappeared.

Alone. She was finally alone.

And not the type of solitude one might find at a single table at a tea ship, or at the end of a jetty. This was true isolation.

She stood upon the beach, listening to the waves beat against the rocks. The wind sighed through trees and grasses. A bird—not an owl—chirped. These were the only sounds. Not the hiss of welding torches or the shouts of dockworkers. Nor the quiet voices of her fellow engineers consulting with one another about their latest projects. No tetrol-powered wagons rattling down the street. No vendors selling everything from meat pies to automated egg cookers.

All silence. And herself.

Kali waited for the iron cage around her to loosen. This was what she wanted. What she'd dreamed of for three months. Surely once she'd arrived here, to this desolate place, she'd finally feel at peace?

Peace didn't come. She felt exactly the same.

Disappointment pierced her like an ether-powered bullet. Had she run this far for no reason?

She shook her head at herself. *Of course I don't feel at ease yet. I've still got to get everything up to the cottage and clean. I'm sure once it's all in place, I'll be fine.*

Picking up the control box from where she had left it in the sand, she guided her pallet of belongings up the hill and toward the cottage, the tether dangling between them.

Anxiety tightened like a steel corset. She wondered if there was anyplace she could go that would make her feel safe and whole again.

CHAPTER TWO

Nothing could be set up until the cottage was reasonably clean. She unfastened her cloak and hung it from the lone peg on the wall, pushed up her sleeves, and got to work as the afternoon stretched out like a pale shroud, though the inside of the cottage was murky with dust and age.

Anticipating the dilapidated state of her new home, she'd packed a few brushes, as well as a clockwork sweeper. It was her own device, constructed of a central brass cylinder with three rotating brushes—whimsically, she thought the brushes looked like spinning dancers—but their purpose wasn't whimsical. They carried dust into a central pan that needed periodic emptying.

Kali carried all the furniture outside, then wound up the sweeper and let it run back and forth across the floor. Several times, she had to shake loose a particularly large clump of grime caught in the brushes. Mice fled in advance of the sweeper, probably thinking it some demon device of the apocalypse.

She felt a little sorry for the rodents. That same fear had

chased her, too. But either the mice would adapt to their new home outside, or they wouldn't. That was the way of things. One adapted, or one perished.

The clockwork sweeper didn't work on walls, so it was with her own labor she scrubbed at the stone, a kerchief pulled up over her nose and mouth to keep out the worst of the dust. Spiders scuttled like asterisks in an annotated manuscript. She knocked out decades of accumulated soot from the chimney—narrowly avoiding a face full of grime as it came sifting down, and swept that out.

Gods and curses, I'm becoming almost domestic. Something she'd never wanted to be. But that was the nature of adaptation. Demands were made, and ideologies couldn't stand in the face of those demands.

There wasn't much to do about the windows. She washed them down as best she could, but wind whistled through empty panes. The sun had begun to dip toward the horizon, and a cold embrace settled around the cottage. She'd need to patch the windows to keep from freezing. Tomorrow, she'd work on a more permanent solution. For today, she tacked up pieces of coated canvas and hoped to make it through the night without succumbing to frostbite.

But she had a means of keeping herself warm. And fed. The two most important elements of survival—or so her father had taught her from his years on long army campaigns.

Not wanting to waste her minimal supply of ether, she dragged into the cabin the large, heavy metal contraption that made up the bulk of her island possessions. She brought in her leather satchel full of tools, as well. Light inside the cabin began to fade, so she lit an oil lamp to help guide her in her labors.

The large metal device folded down for relatively easy transport. Now she loosened the screws and pulled on the steel panels, until the mechanism stood nearly as tall and wide as a cottage wall. She shoved it against the fireplace, then connected a wide vent from the back of the device to the hearth. Knowing that she wouldn't be able to use electricity or even tetrol on the island, she'd made adjustments back in Liverpool so that her cooking and heating device ran on peat—of which there was no shortage on Eilean Comhachag.

Once all the pieces had been put in place, Kali stood back to admire her handiwork. The large machine vaguely resembled a modern stove, with a range, oven, and even a salamander for putting the finishing touch on meat. But her cook-apparatus also used a series of heated glass tubes to purify water. Gears along the side turned a small barrel fan, circulating warm air through the cottage. There was even a timer built into the device so that if she wanted to begin cooking a stew or brewing a pot of tea, she'd only to twist the dial, and she'd have her food or drink at the time she wanted.

"All the comforts of home," she murmured. Though home had become far less comfortable these past months. The island, and the cottage, would be her new home, and if it was more Spartan than she'd been used to, she simply repeated those important words again. *Survival. Adaptation.*

Night was descending quickly. Far from inhabitation, darkness laid its claim with greater authority. She needed to work hastily. The bed and mattress were a loss, as she expected they might be, but her unfolding cot and tightly rolled mattress would serve as her bed. The rest of the furniture she brought back into the cottage, as well as her trunk full of clothing, a brass hipbath, and the wooden crate packed with books.

She might be in utter isolation, but this wasn't a punishment. There could be no life without her books.

Back at South Uist, she'd bought peat-cutting tools. Yet it was already too dark for her to go searching for fuel. She'd come prepared, though, with a few precut blocks, so she laid them in the firebox and set them alight. Soon, the cottage filled with warmth and the glow of a fire. It felt so different from what she'd known. Even with her cook-apparatus, it was a primitive existence she'd lead out here. Liverpool had been at the forefront of technology—it had to be, with the wealth of its ports, the constant ebb and flow of goods that fed the nation.

Exactly why it had been targeted.

But no one and nothing would find her in Eilean Comhachag. In the silence and solitude of her cottage, she exhaled.

Night fell like a curtain. One moment, ashen light marked the horizon. The next, utter darkness.

She cooked herself a simple supper of eggs, toasted bread, and tea. Here would be another challenge. Almost all her meals at home had been purchased. Oh, her mother would cover her head in playful shame that her only daughter knew nearly nothing of cooking, especially the *daal* and *pulao* and *naan* on which Kali had been raised. But there had always been devices to take apart and diagrams of machines to study.

Sitting at the rough table in the cottage, eating her plain meal and listening to the wind and isolation, homesickness formed an ache at the back of her throat. Her father's laugh. Her mother's singing. The din and color of Nagpur—its skies full of silk-draped gyrocopters and gliders. Trees full of jewel-colored birds both real and clockwork. Air full of heat and spice.

This gray and bleached island was Nagpur's barren counterpart.

Kali wiped down her plate and mug. Tomorrow, she'd set up her system that would connect to the water pump, so she'd have hot and cold running water.

Changing into her nightgown, she climbed into her cot, bringing a treatise on developments in tetrol-powered direct current generators with her. She'd read it three times already, but a comfort read was what she needed for her first night on Eilean Comhachag.

But as she settled down and turned the pages, it began.

The owls.

Their hoots surrounded her cottage and punctuated the night like rapid gunfire. Not a sound from them earlier. She'd begun to doubt their existence, despite the island's name. Now, as if to mock her, the nocturnal predators cried out into the darkness, their numbers far too great to count.

Who? Who? Who is this stranger in our cloistered home?

Good God, if this is what her ancestors had to contend with every night, no wonder they'd all fled for other islands. It was a barrage of sound. Eerie and ominous.

Where her forefathers had failed, Kali wouldn't. She'd either learn to endure the sound, or fashion some noise protection—stoppers for her ears, or a muffling head wrap.

Tonight, she'd bear it as best she could.

She studied the treatise, trying to lose herself in the mechanics of internal combustion and electromagnetics.

But after a moment, she lowered the publication. Tilted her head.

There was another sound, beneath the owls.

A humming. An unearthly, metallic humming.

Jumping out of bed, she donned her boots and threw on her cloak. Grabbed her pistol. After checking to make certain it was loaded, she flung the door open and hurried outside.

Stars flooded the sky, undimmed by any city lights. But Kali didn't marvel at them. Their beauty was cold as diamonds, and just as useless to her now. But the humming persisted. She turned in a circle, searching for its origin.

Her breath caught as she faced north. There, at the northern end of the island. Something *glowed*. A pale corona of light pushed back the darkness.

The island was uninhabited. She *knew* this. Campbell and everyone on South Uist had sworn it to be so. They'd no reason to lie.

Then what the hell is that?

Two impulses warred in her. Part of her wanted to run and hide beneath her bed. The other part wanted to race across the island and investigate. She had a weapon. Knew how to use it. But what awaited her? And could she cross the island's rugged terrain in the dark? She could carry her lantern, but only a fool ran around in her nightgown carrying a lantern, like some grease-brained girl in a Gothic novel. Why not simply scream out into the night, "Vulnerable target!"

No matter what it was out there, she had no way off this island. Campbell wasn't coming back for a month.

So either she hid in terror for four weeks, or she learned what it was that made the sinister noise and gave off that unsettling light.

She crept back into her cottage. Doused her lantern and huddled in her bed, her gun across her lap. It had been a long, exhausting day. But sleep kept itself hidden. When the sun rose, she'd have to go investigate.

The owls stopped their infernal chorus at some point during the night, and in the silence, she must've dropped into a fatigued sleep. She woke with a start, a knot in her neck, and a revolver in her lap. For a moment, she stared at the rough stone walls surrounding her, grayish light coming through clumsily patched windows. This wasn't her flat, not even the temporary shelter set up for survivors and refugees. And there was that silence, encompassing everything.

But the gun across her legs and the distant crash of waves upon a pebbled shore reminded her. Eilean Comhachag. And the lonely cottage that was her birthright.

But perhaps the cottage wasn't as alone as she'd thought. There'd been that odd metallic humming and light last night. Something else was on this island besides herself.

Rising from bed, she massaged her left thigh, easing out the kinks in the muscles. She'd need all her mobility today. She set her cook-apparatus to brew her some tea, and as it prepared her beverage, she put on a heavy wool dress, one that could suitably face bogs and brambles. Her boots were sturdy, too. Fashionable little kid boots served no purpose out here. Quickly, she braided her hair, to keep it out of her face.

After she bolted down cheese, bread, and tea, she strapped on a thick leather belt laden with pouches and tools. She tucked her revolver into her belt, then checked the barrels of her shotgun. They weren't ether guns, but when she'd packed, she hadn't expected more than a possible wild dog that might need scaring off. What she carried would have to suffice. She slung the shotgun's strap across her shoulder.

Please let me just meet with a hungry wild dog.

But she hadn't heard any howling last night. Only owls. And that strange humming. Wild dogs generally didn't emit a peculiar light, either. Not in her limited experience. She'd read that there were some experiments being conducted, similar to what they'd done with Man O' Wars, where they took animals and—

Now you're delaying.

She was out the door before she could make any more excuses.

Sometime in the night, a heavy mist had settled over the island. Everything appeared in hues of murk and ash. The field in which the cottage stood. The grassland and rocky hills beyond. Fifteen feet away from her doorway, and she could barely see the little stone house. A newcomer or someone unwary could get lost as a bolt in a scrap heap. Fortunately, she wore a leather gauntlet with a miniscope and compass mounted to it. Marking her position, she headed north, with her heartbeat keeping noisy company.

She kept the ridge of hills to her left, using them as a guide as she carefully picked her way across the uneven terrain. More trees and scrub dotted the landscape. A rodent of some kind darted between the bushes, and she cursed herself for starting in surprise. After all she'd faced, a tiny animal was nothing.

As she walked, she used a retractable pencil to make additions to her old map. The hills rose up more sharply three miles from where the cottage stood, and they continued on in rough peaks, with hardly any access to their summits. No grasses were flattened into trails, not even game trails. A small pond lay four miles from the cottage, its green edges choked with waterweeds and long-legged insects skimming across its surface. If fish lived in the pond, they hid themselves in its silty bottom. She'd have better luck catching fish off the beach.

But her note-taking was another delaying tactic. She had to press farther north to find out the origin of the light and last night's humming sound.

Edging along the gravel-covered base of the hills, she moved slowly onward, telling herself stories of goddesses who'd braved hordes of demons without fear.

Yet she was no goddess. Only a woman, completely on her own.

A shape appeared out of the mists. A large, dark shape. Heading right toward her. It moved noiselessly over the gravel, notwithstanding its size.

She grabbed her revolver, aiming it at the shadow.

It immediately stopped moving. Then it spoke.

"You're not from the Admiralty."

A man. With a deep, rasping voice. As if he hadn't spoken in a long time.

Even through the heavy mist, she saw that he didn't hold up his hands, despite the gun trained on him.

"No," she answered, her mouth dry. "Not the Admiralty." Yet she didn't want to tell him where she was from. She'd no idea *who* this stranger was.

"Anyone with you?" he demanded. He spoke with an air of command, as though used to obedience.

Despite the authority in his voice, she kept silent. Telling him she was alone could endanger her. At least she was armed.

He didn't seem to care about the revolver in her hand. He moved closer, emerging out of the fog.

Oh, God. He *was* big. Well over six feet tall, with shoulders as wide as ironclads. His body seemed a collection of hard muscles, knitted together to make the world's most imposing man. He had black hair, longish and wild, as if he hadn't seen a barber in some time, and a thick beard, also in need of trimming. He stood too far away for her to see his eyes, but she could feel his gaze on her, dark and piercing, hyper-vigilant like a feral animal.

And he stepped still nearer to her.

"My father was in the army," she said, clipped. She raised her gun. "He was a crack shot. He trained me to be one, too. Stay where you are."

She thought a corner of his mouth edged up in a smile, but the beard hid his expression. "I'd knock that Webley out of your hand before you could pull the trigger."

Words poised on her lips that no man could move that quickly—he was still ten feet away—but those words faded the more she looked at him. His massive hands could likely crush a welder's gas tanks. But more than the raw strength he exuded, a palpable but unseen energy radiated from him, something barely contained.

She couldn't tell if she was fascinated or terrified. Or both. "You're doing a poor job of putting me at ease," she answered.

Again, that hint of a smile. "Never said I wanted to put you at ease."

"Not another step," she snapped. Instinctively, she moved back, out of striking distance. But as she did, her left boot caught in the rocks, and she stumbled.

Unseated, the stones tumbled down in a small rockslide. They knocked her down, twisting her leg at an unnatural angle. She sprawled on the ground.

Instantly, the stranger darted forward, a frown of concern between his brows.

She kept the gun pointed at him, despite lying awkwardly upon the rocks. "Back. I'm fine."

"Your leg—"

Her skirts had come up, revealing both her limbs.

The stranger must have been civilized at one point, because he quickly turned his gaze away.

"Go ahead and look," she said. "I gave up on modesty months ago."

He did, and when he saw her leg, he cursed softly. "Mechanical."

Kali studied her prosthetic leg, trying to see it through the stranger's eyes. It was a complex device of brass, leather, and wood, carefully calibrated to move as smoothly and with the same range of motion as a normal leg made of flesh and bone. The apparatus strapped to her upper thigh, kept on much the same way a garter belt held on stockings. Though it wasn't necessary to give the leg the shape and form of an actual limb—all it really needed to do was function properly, and beneath her skirts, no one could truly tell what it looked like—she'd taken pains to shape the metal and carve the wood so that it resembled her other, whole leg. Vanity, perhaps, but when a woman lost her leg, she could be forgiven for a little pride.

Few people had seen her prosthetic leg. She hadn't been eager to show it off. A few doctors had run her through some tests to see how it functioned. They'd looked at her like a science experiment, not a person. Not a woman. Other than the doctors, however, nobody had laid eyes upon the evidence of her broken life, her ruined body.

Until now.

She stared at the unknown man. Waiting. Watching. Her heart slamming against the inside of her ribs. As though this feral stranger's opinion mattered.

It shouldn't. It did.

Slowly, he crouched down. Through the wild tangle of his hair, his expression was . . . fascinated. No disgust or horror. No looking at her as if she were an attraction at a traveling fair, displayed beside the conjoined twins. But genuine wonderment—not revulsion—gleamed in his eyes.

Her head grew light, muddled with confusion.

"Scuttle me," he murmured. "Never seen its equal."

"Have you seen a lot of cripples and their fake limbs?"

His gaze was solemn. "Sailors see many wounded men. With injuries far more severe than yours."

An odd heat crept into her cheeks.

"The sawbones and tinkerers try to fit them with artificial limbs," he continued, "but none that I've seen are so advanced. So elegant."

More heat filled her cheeks to hear her prosthetic called *elegant*. She pushed herself to sitting and dug through the tools and pouches on her belt. "It's doubtful you would see anything like this. Since I made it."

His shocked gaze shifted from the leg to her, the surprise plain in his eyes.

"I planned and built the thing myself." She tugged at her left foot, pinned beneath the rocks.

He lifted some of the larger stones, casting them aside easily. Soon, her leg was free.

"I didn't trust the design to anyone but me." And with many, many weeks of recovery, she'd needed something to occupy her time. She removed her small screwdrivers and pliers from her toolbelt to repair the damage wrought by her fall.

She pulled off her boot and adjusted the screws that joined the foot to the ankle. The sooner she fixed the damn thing, the sooner she could get away from him.

Satisfied with her repairs, she tugged her boot on. She ignored his outstretched hand and clambered to her feet. Carefully, she tested her weight on the leg, and breathed a quiet sigh of relief when it held. Fixing the prosthetic wouldn't be a problem—if she were at her workbench or even using the table at the cottage—but she seldom had to make field repairs. At least it would hold enough to get her back to her little hut.

She examined the shotgun, worried that she'd damaged it with her fall, but aside from some scratches on the barrel and stock, it seemed in good condition.

At least he didn't press her with questions—what had

brought her here, how long she planned on staying. And she wouldn't ask him the same questions.

Still, she couldn't help her curiosity. He wore a long navy coat, patched in places and a little threadbare, with tarnished buckles. Standard naval issue. All of his clothing seemed clean but slightly ragged, from his linen shirt, to the buckskin breeches clinging tightly to his dense, burly thighs, to the scuffed tall boots, stained with seawater.

Was he a disgraced sailor? A deserter? Or one who'd left the navy but kept some of the trappings.

Whoever he was, he continued to stare at her as if she'd descended from the sky on iron wings. Well, he hadn't looked in disgust at her artificial leg, and he wasn't leering at her, either. Two small elements in his favor.

"You've got an odd voice," he said suddenly.

"And you're an expert conversationalist," she retorted.

A slight ruddy color stained his cheeks above his beard. "Been a while since I had company. But"—he narrowed his eyes, thoughtful—"I hear a burr in your accent, and a lilt of Hindi, too."

She tried to hide her surprise. "My father's Scottish. Maa's from Nagpur."

He nodded contemplatively. "Bit of Scouse in there, too."

Here was another shock. She'd only lived in Liverpool for five years, but apparently it had been enough to give her accent some color. A perceptive man, this wild former sailor. Unease crept through her belly. She'd come here to be alone, not to think of the past, but those plans were crumbling apart.

"The last place I lived was Liverpool," she said cautiously. She could turn and flee, ending the conversation, but even under good conditions, her prosthetic didn't let her run fast. This stranger could easily catch her. The length of his stride was twice her own. Maybe more.

He was silent, however, for a long moment. Then, "The Battle of Liverpool. You were there."

Her left leg suddenly ached, and the air in her lungs turned brittle. "And I survived. Which is more than I can say for more than half the people with me on the ground."

Images, sounds, smells—phantom senses assaulted her.

Hapsburg and Russian airships, captained by Man O' Wars, dropping explosive devices upon the city, setting everything ablaze. Flattening buildings and crushing the men, women, and children within them. Screams. Cries. The useless clanging of the fire brigades' bells. Seafaring ships at dock turned to charred, sunken wrecks. The British Man O' Wars and their airships arrived quickly, and they'd fought the enemy in the skies above Liverpool—something mythical and terrible straight from the *Mahabharata*.

Trapped beneath a collapsed wall, Kali had seen it all. The bursts from ether cannons. Airships plunging out of the sky, crashing into the rubble as the men within shouted in terror. She'd watched the world become a fiery hell. She'd seen, too, the remaining British ships destroy or chase off the enemy vessels. Until loss of blood had claimed her consciousness. And her leg.

"It's still a smoking ruin," she said. Just as she was. "There's no Liverpool left in Liverpool. And the navy lost a lot of airships that day." She stared at the man, his face ashen.

"The sun's going down," he growled. "Better get back to wherever it is you're staying."

Without another word, the big man turned and strode away. The mists engulfed him, and in an instant, he'd vanished. She couldn't even hear his footsteps. It was as though he'd never been there.

Kali was many things, but never fanciful. She hadn't imagined the meeting and conversation with the stranger. He'd left giant footprints in some of the mud amongst the rocks. So he *was* real. But her exploration of the island had left her with more questions than answers. Who was he? Why had he run away so abruptly? It had to have been his home casting the light—but why did his house hum?

It didn't matter. None of it mattered. She was here to be alone. He didn't concern her.

Whoever the man was, though, he'd spoken truly. Daylight didn't last long this far north. And the mists still hadn't cleared. The safest thing to do was retrace her steps.

Carefully, she made her way back, taking extra care not to get her prosthetic leg caught in the uneven terrain.

He clearly wanted to be left alone. Just as she did. They could share this island without actually *sharing* it—couldn't they?

Yet if she'd come to Eilean Comhachag in search of peace, she knew now she wasn't going to find it.

CHAPTER THREE

Fletcher had seen the cottage when he'd first arrived at the island. He'd explored it, finding it in worse shape than a dockside strumpet. Nothing that a day's work couldn't fix, but he had to stay at the north end of the island, and so he'd left the cottage to its decay.

Unseen, he'd followed the extraordinary woman back to the cottage. He'd wanted to make sure she got back to wherever she stayed safely, and to prove to himself that she'd been real, not a hallucination born from months alone. But no, she was an actual human being, and had taken up residence in that crumbling pile of rocks. Part of him had wanted to stay and watch her, learn what had brought her to his island. Instead, he'd slunk away, retreating into the isolation he knew best.

Approaching the structure warily now, two days after they'd met, he saw she'd been busy. The cottage wouldn't ever be top class, but she'd patched the roof and did the best she could with the windows, given that there wasn't a glazier for miles. More intriguing was the device attached to the water pump—an assembly of gears and vulcanized rubber belts, and a hose fitted to the end of the pump itself. The hose ran toward the cottage. She'd managed to dig under the wall, and installed a hose leading inside. Some kind of plumbing she'd fashioned?

After seeing the ingenuity of her false leg's design, he could believe it.

Cheerful smoke curled up from the chimney, fragrant with peat. Either she'd brought the fuel with her, or learned how to harvest it. Resourceful.

He stopped on the edge of the field, deliberating. After following her to her home, he'd made sure to avoid her over the past few days—not an easy job, considering the island was only ten miles from the southern end to the northern tip, and six miles wide. She'd stayed out of his way, too, staying south of an invisible border beginning at the pond. He'd missed going down to the beach to watch the waves tumble against the rocks, and the good fishing the bay offered. Yet he could survive without both. He'd learned, these months, just how little he needed for his survival, how spare his life could become. The loss of half the island wasn't much.

And yet, here he was. At midday, standing at the periphery of a field and staring at a little stone cottage. A cottage that housed the first person he'd seen or spoken with in three months.

He wanted to bolt back to his end of the island and stay there, content in his solitude. Another force, bright and demanding, tugged him toward the home, and the woman within it.

And then he stood in front of her door and knocked.

Knocked, for God's sake. An ordinary gesture made odd by the fact that only two people lived on this island, and he'd dispensed with things like knocking on doors and speaking in complete sentences. At least he still wore clothing.

The woman opened the door. She held onto it, as if pretending that she could bar him entrance. He backed up a step, preparing to bolt. They stared at each other silently for a long time.

The other day, he'd been too shocked by her presence on the island to fully look at her, but now that he'd had a few days to get used to the idea, he really saw her.

True to her story about her origins, she had skin the color of spiced tea with milk, and warm brown eyes. Her thick black hair was twisted into a knot at the base of her neck. Little golden hoops adorned her ears. The simple green wool dress she wore revealed ripe curves. But the coolness in her gaze and firm line of her mouth were anything but enticing. He wasn't here for ravishment or seduction, anyway.

Wordlessly, he held out a brace of rabbits. He'd hunted them only this morning.

She gazed at the still bodies of the rabbits, and he realized only then that, as a city woman, she probably wasn't used to strange men showing up at her door with dead animals. Once, he'd been charming with young women, enough to secure a steady sweetheart. All that had changed, though. He had stopped interacting with women and their land-bound ways long ago. Now that he'd been on the island, his meager manners had degenerated even more.

But she didn't scream, didn't faint. Frowning, she simply took the rabbits from him.

"This has to be the strangest present I've ever received," she said.

He liked her voice—low and smoky—but her words were little needles of embarrassment. He didn't think he could *be* embarrassed, and yet here he stood, his face hot, his tongue thick.

"Be sure to eat all of the rabbit," he said, turning away. "Guts, brains, eyes, organs. No squeamishness. You just eat the meat, you'll starve."

"It's fortunate that I'm not a vegetarian."

He began to walk off. He was nearly at the edge of the field, when her voice called out, "Wait."

He stopped but didn't turn around.

"You brought me some dead animals," she said. "The least I can do is offer a cup of tea in exchange." She sounded as though she were forcing the words out.

Tea. His stores of it had run out two weeks ago. Some things an Englishman could go without, but depriving him of tea was tantamount to giving up his own blood.

But he *could* live without tea. He'd done so for two weeks. It wasn't truly essential. Yet he still wavered. Stay or go? It didn't sound like she honestly wanted him there.

Staying meant the possibility of questions he didn't want to answer. It also meant talking with another human being, and a pretty one, at that. A sudden sharp ache hit him in the center of his chest. He hadn't realized that he'd craved company until it—she—had mysteriously arrived a few days ago.

Slowly, he turned back and gave her a brief nod. "One cup. Then I'll go."

She didn't look entirely pleased by his decision. "Go or stay. No one's forcing you inside, Captain."

He tensed. "Never said I was a captain."

"The naval coat and air of command rather gave it away," she said drily. "Captain."

"Don't call me that."

She planted her hands on her hips. "'*Hey, you*' has a slightly impersonal feel to it."

"Fletcher," he ground out.

"Mr. Fletcher, if you'll—"

"Fletcher's my Christian name."

She crossed her arms over her chest. "No last names."

He shook his head. "Don't serve any purpose out here, anyway."

She nodded, as if agreeing with—even approving of—his logic. "I'm Kali."

This time, he was the one caught off guard. "The goddess of death?"

"And creation. I'm surprised you know of her."

"There aren't many places in Britain's empire that I haven't been." Why did he say that? He didn't need or want to tell her anything about himself, but the words seemed to spring from his mouth.

"Still," she murmured, "not many *videshi* bother to learn such things."

He shrugged. It seemed only right to study the ways and customs of a foreign place, if only to keep from offending the locals. And learning about new cultures had been part of his desire for joining the navy in the first place—but he wouldn't tell her that. The less he revealed of himself, the better. For both of them.

"A powerful, feared goddess," he said. "Didn't think anyone would be daring enough to name their daughter after her."

Kali's mouth softened into a guarded smile as she leaned against the doorjamb. "My full name's Kalindi. Father always called me Kali. He said it was fitting."

"Bloodthirsty child."

She waved a dismissive hand. "Ah, I cried when my father killed snakes and scorpions. But I was . . . wild."

The word, spoken in her husky voice, sent an unexpected pulse of sensation through him, like the first stings after a chilled limb began to warm.

She started to speak, then stopped. She looked ready to send him packing. He took a step backward.

But then she pushed the door open wider. "Come in," she said, unsmiling.

Inside the cottage, he felt as if he'd stepped into one of the Admiralty's research facilities. The rough stone exterior of the cottage hid the latest in technology.

After laying the rabbits on a table, Kali moved toward a self-contained cooking apparatus, its different components neatly fitted together, from the range to the fire to a tap, under which sat a kettle on a small metal trivet. She pulled a lever on the side of the contraption, and the tap opened, filling the kettle. Before the kettle overflowed, the tap shut off on its own. The trivet swung out on a hinged arm, setting the kettle onto the range, where a flame automatically sprang to life.

Not even the top-of-the-line naval ships were equipped so finely.

Yet she paid the extraordinary device no mind as she pulled two mugs down from a cupboard—one ceramic, the other of enameled tin.

"I didn't plan on guests," she said, setting the cups down on the table. "Nothing matches."

"You think I'm the sort of bloke who cares about matching china?"

She cautiously eyed him, from the top of his head—barely clearing the beams—to his big scuffed boots. He hadn't been stared at in such a fashion for many years. It shouldn't affect him at all. It did, though. Because he'd been alone. And now he wasn't. His sole companion on the island was *this* woman, with her dark eyes like obsidian blades that cut him into pieces. He didn't know what to make of her.

"I think we've both got our share of secrets," she answered. "But I won't ask about yours if you don't ask about mine."

He debated for a moment, then stuck out his hand.

For a moment, she just looked at it. Then, guardedly, she held hers out as well. His fingers easily enfolded hers as they shook to seal the bargain—she had slim hands, perfect for designing and building wickedly clever devices. Compared to her, he had a beast's clumsy paws. But her skin wasn't soft and delicate. Calluses lined her fingers, her palm, just as they did his.

They comforted him, those calluses on her hand. But at the touch of skin to skin, filaments of light and warmth threaded up his arm and through his body. It had been a long time since he'd touched a woman. Not since Emily.

He let go of her hand, resisting the impulse to rub his palm against his thigh—though he didn't know if it was to scrub the feeling away or push it more deeply into his skin.

Her cheeks darkened, and she turned away to pull a tin down from the cupboard. He knew before she opened it what it held, closing his eyes and inhaling deeply the green and woody scent of tea. His body responded almost as strongly as it had when he'd held her hand.

He opened his eyes and saw her staring at him. Then she spooned some of the dried leaves into a glazed earthenware teapot.

"I . . . ran out of tea two weeks ago."

She gave a small shudder. "My God, I can't believe you haven't gone mad."

"That fact hasn't been established."

Instead of looking at him with fear, she chuckled. A velvety sound resonating from the back of her throat.

"Us being on Eilean Comhachag voluntarily doesn't speak well of either of our mental states." She peered at him more closely. "You didn't know the name of the island."

"Never said that."

"But you blinked quickly when I said the name, so either you got a speck of dust in your eye—which is impossible, because I cleaned the hell out of this place—or you had no idea the island was called Eilean Comhachag."

Bugger, she was a perceptive one. "Not knowing the name of this heap of stone doesn't mean anything. I'd wager you don't know the names of half the islands in these parts."

"Yet *this* was the one I wanted to find."

Why would she come to this desolate pile of rocks of her

own volition? Maybe it had something to do with Liverpool. Or her injured leg. She seemed as cautious as a bird in the snow being offered a handful of crumbs, flitting forward, then back, ready to fly. Yet hungry, too.

The kettle whistled, and the flame beneath it automatically went out. She grabbed a padded square of calico and used it to pick up the kettle, then filled the teapot.

He glanced around the cottage. There was a second table, one that looked like she'd recently built herself. Pieces of brass, wood, and leather lay in a neat jumble atop the table, the sign of a thought in progress. "Got enough here to keep you occupied."

She followed his gaze to the unassembled mechanical pieces. "Tea and inventions. The two things I need to retain my sanity." But her voice was wry, as if she didn't fully believe herself.

Damn. It'd be difficult to hold to their bargain when the glimpses of who she was continued to intrigue him. He thought for certain he'd toss the rabbits at her and leave as fast as he could—which was bloody fast. The tea hadn't been the lure that kept him at the cottage, though. It was her. This sharp, damaged woman, more edged than a cutlass, but with an unspoken, invisible yearning he felt with a surprising instinct.

"I've planned better than you," she added. "The ferryman comes back in a month with more supplies, and more tea."

His muscles tightened. A ferryman. That meant a greater chance of discovery. But Fletcher kept his expression neutral.

She filled the two cups with tea, and only years of rigorous naval training kept him from lunging for his mug when she offered it to him. Instead, he was like a trained bear, he sat at her table and held the cup between his hands. The mug felt small as a thimble, but he nursed his tea slowly, he and Kali sitting in a silence that wasn't exactly friendly, but wasn't hostile, either. She kept eyeing him as if he might suddenly kick down the door and run off into the mists.

He glanced at the cooking apparatus, and she followed his gaze.

"It folds nearly flat," she said. "It doesn't weigh too much, either. I thought it would be good for scientific expeditions. This is the prototype, though."

She'd built *that*, too? "Seems to be working fine."

She shrugged, and there was an economic grace in her movements. "It's been a process. I keep having to make adjustments with the fuel system. Yesterday it smoked up the place so badly I had to sleep outside."

He scowled. "Not safe to do that."

"I had flannels over my flannels, so I wasn't cold."

"There's more to be afraid of than the chill."

"The only predators I've seen on the island so far are the owls."

"I could be one, too," he felt compelled to add.

She gazed at him across the table. "I would've known that by now."

"A fifteen-minute meeting doesn't tell you anything." An odd anger surged, that she'd be so naïve as to trust him on such short knowledge.

"A considerable amount can happen in fifteen minutes."

He saw experience in her eyes. No, she wasn't naïve, but he still didn't care for the idea of her sleeping outside on her own.

"Besides," she added, pouring herself another cup of tea,

"secrets or no secrets, if there's something you want, I'd wager you just take it." After refilling his mug, she looked pointedly at his shoulders. No use in being modest—he had wide shoulders. Everything about him was big, a fact that had taken him some getting used to. At first, he'd kept knocking his head against doorjambs and trying to squeeze into chairs that couldn't possibly hold him.

"There's a difference between a man who's in the navy and a privateer," he answered.

"Out here"—she waved at the isolated landscape on the other side of the window—"nothing can stop you from doing what you want."

"You *trying* to provoke me into ravishing you?"

The moment the words left his mouth, a heated awareness crept between them. Dark and shrouded in mysteries.

"What a high opinion you've got of yourself." Yet she set her cup down, then nudged it around, making tiny adjustments to its position.

He drained his cup in one gulp, and pushed back from the table. She stared up at him, her dark eyes wide. "Three months I've lived on this island, Kali. I don't have all this fanciness"—he nodded at the cooking apparatus—"but even if I did, I wouldn't count on anything. You want to survive, you need to be on guard. Against everything."

"It sounds like you're including yourself in that list."

Threatening a woman tasted acrid. "Everything," he prevaricated.

She, too, stood from the table but kept its width between them. "No need to worry," she said tightly. "You won't find another woman more guarded than myself."

But she didn't act like a frightened person, didn't cringe and huddle into herself. Kali had boldness. Tenacity. Strength. It was easy to forget that she'd been at Liverpool, and that she'd not just seen the battle, but suffered a terrible injury because of it. Sailors and soldiers were only human, and could be hurt or killed like anyone, but they had a bleak familiarity with violence, with blood.

She was a civilian. An engineer. A woman.

And he was an ass.

"I . . ." He bolted toward the door. "Remember what I said about the rabbit," he said over his shoulder. Then he was outside, all but running back to his side of the island.

As he strode across the fields and along the base of the hills, he called himself a long and extensive list of names, none of which he'd say in the presence of women, children, or the elderly.

He shouldn't have gone to see her. He should have known better, and kept away. His steps slowed. Maybe he should go back and tell her that he'd stay out of her way if she didn't bother him.

I won't go to the cottage anymore. I'm a dead man, aren't I? Dead men don't have friends. Even pretty, wickedly clever ones. It's safer this way, for everybody.

But he didn't turn back. He hesitated, then continued striding toward his end of the island.

Tomorrow. I'll tell her I can bring her food if she needs it, but we won't be having tea together. Won't talk or try to cleverly figure out each other's secrets. And she can't tell the ferryman about me.

But he'd do all that tomorrow. With his mind made up, he kept hiking toward his home. Yet his steps were a little slower. Knowing that he wasn't alone on the island—Eilean Comhachag, she'd called it—made his isolation that much sharper.

Sodding damn. She'd ruined his perfect loneliness.

Watery afternoon sunlight spilled across Kali's makeshift worktable. It wasn't the strongest illumination, but she'd always preferred working by natural light rather than gaslight or oil lamps. Her colleagues at the engineering firm in Liverpool had joked that if she kept that practice up, she'd be out on the street, just another blind girl selling poesies. But her eyesight stayed strong as ever, and the lenses of her goggles were only to protect her eyes, not to strengthen her vision.

She was the only one who'd survived, out of everyone at Drogin & Daughters Mechanical Engineering and Fabrication. Not even young Fred Gorman, her assistant—half her age and already thinking of ways to make flight without ether possible. The building hadn't survived, either. After she'd been released from the makeshift hospital, she'd returned to where her workplace had once stood. Most of the debris had already been cleared away by that point, save a smoldering heap of bricks and a few charred blueprints. The bodies had been removed and buried. She'd missed the mass of funerals, laid up in bed and fighting infection.

Kali now rubbed the heel of her palm against her forehead. She made an adjustment on the delicate brass leg of the cricket. When the tiny automaton worked, it was supposed to rub its legs together in a soothing imitation of real crickets, and its abdomen would softly glow. It would help children afraid of the dark—or so she hoped. Normally, she worked on larger-scale projects, things with broader technological and economic uses.

She couldn't bring herself to think of the larger world now. Only these little designs that might make someone's life feel safer—even if it was only an illusion.

When she almost twisted the cricket's leg beyond fixing, she tossed her screwdriver down in disgust. Her thoughts were wayward as welding sparks, cascading everywhere. She stared out the window at the scrubby field surrounding the cottage.

Three days had passed, and not a word or sign of Fletcher. He hadn't returned since he'd rushed out, advising her about how to eat rabbit.

She stood up from her workbench and stretched, then untied her waxed canvas apron and tossed it onto her chair.

Tea the other day had been . . . strange. She hadn't planned on inviting him inside, but the words had leapt from her mouth as if some hidden part of her had summoned them. Having him at her table, with them cagily drinking tea, she'd wondered who would get up and run off first—her, or him. She didn't think him a ghost any longer—more like a feral animal cautiously nosing its way toward the fire, in search of warmth and companionship.

Should she chase him away from the fire, or try to lure him closer? Both impulses wrestled within her. Maybe they were both ghosts, pale shadows of who they'd once been, brought to haunt this island. She'd come here to be by herself, and never had she been in the company of a creature more isolated than Fletcher. He was her dark reflection, and the tea they'd shared had been an education in what it meant to be alone.

Her gaze caught on the cricket. If she focused, she could have it finished within half an hour. True to her calculations, in thirty minutes, the little automaton hopped and chirped, its belly glowing gently.

She threw on her cloak and strapped on her tool belt and tucked in her revolver. She wrapped the cricket in some muslin, and also packed a satchel with a lamp and a few other supplies, just in case she was caught after dark or the weather turned inclement.

Heading out, she saw the mists still lying across the island in patches. Since her arrival, she'd explored her half of Eilean Comhachag, and now recognized more landmarks. The twisted rowan tree right before the ridge of hills began. Where to avoid the scree at the base of the hills so she didn't lose her balance again. The gradual slope upward of the field, leading to the pond.

Strange disappointment twisted in her when she reached the pond and found no sight of him. Then again . . . if she met up with him before she reached his home, she'd have less of an excuse to see where he lived. Would it be a cottage like hers? Some rough lean-to or structure of barest survival? Hell, he could have found a cave in one of the hills and made his home there. But that wouldn't explain the light or humming, which she'd continued to hear every night since she'd arrived.

Past the pond, the terrain opened up into a rocky, rolling moor. Gorse and heather sprung up in surprised tufts, as if unable to believe that they'd endured in such an inhospitable environment. The mists hung lower here, caught in bowls formed by the moorland. She pulled her cloak closer as she trudged over the heath. It brought to mind her father's tales of malevolent fairy folk and monsters—creatures like the hideous Arrachd, lurking on the moors, waiting for the unwary traveler to feast on his or her bones.

Her feet demanded she turn around and go back to her cottage. Fletcher hadn't invited her. He'd made it clear enough that he wanted to be left alone. But she kept walking, hunching her shoulders against the creeping chill. She'd survived a city being destroyed all around her. She could manage something as minor as a stroll across a moor.

The land rose up, a small hillock hiding the next expanse of moorland. Unused as she was to so much exercise, her breath rasped in her throat while she climbed the low hill. But when she reached the very top and looked down into the vale below, she lost her breath completely.

An airship had crashed into the moor.

CHAPTER FOUR

It hadn't been a recent crash. Gorse and grasses poked through cracks in the airship's hull. The ship itself was mostly intact. Some time ago, it had plowed into the moor, stern first, digging a massive trench behind it. The front of the airship had broken off, its figurehead and bowsprit were only jagged shards of wood after gouging through the rocky soil.

To see something as incongruous as an airship in the middle of a moor—she must be dreaming. But the cold air in her tight lungs and the growing wind scraping at her cheeks proved she was awake.

It was a British airship, or had been, before it had crashed. Her experience in Liverpool had taught her that this vessel had the layout of a British ship, with its central support curved in an arc from stem to stern. The ether tanks that would be mounted to that support had broken off, and lay upon the deck. The turbines had partially cracked off, but were still attached to the stern of the ship. The ship wouldn't be going anywhere.

"The hell are you doing here?"

She whirled and found Fletcher standing just behind her. He loomed out of the fog. It amazed her that such a big man could move so quietly—though her attention had been focused on the mysterious airship, and nothing else.

"Pray God the Queen never visits you," she snapped. "You'd run her off with your abysmal manners."

"She won't come here," he answered flatly.

Kali glanced back and forth between the massive man and the crashed airship. "It's yours."

He gave her a terse nod. His eyes were chips of cold blue quartz, his mouth a hard line. He had an ether rifle slung across his wide back and carried a canvas sack stained with blood. Supper.

"I've never seen the inside of an airship before," she said. She'd observed them from the outside, locked in fiery combat, the sight wonderful and terrible, but she knew nothing about the interior of one of these vessels. The navy let no one outside of their ranks learn the layout of the ships, or indeed, much of anything. All nations' navies guarded their ships carefully. They were the key to winning this endless Mechanical War..

Airships had torn her life apart. But airships had kept her and Liverpool from total annihilation. Terrible beasts they were, but fascinating.

"It'd be rude not to offer me a tour," she said.

Fletcher said nothing, only glared at her. Yet she felt something, an almost palpable pulse of energy traveling between him and the airship.

Gods and goddesses. He's a Man O' War.

The captain of the airship, and its source of power and ether.

She took an involuntary step backward. His mouth twisted, as if he expected her reaction.

As extraordinary as the airship was, it was just a thing. Seafaring craft had existed in different forms for thousands of years.

But Man O' Wars—nothing like them had existed until less than a decade ago. They were combinations of man *and* machine. At some point in the past, Fletcher had undergone the procedure to turn him into this amazing hybrid. Telumium plates had been embedded in his skin, with filaments of the rare metal threaded around and into his heart. Not every man could become a Man O' War. They needed to have an *aurora vires* rating of Gimmel or higher. It took an extraordinary individual to make this transformation. And Fletcher had done so.

He muttered something now under his breath. A curse. Realizing the moment that she understood what he was. Beneath all his wild hair, he looked angrily resigned.

So much for keeping secrets. No way to hide this one: he was the Man O' War captain of a British Aerial Navy airship.

"Don't much care if I'm rude or not," he growled. "You're not getting aboard."

She ought to leave it at that. Just turn around and head back to her cottage.

"I saw these ships in action over Liverpool. But this is the closest I've ever come to one. I'm an engineer. How can I not see how they work?"

Fletcher exhaled. Then nodded. He strode ahead.

Kali followed, her heart throbbing with dread and determined excitement.

He had to be a fool. Or mad. He was certain the moment Kali set foot inside the ship, his haven would be gone.

Yet she'd been at Liverpool. She had a right to see what had helped tear her life apart—though she hadn't phrased it in exactly those words.

He paced ahead. He should've known the moment he saw her that his burial on the island was over. She'd drag him back to the realm of the living—to the danger of everyone.

Even worse, when he'd spotted her moments earlier, a jolt of pleasure hit him. As if he'd actually wanted to see her again. Signs of life within him that he didn't want. Easier to be dead, numb.

"What's her name?" she asked behind him.

"*Persephone*."

"Pretty."

"Wasn't me that gave the name to her." They'd gotten closer to the airship, and as they did, he felt it pulling upon him, that slight gripping sensation through his body, as *Persephone* drew on his implants to feed its batteries. He'd grown so used to the sensation, he barely felt it anymore.

The keel had been smashed into the ground, and half the hull had been buried with the impact. But that still left the other half aboveground, its portholes and gun ports staring out at the moor. As he and Kali reached the ship, she frowned at the remainder of the hull. Twenty feet of airship towered above them.

"There's no door," she noted.

"Don't need one." He leapt and grabbed onto the railing at the quarterdeck, then pulled himself up. Standing on the top deck, he braced his hands on the railing to look down at her. Her mouth had dropped open and her eyes were round as cannon shot.

"I'd heard Man O' Wars were strong, but . . ." She shook her head.

"Nothing to twist your wrench about. We can all do that." They'd taken him and other recently-made Man O' Wars and trained them for nearly a year before letting them out into the world. Strength like theirs, unchecked and unknown, proved a greater liability than asset. Still, there had been mishaps and accidents.

He could leave her down there. Keep her from boarding and preserve the solitude of his crypt. Instead, he picked up a rope and tossed one end down to her.

She looked at the rope, smiling darkly. "I used to be damned good at climbing. Not so agile anymore." She rapped her knuckles against her prosthetic leg.

"Grab one end. I'll pull you up."

For a moment, it looked as though she'd refuse. Beneath the spice hue of her skin, she'd gone ashen. But she gripped the rope, then looked at him and nodded.

He pulled. She weighed so little, and his strength was so great, that she practically soared up the side of the ship. She actually let out a small gasp. And then suddenly she flew over the rail. Right into his arms.

She let go of the rope and grabbed onto his shoulders for balance. At the same time, he dropped his end of the rope and wrapped his arms around her to hold her steady. They pressed against each other, chest-to-chest, their faces mere inches apart. Her warm, startled breath fanned across his face. Close as they were, he caught all her scents: wool, tea, machine oil, cool air, and warm woman.

Pulling her up the ship hadn't raised his pulse. Now it thudded through him.

They stood like that for . . . he didn't know how long. Time drifted like the mists as he held her—the first woman in his arms in a long, long time. And he didn't know how long before the Battle of Liverpool she'd been embraced by a man, but the three months since must've felt lengthy to her, as her pupils were wide and dark, her breath not slowing, the flutter of her pulse in her neck speedy.

"Down, please," she rasped.

"Let go," he answered.

She seemed surprised that she continued to hold onto him. So they both unhooked their arms from each other awkwardly, and she slid rigidly down the length of his body. Tender and romantic, it wasn't, yet he'd had no choice but to feel her curves on her way down, and realize she didn't wear a corset.

As soon as her feet touched the deck, she stepped backward and made herself busy looking around. Looking everywhere but at him.

He'd no idea what to say. He hadn't been good at protocol before, and three months of living death hadn't helped his skills.

"Welcome aboard the *Persephone*," he finally muttered.

She walked the length of the deck, studying everything. The ship hadn't landed evenly, so the deck had a small tilt to it. As she examined the telumium panels mounted into the rail, her fingers tracing the punctures from ether bullets, he hovered close.

"You don't need to worry that I'll steal anything, Captain Fletcher," she said over her shoulder.

"I said not to call me *Captain*."

She faced him. "But you're the captain of this ship."

"*Was* the captain. Now it keeps me alive and I keep her from becoming an aviary." Yet even as he spoke, a bird landed on its nest, built on what had been the central support. "Seen enough?"

"Not yet. Besides," she added, hefting her satchel, "I've brought you a present, and it'd be the height of rudeness for me to leave before I gave it to you."

"Present?" When was the last time he'd gotten a gift?

Her mouth curled. "I thought it was something you could use out here, all alone."

"Tell me what it is." He reached for the satchel, and she held it out of his reach. Which wasn't entirely true, since taking it from her would've been absurdly easy. Yet something odd was happening in his chest. Something that felt vaguely familiar. Enjoyment.

"No present until I see it all."

He raised a brow. "We're talking about the ship, right?"

His odd enjoyment gleamed brighter as she actually blushed. Good to see that he unsettled her as much as she did him.

"The ship," she confirmed.

He debated a moment longer—there'd be no turning back once she went below decks and brought her bright energy into the place that he haunted—but he could see the bright curiosity in her eyes, and it pleased him.

Saying nothing, he walked to the companionway and she

followed. The stairs leading below were mostly intact. Despite her insistence that she could manage, he offered her his hand as she descended the steps. To his surprise, she actually took his assistance. She wasn't wearing gloves, and he didn't need to, and he tried not to think about the pleasure of holding her hand again, feeling its delicateness combined with strength. But he let go as soon as they reached the bottom of the companionway.

The passageway sloped to the right, but Kali walked carefully along it, keeping one hand braced against the bulkhead. He followed her gaze as she stared at the metal plates mounted along the bulkheads, small brass canisters were attached to some of them, and copper tubes leading away from the cylinders.

"Batteries," she said. "They power the turbines. And they draw their power from . . . you."

"I run the turbines at night when I'm on the ship to drain the batteries," he explained. "Keeps 'em from topping off."

"*That's* what I hear at night." Her fingers ran along the copper tubes. "I don't know what these do."

"Take ether generated from the batteries to tanks."

She frowned. "You're not flying anywhere."

"Most of the ether I release from the storage tanks, but I keep some of it saved for my weapons."

Kali fell quiet, and as they moved along the passageway, he watched her studying his ship. She winced at the damage the airship had taken, not just the splintered wood and bent metal, but the holes left by ether cannon blasts, the open cabin doors revealing quarters and other work and living spaces that had been smashed apart by enemy fire.

He nodded toward a cabin's open door. A large hole had been torn in the exterior, and the small room was empty. "These were Mayhew's quarters. A lieutenant who liked to tinker. Always spending his free time holed up in there, messing about with wires and gears. Nothing like what you do, though." He peered at the bare cabin. "All his tools and supplies are gone. You could've made use of them."

She patted her tool belt. "I wouldn't have come to this island without being well supplied."

Next, he pushed open the door leading to what had been the officers' wardroom. It still had some of the furniture, and an exterior wall, though the glass was missing from two of the portholes, and all the framed prints that had once hung upon the bulkheads now lay in a pile in a far corner beneath a film of dust.

"This is where the officers ate," he said.

Stepping to the table, she opened her satchel and removed a muslin bundle. Opening the bundle, she took out a small clockwork cricket. She turned the key, and the little mechanical insect hopped cheerfully. Its belly glowed softly, and every few moments, it chirped.

"Should I bother asking if that's your design?" he asked wryly.

"If it's ingenious," she replied, "it's mine. And I didn't bring anything that I didn't build or create."

He scooped up the cricket. A whimsical little thing. Purposeful in its jauntiness. The light from its belly illuminated the roughness of his palm. "This is my present. A child's toy."

Now she shrugged. "A little company is always welcome."

She looked at the broken chairs, the debris littered across the floor. "There were no other survivors."

"No." When she looked horrified, he added quickly, "I was the only one on board when she wrecked. I'd made everyone else abandon ship as soon as I saw she wasn't going to make it."

"You couldn't abandon ship, too?"

"Someone needed to pilot it, make sure it didn't crash into anywhere inhabited."

She stared at him. "But . . . you could've died."

"I did, in a way." He paced over to the heap of broken pictures in the corner and toed his boot through them. Prints of other airships and seafaring vessels—as though he or his officers would ever forget that they were in the navy. Maybe the men outfitting the ships thought images of land would make him and the rest of the crew long for things they couldn't have. But he never missed dry—or solid—land. His home had been the sea, and then the air.

From behind him, she murmured, "You must've been scared."

"As hell." He turned back to her. The ashen light through the portholes traced along the angles of her face, and the golden hoops in her ears. Women had seldom been aboard— the Aerial Navy had a strict policy about spouses on airships, and as the captain of the *Persephone*, he insisted his crew find their pleasures on land rather than bring hired companionship on board. Kali was incongruous here for many reasons.

"Wasn't much choice in the matter," he continued. "And I'd just been in battle. Death's always a possibility when engaging with the enemy. The biggest surprise came when I awoke after crashing." He glanced down at his shirt and coat, covering the telumium plate on his pectoral. "We're durable, us Man O' Wars." But he needed to stay dead. A fate he'd learned not just to accept, but embrace.

Except when she'd arrived on the island. Then his heart had begun to beat again. It had always beat, but now, now . . . he felt the chill of his self-dug grave begin to dissipate every moment in her presence.

"Battle," she mused, walking toward the portholes. She lightly touched the empty brass frames. "And you crashed here three months ago."

He waited. It was only a matter of minutes before she understood.

No, he was wrong. It was a matter of seconds, because she whirled back to face him, color leeching once more from her cheeks.

"You were there at Liverpool," she said quietly.

He nodded.

Her gaze was hot. "You said nothing earlier."

"I didn't know what . . ." He dragged his hands through his hair. "It's not a topic that's easy to breach. And I thought that you wouldn't be much pleased with me if you knew." As if her opinion of him meant something.

"Why the hell not?" She took a step forward, eyes snapping electric fire.

He glanced down at her leg.

She snorted. "As though I'd blame you for that. This"—she tapped the artificial limb beneath her skirts—"was a gift from the Hapsburgs and the Russians when they attacked. I'd probably be dead if the navy hadn't shown. There wouldn't have been any medical teams looking for survivors." Still, she continued to scowl. "Gods and goddesses, it confounds me that you'd think I'd be angry."

Strange. He'd faced brutal combat on sea and in the air, had undergone the incredibly lengthy and painful process of becoming a Man O' War, and had stared down death dozens of times. Yet the potent force of this one woman actually made him edgy, gave him an uncertainty he'd never once known.

"I thought maybe you'd blame us for not getting there sooner. Not doing enough. For being the cause of your loss."

"From the enemy's first fusillade to the appearance of the navy," she argued, "it was a matter of hours. You couldn't have gotten to Liverpool much sooner. As for not doing enough"— she shook her head—"when I was able to watch the skies, I saw the skirmishes. It made me dread the airships. But I also saw the British aerial fleet trying to save the ports, pushing the Hapsburgs and Russians away from civilian targets. One British ship deliberately took Russian fire to keep them from dropping bombs on one of the worst slums in the city. I saw it."

He smiled mirthlessly. "Then we've already met."

Her scowl dropped away. "That was your ship? *This* ship?"

"The same."

"You must've realized that Valentine Grove was just a slum. But you saved it anyway."

He glanced away, then back. "Lives are lives."

Several moments passed with her simply staring at him, looking baffled, angry, awed. Suddenly, she strode out of the wardroom. He set down the cricket, then followed at a distance, not trying to catch her, even when she clambered up the companionway. But when she reached the top deck, instead of trying to scramble down the side, she paced what was left of the quarterdeck. He stood near the ramshackle remains of the pilot's house, watching her. At least she no longer looked frightened of the airship.

"Both of us there," she muttered. "Both of us here. *Kismat?* Is something written in our astrological charts? Fate?"

Though she spoke under her breath to herself, he could still hear every word as if spoken plainly.

"Coincidence, not fate," he said, causing her to stop in her pacing. "A string of choices we both made and now here we are." He spread his hands, taking in the deck of the downed airship, the moors rolling all around them, and the whole of the island, set apart from the world. "You're a woman of science. You know fate or kismat or whatever word you want to call it doesn't exist."

She stalked to him. "Tell me. Everything."

He didn't want to speak of it, to think of those last few hours of his life before he'd come here, to this rocky, wind-swept hereafter.

It was clear she wouldn't be put off. May as well rip the plaster off and get it over with, he thought.

Most of the forecastle had broken apart when the ship had crashed, but enough remained for him to stride to it. He rested his boot on the bottom of the rail and looked out over the moorland as if they were waves or the tops of clouds.

"I was at Greenwich when the telegram came," he said. "The enemy had taken too many defeats—an important munitions plant destroyed a year ago, the failed attempts at incursion in the United States—and they wanted to strike a devastating assault against us. Hurt us. Make a statement. So they went for our most important port: Liverpool. Any airship stationed in Britain was dispatched. We got there as soon as we could, but the enemy had worked fast. Half the city was gone by the time the *Persephone* arrived."

"*My* half," she said, coming to stand behind him. "My offices were near the docks."

He cursed lowly. The docks had been one of the hardest hit. Even from the height of his airship, he'd smelled the burning wood and charred flesh. And she'd been there, in the thick of it. Her leg crushed and death all around her.

He wouldn't have been able to help her, or the people at her offices. The damage had been wrought. Slim comfort in that knowledge, though.

Thoughts like that had haunted him since he'd crashed here. They were always close, like whispers in corners.

"We did what we could to minimize civilian casualties," he said. "That meant chasing the Huns and Russians away from the city, so if their airships crashed, they wouldn't do it on anyone below. The *Persephone* went after a Russian cruiser. Herded the ship north. But we took heavy damage in the pursuit."

He turned his gaze skyward, his mind conjuring images of the Russian ship ablaze, and the ghostly picture of his own airship, barely holding together as she hunted her prey.

"The Russian ship broke apart over the sea in the Inner Hebrides," he went on. "It wouldn't be much longer before the *Persephone* met the same fate. But I had to save my crew and keep the airship from hitting any settlements. So I made them abandon ship."

"And then you were alone," she said quietly.

"A Man O' War is never alone, so long as he's got his ship. Like a married couple, we are."

"So you and your *wife* crashed together. Here."

"Romantic, wouldn't you say?" His smile felt wry while his insides turned cold. "She dies, I die."

"Except neither of you died." She nodded toward the turbines. "I can still hear her humming, and her lights shine at night."

"She'll never fly again," he said. "Poor lady. A bird with her wings clipped. Not much of an existence for an airship. And me . . ." He stared down at his hands. "I'm living," he conceded, "but not."

She eyed him. "You're breathing, talking. Eating. You seem alive to me."

"That's *survival*, but not living." He knocked his fist against the rail. "We're two wrecks who'll never take to the sky again. Which is how it ought to be."

Her brow furrowed at his words, but he didn't want to explain himself.

"There had to be some way to signal for help," she insisted.

"Not many telegraph poles out here."

She threw him a look that said his sarcasm wasn't appreciated.

"All I could do was wait for rescue," he said at last. He looked up at the sky again. "It never came."

"That doesn't make any sense," she complained. "Whatever crew survived abandoning ship had to have made their way back to the Admiralty and give them an idea as to where you'd be."

He shrugged. "If they did, they were worse navigators than I'd believed. Because no airships or seafaring vessels ever came. I was marooned."

"What about swimming to the nearest inhabited island? Man O' Wars are famed for their strength and stamina. I know you can't be away from a battery for too long, not without consequences, but surely a half day's swim to Vatersay and then another day for an airship to retrieve you could be possible."

"Possible, aye."

"Maybe you didn't want to risk it," she said, half to herself. "But," she added, brightening, "the ferryman comes back in three weeks. He can take you to South Uist, and you'll be back in Greenwich in a day."

"There's the catch, Kali m'dear." He gazed at her. "I don't want to go back."

CHAPTER FIVE

"Stay?" Kali asked. She took in the rocky, barren moor, the half-destroyed airship. "Why?"

His expression darkened. "You going to berate me? Shame me for dereliction of duty?"

"I only asked *why*. If you're looking for someone to tell you to rejoin the world," she answered, "you'll have to search elsewhere."

Leaning against the rail, he studied her, his arms crossed over his wide chest. He looked at her as one ghost might recognize another, two spirits passing through the realm of the living, unseen to everyone but other phantoms.

A need welled up in her. Words and images and memories demanding to be let out, when they'd been held inside for so long in a death's grip. In her telegraphs and letters home, she'd been elliptical in her language, sparing her parents the horror of what she'd seen. And there'd been no one left in Liverpool she could speak with—no one she trusted, anyway. There had been brusque, weary doctors and sad-eyed nurses who'd come up from London when most of the medical professionals in Liverpool had been killed. Even hospitals hadn't been spared from the destruction.

How do you feel, Miss MacNeil? Is there anything you'd like to talk about?

I'm perfectly well, she'd always answered. *There's nothing I want to discuss.*

She'd lived, hadn't she? No cause for complaint. But she knew no one would understand. Not even other survivors.

As she'd recovered, she forced herself into numbness. Retreating farther and farther from the world. Talking less. Wincing at the slightest sound. Keeping herself locked tight as a strongbox.

Yet she could speak to Fletcher. He knew. He understood.

She walked along the tilted, partially shattered deck, trying to divert her attention with the embedded panels and their levers and switches, one part of her speaking, the other part distracting herself by attempting to figure out the functions of all the technology on the airship. "The enemy airships were spotted just after luncheon," she said. Her voice sounded far away. "They came in so suddenly, no one thought to take shelter in the basement. People actually stood out in the street and stared at the sky. Nobody could believe that the Hapsburgs and Russians would do more than fire on the shipyards and docks. From my office window, I could see them, the workers hurrying away, probably thinking they'd be safe if they got away from the water. But they weren't. None of us were."

She crouched next to a panel that must have at one time directed more power into the turbines. Without any crew to tend to it, the brass had tarnished, and her reflection in the metal was muddy.

"I heard this . . . whistling . . . from above," she continued, pulling on the useless levers. "But I couldn't believe it. There'd been rumors about experiments with shells and other explosive devices dropped from airships onto the ground. Not just firefights between ships, but actually attacking whatever was below. Factories or military installations. Yet I never believed it. Surely wars couldn't be fought in such an . . . inhumane way. So detached and callous."

"It's a modern era." He spoke with no inflection. "Enemies have always tried to pretend that whoever they fought wasn't human. It's even easier to do that from a mile above a city."

She stared at him. "Tell me that the British Aerial Navy isn't doing that."

His expression was granite. "There've been arguments on both sides about aerial bombing. No conclusions. Yet."

That was something of a relief.

"So you heard them," he pressed. "The bombs."

She plunged back into that day. How innocuously it had started. She'd dressed and eaten a breakfast of tea and toast with no thought to what might happen in a few hours. Wasn't that the way of disaster? It never announced itself well in advance, but like a rude guest, it simply arrived. But this rude guest didn't demand tea and biscuits when there weren't any. This guest tore one's life apart. Or ended it.

"I saw these . . . things . . . falling from the sky. From the enemy airships. And wherever they landed, buildings exploded. I'd experienced earthquakes in Nagpur. Nothing felt like this. The ground shaking. Fire like Hell itself opening up. People screaming and running in every direction. In my offices, we tried to be calm, get out of the building as quickly and orderly as we could. But while we gathered to evacuate . . ." She swallowed past the bile in her throat. "The bomb struck."

She shook her head, staring at the broken panel in front of her. "It didn't make any sense. We were a civilian corporation. Maybe we handled a few military commissions, but not enough to make us a threat. That's what I was thinking as the walls blasted apart and I saw my friends, my colleagues, crushed by debris or literally torn apart. *This doesn't make any sense.*" A harsh rasp resembling a laugh clawed from her. "As if logic had any business in Liverpool that day."

She started at the feel of Fletcher's warm, large hand upon her shoulder. A tentative touch. He didn't know how to offer comfort, but did what he could. Somehow, that uncertainty soothed her even more than practiced words or rehearsed gestures.

Clearing her throat, she went on. "I won't bore you with the rest of the day. I spent most of it pinned beneath a collapsed wall, with a view of the city being destroyed, and my ears full of the groans of my friends, my co-workers, and strangers, all dying. Stayed conscious long enough to see the British ships arrive and light into the enemy. I saw you," she said, glancing up with a tiny smile, which he didn't return. "The sun began to set, and there was so much smoke and particulate in the air. It was one of the most beautiful sunsets I'd ever seen. As if the sky was gold, the clouds amethyst and topaz and smoky onyx. After that, I lost consciousness. I woke up in a field hospital, with my leg gone and the city finally quiet."

She resisted the impulse to rub at her left thigh, which ached from time to time, as if to remind her of what had been lost.

"The doctors told me I'd lain unconscious for three days," she said flatly. "I'd been out of my head with fever. Nobody from Drogin & Daughters had survived. Just me. When I was well enough, a nurse took me in a wheelchair to the Blue-coat Chambers—one of the last major buildings still standing. Lists of the dead had been posted there. On the way, I saw what had happened to the city. It was . . . a ruin. Almost nothing left. The streets still smoking, days later. There were people digging through rubble to look for survivors and bodies. Fights broke out over crusts of bread and cupfuls of water. What the enemy hadn't destroyed, we did ourselves. We turned to animals. Worse than animals."

"The lists?" Fletcher asked gently, his hand still upon her shoulder.

"They looked like banners. Sheets and sheets of paper with the names of the dead, flapping in the wind, torn and dirty from being handled by so many. Everyone who looked at them turned away with tears in their eyes. I wasn't any different." She blinked hard and ran her sleeve across her face.

"Kali—"

She pushed his hand off of her shoulder. "As soon as I could, as soon as I made my leg, I left. I wouldn't go to London or Manchester or Birmingham. I couldn't go back to India and let my parents coddle me back into infancy. So I found the one place I'd be alone. Or *thought* I'd be alone," she added, gazing at him. He stared back at her, and though he made no more moves to touch her or speak, his eyes glinted. Not with pity—which she would've rejected—or sadness. No, what she saw reflected back in his gaze was . . . respect. Understanding. And anger.

"Weeks I waited," he said after a moment. "Thought for certain that if the navy didn't come looking for me, they'd want to at least recover what remained of the *Persephone*. Not cheap, these airships, and there'd be enough to salvage. They wouldn't want the enemy to get hold of one of our ships, either. Give them too much information."

"But no one came." She rubbed her hands together—the sun dipped lower, and the temperature dropped as violet shadows stretched across the moor.

When he reached for her arm, she didn't pull away. Instead, she let him take her back down the stairs, into the passageways beneath the top deck. They went down several more levels in the airship, and he helped her over the debris and wreckage—wooden planks, metal panels, bits of machinery, plates and cups, clothing. A small attempt had been made to clear away some of the detritus, but those efforts must have been restricted to pushing the biggest items off to the sides of the corridors, leaving a kind of path through the ruins. Men had worked and dwelled here, likely some had died, and now it was broken and littered with the remains of lives.

A ghost ship.

Haunted by the living.

Fletcher reached the end of a corridor and pushed a door open. The chamber inside had to have been his quarters, since it was a generous room that covered the width of the ship. Large windows faced the back, though the glass had all broken. The furniture was minimal—a repaired desk, a tilting bookcase holding a few volumes. A bolted-down bed stood near a bulkhead, blankets strewn across it. Some articles of clothing draped over a chair. One of his shirts looked big enough to use as a sail.

She felt herself unaccountably flustered. This was where he slept. He'd made it as domestic as possible—though it still had the air of an animal's den.

He left her standing in the middle of the chamber and walked to the windows. Crouched just beneath the empty panes was an iron stove. The chimney poked out the window. It was unlit, but in a matter of moments, Fletcher had a goodly peat fire burning. She stepped to it and warmed her hands, waiting for him to speak again.

"Better?" he asked.

She nodded. More silence fell.

"Nobody appeared," he finally said. He watched the flames through the stove's grate. "I thought it strange, but figured either they were too busy finishing off the enemy, or they assumed I was lying at the bottom of the Sea of the Hebrides. So I started to think of all the ways off the island, just like you said. A swim would be arduous, but possible."

"Or you could build a boat."

His teeth flashed in a white smile. "I'm a better swimmer than boat builder."

"But you're the captain of this ship," she objected.

"Didn't build it, only commanded it. Same when I was a seaman. I knew the ways of a seafaring ship, but not the making of one. We had carpenters for that."

She glanced around at his quarters. "From what I've seen, I could put together a boat for you in a matter of days."

Again, he smiled, and it lit a small flare in her chest. "I didn't have you around then. It was either swim for it, or stay. But as I started thinking, planning, figuring out which would be the best direction to head in, I realized something."

"You were afraid of water," she guessed.

"Been in the navy for twenty-two years. Sixteen of those years were at sea. Water doesn't scare me." He shook his head, his expression thoughtful. "I hadn't actually survived the crash. Like you said, I lived. My heart beat. I needed food and sometimes sleep. But the man I'd been had died in the wreck. And I was glad of it."

He paused, as though waiting for her to object, but she didn't. Only felt his words like a chilled wind. One that had scoured her own heart many times.

When she said nothing, he went on. "I thought, didn't I owe it to Britain to find my way back? We'd beaten the enemy badly at Liverpool, but they could always rally. Man O' Wars aren't like spare pairs of shoes just lying around. There aren't many of us, and we cost a bloody fortune to make. We're powerful weapons in this war. Britain couldn't afford to lose me."

There was no arrogance or boasting in his words. He stated a simple truth. Even civilians like Kali knew the importance of Man O' Wars. Only they could power and captain airships, and the Mechanized War would only be won in the air.

"But they needed to lose me," he went on, his gaze distant. "When I first became a Man O' War, it was . . . the greatest honor. Not everyone thought so." A shadow crossed his face.

She'd read a handful of newspaper opinion pieces that decried Man O' Wars as abominations, unnatural farragoes of man and machine. Yet she knew he wasn't speaking of those faceless newspaper hacks stirring up sentiment for the sake of readership. Someone close to Fletcher had hurt him after his transformation. Family? A sweetheart?

But she kept silent. He wouldn't want to speak of that now.

"I threw myself into being a Man O' War," he continued, his voice sounding hollow. "It was all I had. Fought in God knows how many battles. All of them brutal. And I started to wonder . . . were we the cause?"

"We?"

"Man O' Wars. Truth is, we're just weapons. Bringers of death and destruction. The whole damn war wouldn't exist if it wasn't for us. Nations want telumium to create more Man O' Wars, so they fight over territory with telumium deposits. But they need Man O' Wars to do the fighting. A goddamn unending cycle."

His jaw tightened. "Liverpool just proved what I'd come to believe. Man O' Wars are the bloody problem. *We're* the danger."

She stared at him. "You and the other British Man O' Wars, you *saved* Liverpool. Without you, no one would've survived."

Yet her words seemed to glance off him like gravel thrown at the hull of an ironclad. "The battle never would've happened if Man O' Wars didn't exist. I didn't think I'd survive the *Persephone* crashing. But when I did, and when no rescue came . . . it was for the best. If I went back, if I rejoined the fight, how many more would die?" He shook his head. "Better that I stay here. One less weapon. One less chance for someone to meet their death at the hands of my kind. So I needed to stay dead, and so I have."

Angry pain glinted in his eyes. Rage directed at himself. An ache spread from her heart, radiating through her.

Words seemed useless. Liverpool had stolen everything. Her leg, her sense of self. It had taken from him, too. They were both empty husks. And yet ... when she was with him ... she didn't feel quite as empty. As though their hollowness somehow created substance. Two negatives making a positive.

Despite what he said, energy pulsed around him. He wasn't dead. He was alive and vital, and there was a sympathy between them, a shared understanding. And that roused sensations within her.

But she didn't want to feel anything. It was easier, safer, to be numb.

Whirling away from the stove, she strode to a different window and looked out. "The sun's going down. I shouldn't be out after dark." She glanced out at the distance from the window to the ground. Less than six feet, since the remainder of the lower decks had been crushed.

She checked to make sure there was no glass left in the window casing. Then sat herself on the sill and swung her legs around, so she faced the outside. Fletcher made no noise of complaint or move to stop her.

"I'm not going to disturb your peace again," she said. "It's scientific method, really. Try something, and if it fails, you move on. Repeating a failed experiment is just an exercise in folly."

And then she dropped to the ground. The landing wasn't

as smooth as she would've liked, her artificial leg taking the impact hard, but she didn't fall and she could walk, and she wasn't on his ship anymore, in his presence. Sensing his energy, feeling herself being pulled back from the realm of shadows into the light.

Without looking back at him, she strode away from the ship. Back to safety.

Kali stood on the rocky beach, watching the waves curl and tumble onto the shore. The water was the color of blued steel, the sky the hue of pale ash. She didn't know how long she'd been standing here. Minutes. Hours.

Answers and calm were always found at her worktable, or as she sketched and planned ideas for new devices. But since yesterday, it was as though her eyes and mind couldn't focus. They'd try to sharpen on a particular issue related to a design, then blur. In frustration, she'd abandoned her work—it wasn't as though anyone was waiting for it, or she had deadlines to meet—and done something she hadn't done in a long while. Deliberately let her thoughts drift.

Her mother used to take her to Maharaj Baug garden when she'd grow too monomaniacal about her schoolwork and extracurricular projects. Maa' had always hoped that the lush garden would distract her, or calm her fevered brain.

When your thoughts are like a monsoon, Maa' had said, *remember, there is more to this world than the one inside your head.*

Her poor mother, saddled with not just an engineer for a husband, but a daughter who also lived most of her life within the confines of her mind. Maa' had done her best, and Kali usually returned from their outings to Maharaj Baug with a brain that, if not entirely calm, had settled somewhat.

She tried to find that peace now, but she couldn't forget yesterday's surprises. Fletcher, a Man O' War. Who had also been at the battle of Liverpool. Who'd given his life for his country. As he'd said, to the British Aerial Navy, he was a dead man. And he'd decided to stay dead—for the safety of others.

The biggest revelation of all had been the discovery of what tied them together. Not simply his presence at Liverpool, but that they were each, in their way, only partially living. They shared a connection, when she'd run from them so fiercely.

Bending down, she gathered up handfuls of rocks. One by one, she tossed them into the sea, testing how far she could throw them. Each splash punctuated her thoughts.

She couldn't blame him for wanting to stay dead. After what she'd seen, what she'd endured, she herself wanted nothing to do with the world. A Man O' War might be enhanced through technology, but they were still men, with needs and fears and hearts—even if those hearts had telumium filaments attached to them. He hadn't questioned her own need to flee from the world. And if he so firmly believed he was only a weapon, what could she say to convince him otherwise? The damage he bore went much deeper than Liverpool. There was that someone who'd damaged him, planting the seeds of his self-hatred. Seeds that had taken root and grown into a thick, twisted vine, knotted around him, binding him.

Both Kali and Fletcher had hidden themselves away, each of them the walking wounded.

They were fugitives.

The stones in her hands were worn smooth by countless years of rolling up and down the beach, tumbling in the surf. After so long handling metal and wire, it was primal and satisfying to touch organic material, something created not by man but the earth itself. So easy to forget that this planet would outlast them all, and all their buildings and technology would crumble and rust long before the earth stopped existing.

She didn't know what to do with the feelings he stirred in her. This wasn't a simple problem of getting a tetrol-powered ship-loading device to work. There weren't clear answers, defined methodologies. No flow chart telling her *If A, then B. If C, then D.*

Crouching down, Kali arranged the stones in order—largest to smallest. Then by color. Then shape. This she could control, but her own heart proved maddeningly unruly. Anger and grief . . . even threads of happiness deluged her, as if months of packed away emotions all rose up at once.

Standing, she kicked the orderly rows of stones apart.

Damn it, he did *this. He made me feel* again.

And they were bound together. Through circumstance and history. Through an invisible link that made her acutely aware of him. And being in his company gave her an odd, unexpected pleasure. He was gruff. Unmannerly, at times. But he never treated her with pity after he'd learned about her leg. He'd shown up with dead rabbits to make sure she had enough to eat. He had no obligation to her, but he'd done her a kindness.

His sense of humor was dry enough to soak up an oil spill, and she liked that. No desire to bend over backwards to please someone. *Take me as I am*, he seemed to say, *and I'll do the same for you.*

Not many had offered her the same acceptance. Even the men she'd taken as lovers had tried to shape her in subtle, small ways. How to wear her hair. Suggesting that she not talk of her mother's Hindu beliefs—superstition had no place in the modern world, and it only reinforced the fact that Kali had mixed blood. As though her skin wasn't damning evidence enough.

Those men hadn't shared her bed for long. Better to be alone than endure that kind of gentle, well-meaning idiocy.

Looking at the waves hadn't calmed her. Nothing had. Before she'd lost her leg, she'd taken walks to clear the whirlwinds in her mind. Her pace might've slowed since, but it could feel good to let her body take over and give in to the sensation of muscles moving, heart pumping, blood coursing through her. So she turned away from the beach and climbed the slope toward the cottage. Then kept going.

She knew the island better now, and she was getting stronger and more used to her artificial leg. So she found herself in short order by the pond that marked the midway point between her cottage and Fletcher's ship.

It surprised her and it didn't surprise her to discover he was already there. He'd fashioned a fishing pole from materials salvaged off his ship, and a pile of small silver fish lay in the grass beside his boots. He didn't move at her approach.

Doubtless he'd heard her coming from a mile away, with his acute hearing, and the fact that her leg made her less than gazelle-like.

From a distance, she was struck anew by his size. Either he'd been a big man before he'd undergone the Man O' War procedure, or something about the process had transformed him. But she'd never seen a man so physically imposing. The wild hair and beard only added to the sense of barely tamed power he exuded.

Though it wasn't necessary, she approached him slowly, as one might sidle closer to a tiger. She positioned herself on the other side of the pond.

"Will it scare the fish if I talk?" she asked quietly.

"Only if you talk while jumping into the pond."

"I haven't tested my leg in full immersion, so that's an unlikely scenario."

"Then chatter as much as you want." His voice was deep and unyielding, his expression opaque. He didn't look at her.

She was silent for a moment. "I left quickly yesterday. Rudely."

Finally, he raised his gaze to hers. "It wasn't rude."

"I jumped out of your ship and ran away," she said drily. She contemplated the surface of the water, green and murky. "Though I'm not much of an expert on etiquette, that seems to qualify as unmannerly."

"That rot doesn't matter out here." The line on his fishing pole tugged, and for a moment, he was busy pulling a fish from the water. He held it up, wriggling, on the end of his line. The creature was miniscule, barely the size of a child's finger. With a sigh, he unhooked the fish and tossed it back into the pond.

"Hardly a nibble, that one," he muttered.

"Those others don't look much bigger." She glanced at the fish he'd already caught.

"But they aren't all bone. Don't fancy choking on my supper." He cast his line back into the water. For several moments, the only sounds came from the drone of insects hovering over the pond and the rustle of wind in the treetops.

Then, "Think I know why you ran," he muttered. "Yesterday. It's . . . not easy. Being who we are. Living through what we have. And then have it all come back, right in your face, like a keg of powder exploding."

"Did it for you?" she asked quietly. "Explode?"

He gave one terse nod. "I could put it all away when I was alone. Forget, in a way, what I was. But then you showed up. Now . . ." He exhaled. "There were crewmen's bodies that were still aboard when I crashed, I buried them in the woods behind the ship. Hadn't visited their graves since that day, but after you'd left, I went to them." His voice roughened. "Pulled up some weeds. Said a prayer."

She hadn't noticed the graves the other day, but she hadn't gone into the woods to see them, either. It wouldn't be a pleasant task, digging the final resting places for one's crew. Men who you'd commanded, perhaps even took them into the paths of their deaths.

She couldn't imagine that responsibility—the lives of dozens, perhaps even a hundred men, balanced in her hands. And then all the lives he'd saved by facing and hunting the enemy. Though he didn't see it that way.

"In Liverpool, there were too many dead to bury them individually," she answered. "Mass graves were dug, with granite laid over them, and all the names of the dead carved there. Crudely. Before I left, I'd heard plans to bring in marble to replace the granite, and a craftsman to inscribe the names of the deceased. But money and supplies are in short supply. It might never happen. It's a resting place, at least." She looked at him. "There would've been many more graves if you hadn't been there. My own, perhaps."

He didn't answer her. Only gave a barely noticeable shake of his head, as if dismissing her words.

They were quiet for a time. Until he said lowly, "I like the cricket."

Chips of ice fell away from around her heart, imagining the large, powerful Man O' War with the little clockwork toy. "Don't overwind it," she cautioned, "or it'll break."

"If it does, maybe you'll come and fix it," he said with the tone of a man unused to uncertainty.

She skirted the pond until she stood beside him. "It might need maintenance, too. Not just repair."

Again, he fell into silence. Either he was a taciturn man by nature, or these solitary months had taught it to him. "That would be . . . good. The mechanics and engineers on the ship, they were always busy with maintenance. Kept her flying smooth."

"That's a good plan." She tilted her head. "I think you and I might . . . become friends."

One of his brows rose. "Think, but don't know."

"It's just a theory, at this point." After Liverpool, she hadn't wanted friends. She hadn't wanted anything but solitude and survival. Yet talking with him now, she craved more than that. "The best way to test a theory is through experimentation. So, we'll conduct some experiments."

"I've already been someone's experiment," he said, glancing at his chest. "The end result was a disaster."

"These experiments will be much more pleasant," she answered. "And they'll have a far different outcome. We'll start tomorrow. Meet me here at noon. And bring an ether rifle."

Chapter Six

Just as she'd promised, Fletcher found Kali at the pond at noon the following day. She checked her timepiece as he approached, his ether rifle slung across his back.

"You're late," she said.

"Since the crash, I keep track of time as the Creator intended." He glanced up at the watery sun, then back at her. Today she wore her dark blue dress, the one with two rows of buckles along the bodice, and a round collar that gave the smallest glimpse of the dip of her throat. Her belt with tools and pouches slung around her hips, and she also wore her compass gauntlet. Ready for anything.

"In Liverpool, it was all regulated time," she answered. "The horns of ships as they steamed into the harbor told us what time and day it was. It was so strange when those horns stopped." A shadow passed over her face, but it was brief. "I suppose I ought to get used to Eilean Comhachag time."

He strode toward her. "And I've got to get used to the island having a name. Always thought of it as *this place* or *this rock*."

Though his implants made him less susceptible to cold, her smile still warmed him. "It's a good thing you were never a cartographer. 'Where are you from?' 'Over There-istan.'"

His brief laugh surprised them both. It felt and sounded like long-rusted machinery grinding back to life. "Buckinghamshire," he said, before clamping his mouth shut. *Jesus, where the hell did that come from?*

Silence fell.

"Though," she continued, glancing up at him with her impossibly deep brown eyes, "we don't really know each other's names, either. Your crewmen didn't call you Fletcher."

"That'd be insubordination and subject to punishment."

She looked appalled. "I can't believe you'd flog anyone."

"Flogging and whipping were halted decades ago—doesn't stop some captains, though. I didn't flog my men, but a good captain can't let misconduct slide. Makes the whole ship unsafe."

"Sensible," she murmured. It caught him off guard, how much he didn't want her disapproval. As though her opinion of him mattered. Yet it did. She wasn't disgusted by the fact that he was a Man O' War. A look of horror hadn't crossed her face.

He'd never forget that expression Emily had when he'd revealed his transformation to her. The absolute revulsion.

My God, what are you?

He pushed Emily's face and voice from his mind. There was one woman, at least, who didn't consider him a monstrosity, and he stood with her now.

"Usually," he said, "I'd make them pump out and clean the septic tanks instead of having the automatons do it, or scrape the copper dust buildup from the battery terminals."

"And order was restored." She nodded. "I like order, myself."

"Can't build anything mechanical if everything's a muddle."

She smiled again. "So you understand." While he warmed further from another of her smiles, her gaze narrowed. "Despite the damage taken to your ship, it looked like it had been clean and orderly. And that's because of the captain. So you like to be in control. In command."

Straightforward words, but the faint husky tone that crept into her voice, and the glint in her eyes gave them a rosy suggestiveness.

"I do." His voice had deepened. "It's why I was such a good captain."

Her cheeks flushed. The air shifted between them, tensing with dangerous promise.

Haven't seen a woman in three months, and haven't touched one in six, at least. No shock that she'd get under your skin.

That's not the reason, and you damned know it. It's her. This thing linking us.

Pale sunlight gleamed on her silky black hair, and her slim fingers toyed with the pouches on her belt. Her belt slung low on her hips, emphasizing their curves.

What would her skin feel like? Her hands were callused, but she wasn't a laborer. He'd felt strength in her arm when he'd held it, and when she'd been in his arms she . . .

He shook his head. They might not be the last two people on Earth, but they were the only two on this island. All the more reason not to entertain thoughts about her skin, or her body, or the intellect shining in her eyes that could be applied to more than just mechanical engineering.

Even before he'd undergone his change into a Man O' War, he'd been an oaf where women were concerned. Oh, he was confident and brash on the ship, but not on land. Not with the ladies. Never said the charming thing. The clever thing. Just blurted and blundered. His first mate had ribbed him relentlessly whenever they'd had shore leave and Fletcher would yet again botch talking to a lady. Then he'd met Emily, and he thought he'd found the one woman who made him feel comfortable. He could be himself when he was with her. But the implants changed all that. After her, he knew he could never have a woman of his own. He didn't socialize at assemblies, and found ways out of invitations to events where ladies would be present.

It was easier, safer to pay for female company than risk heartbreak. Even then, he made sure to visit the courtesans that specialized in attending to Man O' Wars. None of them had been taken aback by his size, his power. But then, they were paid professionals.

He didn't want to think of those women. He didn't want to think of Emily. Not when he was with Kali.

Fletcher was growing to care for her. He didn't want to scuttle the friendship they'd just started, all on account of the wreck that had been his intimate life.

She cleared her throat. "Let's head toward the moors. I've got use for you."

His goddamn heart beat hard at those words, but he only nodded and trekked toward the rolling fields.

"Did you bring your ether rifle?" she asked as they ambled. He had to adjust his stride, shortening it so they could keep pace. He noticed it more now, the slight hitch in her step as she walked, especially when she tried to go faster. He short-ened his gait even more.

He tugged on the strap slung across his chest. "Planning on shooting me with it?"

"Not *you*, no." Then she glanced down at his legs, and scowled. "Don't do that."

"Do what?"

"Change the way you walk on my account. I can keep up." As if to prove it, she strode ahead. But she tilted as she walked.

He caught up easily. "You'll wear yourself out."

Her expression was set, determined. "I can't get stronger if I coddle myself."

"It's not coddling," he growled. "It's being smart. You've got new equipment. Things aren't going to be the same for you anymore."

She stopped in her tracks and glared up at him with fierce resolve. "Thank you kindly for pointing out that I'm crippled. I would've forgotten, otherwise."

"That's not what I said, bloody woman." Most people would be afraid to stand toe-to-toe with a Man O' War, but she didn't back down. Neither did he. "I've had crewmen who've lost legs, arms. They still do their duties, and no one thinks less of them. But they make adjustments. And it takes more than three damn months to get used to the changes. You push yourself too hard, you'll burn out like a turbine running too fast."

Her expression became tetchy. "I can't get stronger if I don't test myself."

"Never said not to test yourself. But don't try to keep up

with me, because you can't." He glanced away. "Nobody can. Except other Man O' Wars. *We're* the strange ones." He'd always gotten looks whenever he was off his ship, and crewmen with no experience with Man O' Wars gaped like children at a clockwork menagerie. It wasn't difficult for him to command a ship, but he didn't like attention in other ways, coming to reinforce what he'd started to believe about himself and those like him—that they were oddities, aberrations.

Finally, quietly, she said, "All kinds of things in this world are strange. But they're a hell of a lot more interesting than the mundane."

Something eased in his chest, as if bolts had been loosened.

She grinned suddenly. "Do you know what they call a woman with one leg?"

"Peg," he answered.

She scowled. "If you steal my punch lines, then we most assuredly can't be friends."

"Promise to let you get in the last word." He pressed a hand to his chest.

"Good."

He added, "Next time."

She laughed again, and they resumed walking, this time at a more moderate pace.

Sometimes, on airships, they had to vent the ether tanks in order to make a fast escape from the enemy, or to give chase at a quicker speed. But venting the tanks always meant the ship dropped steeply as it shot forward. It was a sensation that took getting used to, but he learned to like it, the drop and plunge forward. Being with Kali felt almost exactly the same way, as if at any moment he could crash or fly.

"This should do it," she said.

Fletcher glanced around. They stood in the middle of the moors, the *Persephone* a dropped toy in the distance. Twenty-five yards to the right of the airship rose a copse of trees. The moors remained as empty as always, only scrub and rock and stretches of nothing—a landscape he'd come to enjoy. But as to what he and Kali were doing there now, he'd no idea.

"Time to let me in on your plan," he said.

She pointed to the ether rifle hanging on his back. "I want to fire that."

He was starting to get used to her enigmatic turns of thought, but this still caught him off guard. "First time we met, you had a Webley in your belt and a double-barreled coach gun on your back. You seem well-armed to me."

Spreading her hands, she said, "There's a reason I didn't bring any of my guns today. I've never fired an ether-powered firearm."

"And you want a go at mine."

"Like I said, I've never shot an ether rifle before. They usually don't put them in civilian hands."

"Because they're sodding dangerous if you're not trained to use them."

"So train me."

He tried to think of all the reasons why he shouldn't. Most civilians couldn't be trusted with the might of an ether-powered gun, but she wasn't most civilians. She wasn't much like anybody he'd ever met. "There's no need. You'll never own an ether pistol."

"Probably not." She shrugged. "But don't you ever want an experience just to have it?"

He felt himself reluctantly smiling. "Didn't join the navy for the handsome pay."

"A farm boy wanting to see the world?"

The idea of him on a farm made Fletcher snort. "More like a factory boy from Wycombe turning chairs who wanted to see the world." As she continued to look at him, a hint of entreaty in her gaze, he scratched thoughtfully at his beard. He couldn't fault her for wanting to try something new. "There're women who can shoot ether-powered weapons—intelligence agents, mostly—but they're also taught how to balance their lighter weight against the guns' kick. It'll knock you on your arse if you aren't strong enough. Or if your balance isn't altogether there, both feet planted firmly on the ground."

Her mouth firmed into a line. But at least she didn't seem insulted. Then her lips softened. "We'll compromise, then. You stand behind me, brace me, and if I get knocked back, you keep me from falling on my arse."

Hell. Hearing her say that word shot heat through him. Forced him to think about what kind of arse she had. If it was rounded or had a subtle curve. And if she had those intriguing little dents just at the base of her spine. Walters, his first mate, had once called them *dimples of Venus.* A bit of a poet and a self-made aesthete, that Walters.

Fletcher ought to refuse. He'd be rattled like a sail in a typhoon if he had to press himself tight against her.

Then again . . . he wasn't an idiot, either.

"You do everything I say," he said sternly as he handed her the ether rifle.

She took the gun, giving him a salute. "Of course, Captain Fletcher."

"To start, don't call me *Captain Fletcher*. Just Fletcher."

Glancing up from studying the weapon, she noted, "We're still not on last name terms. Usually, it's the other way around."

"We do things differently on Eilean Comhachag. It's better with us being just Kali and Fletcher. We've got no history. We're . . ." He struggled to find the right words.

"We're simply us," she filled in. "As we are at this moment. No past. No thoughts of tomorrow. Only now. Only here."

Damn him, he didn't know how he'd met the one woman who seemed to understand him on this isolated lump of rock. But somehow he had, here, on this lonely slab of rock.

All he could do was nod in response.

She returned her attention to the ether rifle, hefting it. "It's lighter than a regular rifle. I'd wager it's because of the ether tank on the side." Studying the brass tank fastened to the right side of the gun, she noticed the small metal disk on the ether tank's butt cap. She slid the disk to one side. Even in the daylight, the green glow of the ether was unmistakable. "The tank's full. But what's this piece for?" She pushed the disc back and forth on its pin hinge.

"Firing at night," he answered. "Keeps the shooter from having their night vision muddled."

She nodded. "And you won't give your position away to the enemy."

"Catching on fast," he said, smiling. "But I wouldn't expect anything else from that sharp engineer's mind of yours."

Kali grinned. He was glad she didn't try to hide her

pride. She seemed to know how extraordinary she was, and it pleased him that not only did she know her worth, there wasn't any feigned modesty.

"Someone had to learn that lesson about the tanks the hard way," he continued.

"That's why you need engineers like me." Her expression clouded a little. "Though I've never done much work with weapons."

"It's work that's got to get done—I used to believe that. That we need guns and cannons. War's as old as history."

"I won't argue that. But dropping incendiary devices from the sky onto an unsuspecting target . . ." Old, dark memories flickered behind her eyes.

Hot anger crawled up from his chest. "War isn't always honorable. I hate that we've come to such shame. The Admiralty's been debating using such bombs on the enemy. I pray to God it never comes to that. Soldiers, seamen, and airmen—they know they're signing on to fight. Maybe to die. But it's too damn easy to make a mistake and drop a bomb on the wrong target. A school instead of a munitions plant. A village instead of a cantonment."

"Maybe the airships dropping the bombs don't care that they're killing civilians. The Hapsburgs and Russians surely didn't."

He held her gaze. "The men who killed your colleagues and your friends, the ones that caused you to lose your leg—they're dead. The *Persephone* shot one down, chased another until it broke apart into the sea."

A sad smile touched the corner of her mouth. "Thank you. But I'll be happier when no one has to die for the sake of telumium and tetrol."

He'd dug six graves after crashing on the island. Buried six good men—Vane hardly out of boyhood—the cost that followed every battle. He'd grown used to it, yet it never grew easier.

"I'd joined the navy to leave Wycombe and turning chairs," he said gruffly. "To keep Britain safe. Not to kill. But that's what I became. A dealer of death."

Her smile this time was gentle. "You saved lives, too."

The steel cables that felt knotted into his muscles loosened slightly. She saw him as something other than a weapon. Even when other Man O' Wars had destroyed most of Liverpool. She had every right to despise his kind. Yet she didn't.

These thoughts and sensations she stirred up in him—he didn't know what to make of them. How to act. What to say.

"The, uh, ether intake is controlled by this valve," he said, turning his attention back to the rifle. He pointed to the small brass piece attached to the tank. "You can shoot the rifle like a normal weapon, but if you release the valve, it adds ether to the chamber."

Maybe she found his sudden change of topic strange. If she did, she kept silent. Instead, she examined the valve. "It adds ether to the rifle's chamber, lightening the air and adding velocity to the round. So it can go faster and further."

He grinned. "You hardly need me here. Seems like you can figure this out all on your own."

"I might," she answered with a cheeky smile of her own. "But I like the company."

Damn. When was the last time a woman flirted with him? He'd kept himself apart for so long, he didn't know the ways of it anymore.

"The rest of the gun works just like any other bolt action rifle," he muttered.

"Let's give it a try." She turned the release valve on the ether tank, then raised the rifle.

"Hold your fire." He pulled a clip of rounds from his pocket. "Might need these if you want to actually hit something."

She pulled a face at him, and he couldn't stop his laugh.

Taking the clip, she then threw the rifle's bolt back, and loaded the bullets into the fixed magazine. She threw the bolt forward, loading the first round. All damned fast and efficient. "My father taught me," she said when she caught Fletcher's astonished look. "He said any soldier's child worth their pepper needed to know how to use firearms without fear. That went double for his daughter."

"Smart man, that father of yours."

More pride shone in her face. "My mother, too. She wasn't an engineer, but she'd a devilishly clever mind." From the moment he'd seen Kali, he'd thought her pretty. But her unfettered delight in her family made her beautiful.

"You miss them," he said quietly.

Her beauty didn't fade, but her happiness quieted. "I send letters and telegrams. And they write back as soon as they can. But I do. Especially since . . ." She glanced down at her leg.

"You stayed in England."

"They'd fuss over me if I went home. I hate fusses. I just want to . . ."

"Move on," he finished. "Be alone."

She gave him a wry smile. "That plan didn't quite work out as I'd thought."

Maybe he just needed another person's company after three months alone. Maybe anyone would've been welcome. But he didn't think so. "Now it's time to shoot."

"Hold on to me, so I don't go toppling arse over teakettle." When he hesitated, knowing what a sweet pain it would be to touch her, she looked impatient. "Don't turn prude on me."

What could he say to her? That his hands had begun to ache with wanting to touch her? That he'd started to long for a connection—any connection—they could have? Touching her would only give him a taste of what couldn't be his. But he didn't back down from challenges. So he stood close behind her, bracing his chest against her shoulder and upper body. He placed one hand on her waist. Warmth from her body soaked through the wool of her dress into his hand, and right up his arm.

"You're hands are so hot," she exclaimed, glancing over her shoulder. "Are you ill?"

"Man O' Wars have higher body temperatures than normal men," he said roughly.

Her eyes widened. "Oh," was all she managed to say, her cheeks turning that rosy spice color he liked so much. This time, it was she who chased the topic back to shooting the ether rifle. She lifted the gun. "So, um, you've got me."

"I do." In fact, he had to make an effort not to hold her too tightly. He'd learned back in training how to keep control of his strength, but this tested his training and control. Considerably.

Yet she didn't lift the weapon yet. Instead, she examined the gun's sight. It was longer than a normal rifle's sight, adjusting to different target distances. "Can this really shoot to a thousand yards?"

"A thousand yards for top accuracy. If a sniper really wanted to try their luck, they could go for twenty-five hundred yards. "

"Good God. And if I wanted to shoot a leaf off of one of those trees over there"—she indicated the copse—"that'd prove no trouble."

"A standard rifle could do the same. If you truly desired to test what an ether rifle can do, give that a go." Releasing her, he pointed toward a rise in the hills, two hundred yards away. A mound of stones was piled at the top of the rise. "Aim for the rock at the top. The one that's the size of an apple."

It looked like she was about to object or insist that she couldn't possibly make the shot, but she visibly pushed away her doubt. She turned to face the rise and her intended target. She started when he placed his hand on her waist again, and shored her body against his.

"Arse over teakettle, remember?" he murmured.

"I remember." She swallowed hard, but whether it was his touch or the possibility of shooting an ether rifle that seemed to put her on edge, he didn't know. Yet she raised the rifle and took aim, grounding her footing to keep stable.

As she lined up her sights, his attention strayed to the coarse black silk of her hair, pulled back into a simple knot, fragrant with something both floral and musky. Was it her soap? Her natural scent? All of his senses had been heightened with his telumium implants, and right now, they all focused on her.

But he forced his concentration back to her and the rifle.

She was handling a dangerous firearm. Either of them—but most likely her—could be hurt if he wasn't vigilant.

"I'm firing now," she whispered. "In three, two, one—" She pulled the trigger.

Two things happened at once. The kick from the gun threw her back, but his body kept hers steady, his grip at her waist tightening, and she barely moved. At the same time, a rock at the base of the pile of stones exploded from the bullet's impact.

"Damn it," she muttered, lowering the rifle.

"Try again. It's a tough shot."

She nodded and reloaded. Without hesitation, she lifted the gun again, and aimed. This time, when she fired, a rock closer to her target shattered. She drew a steadying breath, in and out, but it didn't steady him, feeling the expansion and contraction at her waist, the movement of her muscles along her back and shoulders.

After reloading, she paused, then shot again. The rock atop the pile of stones turned to dust.

She didn't shout or squeal or make girlish exclamations of success. Instead, she nodded once—a quick confirmation that she'd done what she'd set out to do—then lowered the rifle.

"Good showing," he said.

She turned to face him, his hand still at her waist. "I'll never make for a prize sniper, but I shot the damn thing, and I finally hit my sodding target. *Take pleasure in small victories.* That's what my father would say to me."

"I like my victories big," he said.

Her lips pursed. "Of course you do."

"How'd it feel?"

Finally, the opaque look on her face broke apart with her radiant smile. "Brilliant. I could feel the power of it, and I certainly would've been right on my bum if you hadn't been there to shore me up, but a person could get to like the feel of that strength. They could like it immensely."

"I've created a fiend."

She laughed. "I'd rather build things than shoot things. Still, I'm pleased I gave it a try. To truly know what it's like."

"Glad I could help you feel that."

Awareness hit them at the same time. He still held her. Less than a foot separated them. If he stepped forward just a little, they'd be pressed against each other. There were no witnesses, no one within miles to see them.

His gaze fell to her mouth. For all her sharp words, he didn't doubt she'd have soft lips, lips that would yield and take.

Glancing up at her eyes, he mentally groaned. She was looking at *his* mouth, too. And damn him thrice if she didn't lick her lips.

Instantly, he let go of her. Though his body was naturally hotter than hers, the imprint of her warmth lingered in his hands.

For several moments, she just stood there, still holding the rifle, staring at him as though he was a piece of machine's design she just couldn't figure out. He didn't understand himself, either.

Once, he'd thought himself an uncomplicated man. He'd basic needs like anyone: food, some sleep, a drink and a laugh now and then. He wanted to serve his country, protect the land he considered home, and the people who lived there. He'd loved the sea, and then he'd loved the sky. The sky had come at a price, though. He'd lost Emily. So his duties as a Man O' War became the definition of himself. Until he learned to hate even that.

Since crashing here, however, he'd changed. Continued to evolve. He'd learned he could endure silence and isolation. Paring life down to its most essential components. The sky wasn't his any longer. He became earthbound. Not a captain. Not a weapon. Only a man scraping out a means of survival.

Then she'd arrived. And everything changed again. Like all Man O' Wars, he didn't need much slumber, but when he lay down in his bed, her clockwork cricket shedding a soft glow from its place on his desk, he did sleep and he dreamed of her. Nothing specific. Only glimpses of her, or the sound of her voice. Yes—his body wanted a woman. But something else about her haunted him as he slept or prowled his empty, flightless airship.

And here they stood, an ether rifle and uncertainty between them. He *never* felt unsure. Except with her.

Finally, she spoke. "Show me what you can do, Fletcher."

CHAPTER SEVEN

Kali knew from experience that one was never reckless with volatile components. Even a single drop of the wrong chemical could cause an explosion. Every step of the engineering process needed to be carefully monitored, thoroughly contemplated, the various outcomes considered.

She'd felt the tension in Fletcher as he'd held her while she shot. He'd kept himself perfectly still, but she sensed it like a low frequency humming through her body. And he wasn't alone. His nearness made her heart race, like an overheating engine. It wasn't just his size, his tightly controlled strength, his *otherness*. They shared something, the two of them. Histories that were unalike, echoed each other—as if a composer had taken the same notes of a melody and rearranged them into a different tune.

Fletcher stared at her now, a bright fire in his aquamarine eyes. She hadn't meant her words to sound provocative—or maybe she had. She'd lost the blueprint to herself three months ago, and this island—and the man she shared it with—left her without a pattern or plan.

But there was one thing she knew she wanted.

She held the gun out to him. "In my hands, this is still little better than an ordinary rifle. But if wielded by a Man O' War . . ."

"So, it's a scientific experiment." The fire in his gaze banked. He took the weapon from her, handling it with the ease of a trained warrior. "See what both machines are capable of: the ether rifle and me."

"I never said you were a machine. But you and the weapon are each extraordinary. You can't blame an engineer for her curiosity." She laid her hand upon his forearm. "If it makes you too uncomfortable . . ."

To her surprise, he offered her one of his rare smiles. "Pass up an opportunity to swagger and show off in front of a pretty lady? Not bloody likely."

Her pulse fluttered at the compliment. Maybe he was lonely. After three months without seeing another human, let alone a woman, a toothless, pockmarked crone might look pretty to him. Still, he'd been nothing but respectful of her person since they'd met. He couldn't be that desperate.

Perhaps he really does think you're pretty. Ever consider that, Miss Clever Knickers?

"Impress me," she said, crossing her arms over her chest. "I'd wager you could hit that pile of rocks on the first try."

He snorted. "You trying to be insulting? No, I'll need a better target than that." He scanned the landscape, his eyes sharp. Most of the terrain around them was the moor, offering few worthwhile targets. He turned toward the southwest where the ridge of rocky peaks began. At the summit of the nearest peak stood a coppice of alders.

"The tree closest to us," he said, lifting the rifle to take aim. "I'll shoot the top leaf off."

She gaped at him. "That's nearly a mile away. I thought you said the ether rifles were only accurate to a thousand yards."

"In the right hands, they can shoot up to twenty-five hundred yards. The accuracy might not be perfect, but hell"—he grinned—"I'm up for the challenge."

From her satchel, she took a brass spyglass and pulled it open. When one of his brows rose, she explained, "Not everyone's got a Man O' War's eyesight. You could shoot and miss by a mile, but I'd never know. This is simple empirical method."

"You can take the woman out of the laboratory . . ." he murmured.

She shrugged, but it wasn't an apology. "Let's begin." She aimed her spyglass at the copse of trees. Even though her glass was highly advanced, manufactured in Scotland by the best opticians in the world, the spyglass could only do so much, and she couldn't make out each individual leaf. Still, it was better than trying to see with her naked eyes.

"Ready?" he asked.

"At your discretion, Captain—I mean, Fletcher." Difficult to call him by his Christian name when he could sound so very authoritative.

"I'll count off so you know when to look. Three, two, one—" then he fired.

For a moment, nothing happened. The trees didn't move. No branches shook or leaves flew into the air. Disappointment weighted in her stomach. She'd hoped, perhaps foolishly, that he'd be something grander than life. A myth come true. But she already knew that, despite the telumium implants, he was truly just a man, with any man's limitations—

A leaf at the very top of the nearest tree flew into the air.

Slowly, she lowered her spyglass. She'd forgotten to take into account how long it might take a bullet to travel that distance. But it had. And hit its target.

Turning, she found Fletcher watching her. He wasn't smiling. In fact, he looked wary.

"That was . . ." She searched but couldn't find any words to match what she'd just witnessed.

He turned away, his expression weary. "Serves me right for showing off. People say they want to see what a Man O' War can do. Then they learn. We're not normal."

"Of course you aren't," she said.

He threw her a glance, both accusatory and accepting, as if such comments were familiar, but unwelcome.

"You're *extraordinary*," she added. "There's nothing to be ashamed in that."

"I'm not ashamed," he said flatly. "I knew what becoming a Man O' War would mean. Everyone else had trouble with it. Even you. Looking at me like I'm a monstrosity."

She stepped closer to him. "Am I shocked that you could make that shot? Bloody hell, I am. You've got an amazing ability. And I won't pretend that the implants don't make you different from everyone else. But look at me. Look me right in the eye and tell me what you see." She put her face close to his—as close as she could, given the height difference. "Do you see disgust? Fear?"

His gaze searched hers for a long moment, the air between them hot and electric.

"No," he finally said.

"It's *wonder* and *admiration*," she said hotly. She snapped the spyglass shut and stowed it away. "Both for the technological achievement, and for who you are as a person. As a man. And you'd better damn well not forget that."

"I won't," he said softly.

"Good." She wondered—when he looked at her, what did *he* see? The color of her skin? A damaged woman? Or was she, as he'd said earlier, only herself? Kali. She wanted that—to be seen not as crippled or a cultural anomaly but as a person.

Even more shocking: she wanted to be *seen*. All she'd wanted before was to hide herself away, turn invisible from the world. But not with him.

"Who was she?"

Her question seemed to catch him off guard. His head snapped back as if dodging a punch. "Who?"

"The woman who said you were a monstrosity." It was a guess, born from pure speculation, and she half expected him to sneer at her theory.

For a moment, he was silent. Affirming her belief that she'd been foolish in her deduction.

Then, "A shopkeeper's daughter in Portsmouth." He didn't look at Kali as he spoke. "Met her when I was still a lieutenant on a seafaring ship. We'd walk out together whenever I was in port."

"Oh," was all Kali could say. It was one thing to speculate on the existence of a woman in his life. Another thing entirely to have proof.

"I became a captain," he went on. "We talked of the future. Then I was presented with the chance to become a Man O' War. There wasn't a greater honor to be had in the navy. So I took the offer."

"Against her wishes."

"Emily didn't know. I wanted to surprise her. It was such a privilege, having that opportunity. I thought she'd be happy for me. For us."

The naked pain in his voice and the stiff set of his shoulders made it clear that this Emily was anything but happy about Fletcher's transformation. "I don't have a particularly high opinion of this woman," Kali said tightly.

"She fell in love with a man." He stared down at his clenched fists. "But got a monster instead. That's what she said."

"I maintain that Emily's an idiot." She moved to stand in front of him. "You did change. Dramatically. But the core of who you are, that didn't alter."

He scowled. "You don't know that."

"I know that you've got honor and courage." Perhaps more than she'd ever known in any man. "That doesn't suddenly start or stop. It's something here." She placed her hand on her heart. "And no amount of telumium alters it. If Emily couldn't see that, if she made you feel like an abomination . . . My father showed me how to inflict very painful injuries with nothing more than my elbow. I'd be happy to test them out on that foolish woman."

Fletcher's gaze burned into hers. "You'd snap her in two. Emily's fragile."

"That'll make my job easier."

He gave a soft, sharp exhalation and planted his hands on his hips. The raw pain in his eyes had retreated. It wasn't gone entirely, but it had faded. "You're the damnedest woman."

"I've heard that before."

"Doesn't surprise me."

They stared at each other for a long while, and she felt it—another shift between them. He'd bared himself to her. An act of trust. And she was willing to take the burden of his past, rather than run from it, and what it implied about their connection.

"Hungry?" she asked.

His brow furrowed at the abrupt change of topic. "Always."

"The implants," she surmised. "They make you require more fuel than an ordinary man."

He slung the ether rifle across his back. "Doing my best not to decimate the animal population on the island. I've had to cut back my rations. Been dropping weight."

Good God. How much bigger had he been when he first crashed on the island?

"I can't promise you a feast." She rummaged through her satchel and produced two cloth-wrapped packets, then handed him one. "Fish pies," she explained as he uncovered his bundle. "Cookery isn't my area of expertise, but I'm fairly certain that's edible."

"You brought a picnic," he murmured. The normal-sized pastry looked like a petit four in his hand.

"I imagined that shooting ether rifles would be hunger-inducing work. I brought this, too." She held up a canteen. "It's only water, but I purified it. And there's an apple tree not too far from the cottage, so there are apples in here, also."

She started to lower herself to the ground, though her artificial leg made the process a little awkward. Still, she waved off his outstretched hand, offering help. Finally, she situated herself on the grass, her legs stretched out in front of her in a way that would make an etiquette columnist faint. But etiquette columnists seldom covered the topic of women with prostheses attempting to eat luncheon on deserted islands, and Kali never gave a cobra's spit what those fussy writers thought, anyway.

Fletcher remained standing, looking at the pie as if he'd never seen such a marvel.

"Didn't you say you were hungry?" she asked. "Sit your arse down and eat."

He did sit, and with far more grace than she'd shown, crossing his long legs. "It's been a long time since I've been on a picnic. And even then, I didn't have much experience with them."

"That's a shame."

"In the chair factory in Wycombe, we had half days on Sundays. A little church. Time for a quick game of football on the tiny green in the square, then back to work. And before I met Emily . . . seamen on leave aren't interested in picnics."

She didn't want to think of that incredibly stupid woman. But Kali couldn't stop her face from warming when she thought of young Fletcher, fresh off a ship and eager for pleasure. "Too busy visiting museums."

More than just her face heated when he chuckled, a low, raspy sound that stroked along her arms and down the center of her chest. "I've always had a love of culture."

She grew up in a city filled with soldiers. The sight of

groups of them ambling toward Nagpur's pleasure quarters wasn't unfamiliar. Still, it was different to talk about it with Fletcher. To imagine him in a courtesan's arms. Imagine what it would be like were she to trade places with that courtesan . . .

"But I still don't know much of picnics," he added. "Emily wasn't keen on them. And they weren't part of my childhood, short as it was."

For some reason, that saddened her a little. Perhaps she'd been spoiled with the gift of attentive parents, and the luxury of not having to work through her childhood and adolescence. Nagpur had its share of young workers, selling marigold garlands, serving as chai-wallas with steam-spewing carts, and children who crouched by the side of the road, begging.

She'd been lucky. Her father had actually fallen in love with and married her mother. Only a handful of other British soldiers did the same. Had it not been for her father's romantic heart, Kali could have been one of those bastard children of mixed blood, their mothers cast out by their families. And so Kali got to have a family, attend school. Even go on picnics.

"Well," she said, "the ground can be damp, and insects can pester you, or you drop your food and it gets covered with dirt. Picnics are more trouble than they're worth, honestly."

"The ground isn't bothering me," he answered. "The bugs are staying away, and there's no way in hell I'm dropping this pie. So I might like this picnic business after all. But, ah, what do we do now?"

"The standard procedure is eating, remarking on the scenery, speculating about the weather. Children generally like to throw bread crumbs to birds."

Though the owls stayed away, resting up for their nocturnal hunt, a trio of little brown birds did appear nearby. They hopped on stick legs and, peeping, turned bright bead eyes to the humans.

She snickered. "There must be some kind of bird telegraph so that even wild creatures like these know that humans sitting on the ground means they'll get something to eat." She broke an edge off of her pie and tossed bits of pastry at the birds. They quickly pecked them up, then looked to Fletcher for more.

"Sod off," he rumbled. "This is mine." The birds obeyed his command and fluttered away.

He took a big bite of his pie. His eyes closed as he chewed, and he sighed.

Like a nervous newlywed, she studied his expression. "It's terrible."

"It's the most delicious thing I've eaten in months."

"That's not much of a compliment," she said, "since you've been probably subsisting on plain rabbit, fish and roots."

"It's good, damn it. And don't angle for compliments. You're better than that."

She never wanted to be the kind of person who begged for approval. But she hated to think that his first bite of food not cooked by his own hands would be barely palatable. Up until today, she hadn't tried making pies—only the stews and curries her mother had taught her. But a curry didn't travel well over the moors.

She bit into her own pie. And was pleasantly surprised to find it rather tasty, if a little over-salted.

"See?" he asked, watching her face. "No need for false modesty." Three more bites, and he finished his pie.

It was impossible that he could be sated. But before she could break the remainder of her pastry in half, his hands closed into fists.

"I'll ruddy leave if you try to give me that," he growled.

"You can't have had enough—"

"The day I take food away from a woman is the day I throw myself into a vat of molten steel."

She glanced around. "I don't see any vats of molten steel nearby, so you can't refuse."

"I can and I do. Don't press me, Kali," he rumbled when she started to object.

"Bloody obstinate man." But seeing that he wouldn't be moved, she finished the rest of her pie.

He reared back when she stretched a hand toward his face. Like a wolf unused to touch.

"You've got crumbs in your beard." Slowly, she reached for him again.

He looked at her hand, then at her. And held himself still.

She brushed the crumbs away. Her movements were halfway between caution—afraid he might snarl or bolt at her touch—and pleasure. As she tidied his beard, her fingers grazed his lips. They were soft and firm, and his breath was warm against her skin.

The urge to trace his lips with her fingertips surged through her. She wanted to glide her finger into his mouth, then put that same finger into her own mouth so she might taste him.

Instead, she snatched her hand away. Curled it up and pressed it tight to her thigh. Why hadn't she just told him about the crumbs and let him take care of them, instead of acting like a woman eager for an excuse to touch him?

Because that's exactly what you are.

At least he looked as befuddled as she felt.

"I think we're supposed to talk about the scenery, now," she said.

He blinked. "Not much to say about moors," he finally said. "Empty stretches of land. A few bits of scrub. That's it."

Her school years had been spent studying the mechanical world, not the natural one, so she had no interesting facts about moorlands. "It's pretty, don't you think?"

"Pretty? Hadn't thought about it."

Something about the way he spoke, a slight edge in his tone, told another story. "No denials. I can hear it in your voice."

He frowned. "Man O' Wars and sea captains don't think about whether a place is *pretty* or not."

"But *you* have."

He swore, then exhaled. "Fine. Yes. I think it's pretty."

"Why?"

Another florid curse from him, then, "Hell, woman. You're trying to spin my head like a globe."

She didn't understand the reason she needed to know why he thought the moors were pretty. Only that she did. That she wanted inside his mind, his thoughts. That itself shook her. She'd tried to fashion a haven for herself, a place where she could exist in cold nothingness, like an automaton. Yet the more time she spent with Fletcher, the more she became aware of things like movement and thought and the feel of brisk island air against her face. Things an automaton would never want or know.

He raked his hands through his hair, and it stood up in tufts that ought to be ridiculous, but instead made him appear piratical. Wild.

"Because," he finally said through clenched teeth, "it looks like the sea. Like someone had turned the sea into land. The hills are the waves and the gorse is the foam on the waves." He glared at her. "That damn well better satisfy you, because I won't say another bloody word."

Appreciation for natural beauty didn't seem to be cultivated in the navy. Neither were poetic notions. But his spare, resentfully-given thoughts still touched her. Buried beneath layers of gruffness and strength, he did have a bit of a poet in him. And that pleased her.

"We'll make a picnicker out of you, yet," she said with a smile.

Apparently, the idea wasn't entirely unpleasant—he grumbled at her words, but she caught the flash of his own smile. At that same moment, the haze in the sky broke apart, and golden sunlight flooded the moor.

"Now you can't begrudge me thinking *that* is beautiful," she said.

"Aye, it is," he rumbled, looking at her. "Beautiful, indeed."

The days fell into a pattern. She worked until noon, then walked to the pond, where she'd find Fletcher. Sometimes he'd be fishing. Other times, he'd be whittling. And sometimes he did nothing, only seemed to be waiting for her. He didn't always smile when she appeared, but his shoulders straightened and he stood taller. Her heart would kick every time she saw him, no matter how much she'd come to expect to find him there.

Neither of them had said anything specific. They'd made no plans after parting ways on the day of their shooting practice and picnic. But from that day forward, they met at the same place, at the same time.

Anticipation would build from the moment she woke, and there were times when she discovered herself simply staring out into nothingness instead of working on her latest designs, or checking her timepiece to see if it was noon yet. The hands on the clock moved with glacial sluggishness those days, and she could've sworn there were times the hands actually moved backwards. She'd even disassembled the timepiece to make certain it worked properly. It did. But time moved slower and slower each morning.

They never wasted time on meaningless pleasantries or inane conversation. No inquiries into each other's evening—though she did wonder what he did at night, all alone in that airship—or breakfast, or discussions of the weather. They'd nod at each other and then, in silent agreement, walk. The destination wasn't planned. Wherever their legs took them, they'd wander.

Together, they explored the island. Its eastern coast, with its two-hundred foot bluffs that sank into the sea. The moors of the north, and the small wooded areas at its fringe. Fletcher showed her the graves he had dug for his crewmen, the rough wooden crosses marking their resting places and their names carved into the wood. He must've used the ship's register, because the crosses bore the fallen men's full names, dates of birth, and death. One of the dead had been only seventeen. She'd placed wildflowers on their graves—she hadn't been able to bring herself to do the same at the mass graves in Liverpool, and flowers had been in short supply—so she honored the fallen now.

He'd watched her do this, his expression stony. But he'd nodded in approval, and they'd moved on.

They traversed the whole of the island together. Sometimes in silence, sometimes talking. Pointing out birds or animals or plants. Or even discussing their lives before they'd come to Eilean Comhachag.

He asked of her life in India and why she'd moved so far away, all the way to chilly Liverpool. She hadn't wanted to leave Nagpur, but in some ways, India hadn't embraced modernity. Work for female engineers was scarce, and those positions that were available offered no room for advancement. She'd had to make a choice: her family, or the chance to truly make developments in technology.

"Still hurts," she said on one of their rambles. "Sometimes, my leg pains me, even though it's not there anymore. It's the same with my parents. It's an ache in me, their absence."

"Yet you left them. Left your home."

"Because I knew I had more to offer the world than acting as some engineer's glorified amanuensis."

"Not everyone's got such a sense of purpose," he said admiringly. "Most people are full of fear."

She snorted. "Oh, I was afraid. Terrified. Booked my ticket to sail from Bombay. Three times I changed the date of my departure. I kept finding excuses not to go. I needed to stay for a cousin's wedding. Maa' wasn't feeling well and I ought to help around the house while she got better—never mind that we had servants who loved her and would do anything to help her. I was a hairsbreadth away from consulting an astrologer who could tell me not to leave. All the while, I hated the work I was doing for a civil engineering firm, if you could call fetching tiffins and tea *work*."

"The fact that we're here now means you did leave," he pointed out.

"My father." She smiled at the memory. "He took me aside and said, *I love you, my dear, but if you don't get your arse out of Nagpur and show the world what you can do, you'll taste regret for the rest of your life. And it's a bitter flavor.*"

"Wise man, your father," Fletcher murmured, pushing aside a patch of overgrown gorse so she could pass through.

She emerged on the other side of the shrub, and they continued on their walk toward a stream. "Usually. But this is also the man who tried to invent a device that sounded an alarm whenever a baby's nappy needed changing."

"I'd think the crying infant would be enough of an alarm."

"Thus the failure of the invention. But after he gave me that bit of advice, I finally left." She sighed as an ache of homesickness swelled.

"Advice or no," he said, "not many would take the same risk. Did you even have an offer of work in Liverpool?"

She grinned. "Not a one. Just my diploma from the university and a portfolio full of designs. I arrived in Liverpool knowing nobody, without a job or a place to stay." Those first weeks in a dingy boarding house had been brutal, with her literally knocking on doors during the day and stifling her sobs into her pillow at night. Until Drogin & Daughters decided to take the gamble, and had hired her.

These past few months, she felt as though she'd become nothing but longing. Missing her family, her friends. That grief never vanished, but the scar was fading, more and more with each moment spent in Fletcher's company.

"You're a bloody brave woman," he said.

She laughed. "Not brave. Just egotistical. I couldn't stand the thought of languishing in obscurity."

"I know bravery," he said, abruptly solemn. "I've seen it in dozens of battles. So if I say you're brave, then you'd better listen."

His vehemence stunned her into silence, and they'd been quiet the rest of their walk that day.

He had stories in abundance. It took some work on her part to pull them out of him. Fletcher radiated strength, but he was a modest man, reluctant to talk of his own heroism. When once she even used that word, *heroism*, he snorted and fell into a moody silence. But there was no other word for it.

As a sailor, he'd defended British outposts and their native populaces from warlords and other European nations trying to stake their claims. He'd run into collapsing, burning towns to pull people to safety. He'd risen quickly from a common seaman to an officer, proving again and again his courage and steadiness in the midst of battle. In one fierce battle, the captain of his ship had been badly wounded, and the next in command crumbled beneath the pressure, so he'd stepped in to command the crew to victory.

She already knew his valor as an airship captain—she'd watched him in the skies above Liverpool. And he'd sacrificed himself so his crew might survive, and no one would be injured by the crashing *Persephone*.

But these were tales that had been as difficult to extract as rusted bolts. He wouldn't speak of the procedure that had transformed him into a Man O' War, either, though from the small grains of information he'd accidentally dropped, she learned it had been painful, and long. He couldn't be away from his ship, or one of the specially-designed batteries, for more than a few days without his energy building up to dangerous levels, provoking a frenzied, mindless rage. Thus the reason why he kept the turbines running at night, to drain the batteries so his energy had somewhere to go. And he couldn't have children.

He'd given away all chances of a normal life when he'd laid himself down on the operating table. Deliberately changed himself into an amalgam of human and machine. Though he never spoke of Emily again, it was clear he thought he would have some chance of normalcy with her. And been wrong.

When Liverpool had been attacked, Kali had been without a lover for some time. In the aftermath of the battle, there'd been no man to look at her or her prosthetic leg with disgust. She bore her transformation alone. All she'd written to her parents was that she'd been injured, but not fatally, and she would recover from her injuries in England. She refused their offers of help.

One day, she met Fletcher by the pond. In his hand, he held a long, smoothly-polished stick. Wordlessly, he held it out to her.

"What's this for?" she asked, taking it. The stout piece of wood was four feet long, with a tapered end, and a wider top. A strip of leather looped through a hole near the top of the stick.

Silently, he gazed toward the ridge of peaks to the west. The one part of the island they hadn't explored. She'd always been afraid of those sharp hills. They weren't mountains, but they were steep, and rocky. She didn't know if she had the strength or balance to attempt them. Before she'd lost her leg, she would've challenged him to a race to the top, but now . . .

"It came from the *Persephone*," he said. "The wood. Took it from the engineering deck."

"Fletcher," she said, eyeing the walking stick dubiously. Her heart contracted, thinking of him patiently carving the walking stick just for her. It was well balanced, too, and just the right height. Considerable thought had gone into its making. And he'd made it from a piece of his ship. "I hate disappointing you—"

"Then don't," he said. Without another word, he strode toward the steep hills, leaving her alone.

Go after him? Or stay? Risk injury and humiliation, or watch him climb the hills while she felt sorry for herself?

She hefted the walking stick, took a deep breath, and followed.

CHAPTER EIGHT

He was patient. Kali had to credit him that. Doubtless he could have bound up the steep hill, powerful and fleet as a tiger. Or he could have shouted at her, urging her to be stronger, go faster. Of course, if he'd tried yelling at her, she would've taken his carefully carved walking stick and swung it at his head—or his groin.

Yet she didn't have cause to use the walking stick as a weapon. Fletcher hiked slightly ahead of her, but from the set of his shoulders, and the tilt of his head, it was plain his senses were tuned to her. He slowed whenever her steps faltered. Yet he didn't once turn around to offer her help or suggest that she'd gone far enough for the day. As if he knew she'd push him away or insist she was fine. A compliment of sorts. He believed she could make it up the hill, and his belief shored up her own.

But it wasn't easy. Her leg of flesh and bone protested at the amount of work it had to do. The long walks around the island had strengthened her, true, but a steep slope presented a new challenge to her muscles. It took some finessing of her artificial leg, too. She had to stop once to loosen some of the pins, enabling a greater range of movement. And there was a rhythm to hiking, a careful calibration of balance and weight.

Sweat filmed her back, and she wiped her forehead with her sleeve. Breath was like a furnace in her chest. She hurt all over.

The summit seemed miles above. How could she ever make it?

"I stole the captain's brandy once," he said, breaking the silence.

His unexpected words pulled her out of her misery. "Didn't peg you for a thief."

He continued climbing upward as he spoke over his shoulder. "I was a petty officer, and a right swaggerer. Thought I knew everything about everything. Got a few lashings back when they were still handing them out, but that didn't stop me from pushing back whenever the warrant officer gave me an order. What a strutting bastard I was." He chuckled.

She stared at his wide back. "I'm having . . . a hard time . . . picturing that," she gasped.

"A miracle that I made it above the rank of seaman." He didn't sound breathless at all, the demon. "One night, I got to boasting with the other lads, telling 'em all how I was so ruddy clever, and that the officers didn't know anything I didn't know. So one of the boys—Browne, I think—tells me to prove it. Show everyone that I'm really smarter and quicker than the officers. Somebody got the idea that I should steal something from the captain's quarters."

"How . . . would that prove . . . anything?"

"The lot of us couldn't have been more than seventeen

years old. Had more come than brains. I mean, ah . . . we didn't think clearly."

She panted a laugh as she dug the walking stick into the hill and dragged herself higher. "Quite a . . . feat to . . . manage."

"Nothing's more steady than a naval ship. Everything happens at the same time every day. I knew when the captain would be out of his quarters, and when the midshipman who patrolled the passageway would go by. All I did was wait for the right moment."

"The door . . . had to be . . . locked."

"I nicked a few of the sailmaker's awls and needles and used those to pick the lock. Got inside in a trice." A large boulder blocked their path, so Fletcher veered to the side. He could surely have climbed over it, but she didn't object that he changed their path to accommodate her.

"You . . . clever rogue," she mock-admonished him.

He chuckled. "Here's where my cleverness ran out. I found the brandy and instead of just taking it and leaving, I decided to have myself a drink right there in the captain's quarters."

"Oh, no," she groaned.

"We had our share of grog, and I'd drunk plenty of ale, but strong spirits were new to me. New, and tasty. Finished the whole bottle."

She groaned again at his foolishness.

"When I came to," he continued, "I was in the brig. They wanted to make sure I was conscious for my lashing. Before they dragged me out on deck for punishment, the captain himself came to see me. He said that if I wasn't such a damned idiot, I'd make a fine officer. But I was going to have to make a choice. Keep up my blustering ways, or actually make something of myself. Bled more brandy than blood from the lashing," he added.

Clearly, he'd opted to reform. Yet it stunned her that this modest, honorable man had once been so young and stupid, so arrogant. The intervening years must've shaped him a good deal—or he'd chosen to change himself. Something few people could accomplish.

Her thoughts scattered when he began to sing a seafaring tune. His baritone was low and rang like a bell.

My comely lass, it's back to the sky,
For the Hun has come calling, but never you cry.
With ether and courage, we'll send 'em to Hell,
And then I'll be home, in your arms to dwell.

"Ah," he said. "Here we are."

Kali had been focused on putting one foot in front of the other, taking each step in turn, and listening to his shanty. Only now she looked up and realized they'd reached the summit.

"You distracted me," she said, almost accusing.

"You made it to the top," he countered.

Her first look at the island in its entirety. It was a patchwork of gray and green, a rumpled blanket of stone and grass in the middle of a shale-colored sea. From this vantage, she spotted the roof of her cottage, miniscule from this height, and the rolling expanse of the moors, which truly did look like the ocean made solid. The *Persephone* lay in her permanent berth, dug into the earth. Shadows from clouds speckled the island. It wasn't a lush place, but it held a raw, uncompromising beauty. Now, from the top of this peak, she could see it all, feel the cool wind nip at her cheeks and tug at her unraveling braid.

And she had Fletcher to thank for it.

But she didn't want words. *Thank you* felt so pallid. She'd thought her leg would never allow her to have such a view or know this soaring freedom.

So she reached down between them. Took his hand in hers. Gave it a squeeze.

He squeezed back. A silent acknowledgment of what this meant.

They stood like that, hand in hand, as if they'd made the world and now stood back to admire their handiwork.

And she realized at that moment that for the first time in three months—for the first time in *years*—she was truly happy.

Fletcher stared balefully out the window in his quarters. Nearly through the morning and the rain hadn't let up. It had been coming down since the middle of last night, beating on the top deck like drummer boys announcing an admiral. He'd hoped it would clear by midmorning at the latest to give the ground the slightest chance of drying out. No luck.

He glanced at the clockwork cricket, sitting quietly on his desk. He was careful not to use it too much, in case he should break it. But every night, he turned its key and listened to its musical chirp while it softly illuminated the darkness of his quarters.

Turning back to the window, he cursed. He didn't want Kali out in that muck. It made for treacherous going. Had they been in a city with paved streets, or even a village with packed earth lanes, he wouldn't worry. But there was no town planning commission for Eilean Comhachag, unless you counted the rabbits' warrens.

She shouldn't risk it. But the damn stubborn woman would probably show up at the pond anyway. What if she got hurt between the pond and her cottage?

He threw on his coat and jumped down from the window to the ground. Then he ran. He reached her cottage in fifteen minutes.

Kali frowned in confusion when she answered his knock. She stepped back to let him inside, out of the rain. The cottage smelled of tea, solder, and wool, with the sweet spice of her beneath it all. The windows had all fogged from the warmth of the cooking apparatus's hearth. Though crowded with equipment and tools, everything was neatly organized and clean, a far cry from the chaos of the *Persephone*.

"Something wrong?" she asked.

He glanced up at the roof. "It's raining."

A corner of her mouth turned up. "Here I thought Vishnu's lemon ice was melting and dripping on my roof." She took out her timepiece. "I was just about to head out for our meeting."

"That's why I'm here." He stood completely still, afraid he might turn and knock over some delicate piece of equipment, or accidentally crush a tool beneath his boots. The cottage had been fitted perfectly for someone Kali's size. Fletcher, however, felt like an ironclad trying to dock in a sloop's berth.

She looked taken aback, and hurt. "You don't want to meet today."

"Like hell." He didn't realize how heated his voice was until he saw her take a step back. "I mean, I do want to. But with the rain . . ." A frown began to gather between her brows, and he realized he couldn't flat out tell her that he feared she'd injure herself in the mud and slippery terrain. They'd been hiking the hills for a week, and her strength had grown daily. She no longer gasped for breath on the climb, and her movements were smoother, faster. Still, he didn't like the thought of her tromping around in the mud and over slippery rocks.

"It's, ah, cozier here, don't you think?" he managed.

She looked at him as if he was missing a few wires in his circuits. There were more bits of metal and half-completed apparatuses than furniture. It might be clean and organized, but cozy, it wasn't.

Then her brow cleared with understanding. He tensed. She'd guessed his reason for not wanting to go outside, and in a minute, she'd give him a thorough telling-off for coddling her.

"I never knew a Man O' War could dislike the rain," she said, smiling.

He'd stood watch in the middle of hurricanes without complaint, but he said now, "Hate the stuff."

She pointed to an empty corner of the cottage. "Go dry yourself out."

Feeling like a giant, shaggy wolfhound, he went to the corner and shook his head. Heavy water droplets flew from his hair and even his beard. He threw his dripping coat onto the back of a chair.

"Take a seat and I'll get our luncheon together," she said.

"Don't wait on me—"

"I'm hungry," she countered. "You don't know where anything is, and I'm half afraid you'll topple the whole cottage if you take a wrong step."

He couldn't argue any of those points, but it felt odd to be served as he'd been when a ship's captain. Then, it had been natural, the proper order of things. But after what was nearly four months of self-sufficiency, having anyone wait on him—Kali especially—nettled. But he took a seat at the table and tried not to knock it over from the restless bouncing of his leg.

Finally, she set soda bread and two bowls of stew on the table. In truth, she put a bowl of stew in front of her chair, and then a pot of it in front of him.

Before he could object, she said, "My mother would drown herself in the Nag River if she thought her daughter let a guest go hungry." She sat down opposite him. "Besides, you brought me the rabbits, so most of this stew is yours." Without ceremony, she picked up her spoon and ate.

Nothing for him to do but follow suit. So he ate as well, tearing off hunks of the soda bread to share. They fell into a companionable silence, with the rain and crackle of the fire and the scrape of their spoons the only sounds in the cottage.

She chuckled. "Aren't we a regular portrait out of *Mrs. Abelard's Domestic Journal for Women*?"

"Thought you'd be too busy reading the latest engineering journal to bother with such tripe."

"I didn't make a habit of reading them. If one of the amanuenses happened to leave a copy around, I wasn't above a perusal. And I object to the word *tripe*," she added hotly. "You don't call men's periodicals full of adventure stories *tripe*."

"I don't read 'em."

"But you never thought less of the men who did read them."

He stared at her, mystified. "What's got your engine over-heating?"

She set her spoon down with a clatter. "It doesn't matter how far we've come. Women can be engineers, doctors, professors now, yet we're still not thought of as fully equal. I thought it would be better in England than in India, but I was wrong."

Lifting his hands, he said, "Don't pin the stupidity of other men on me. I called that magazine *tripe* because I read a copy once, and it was full of the most asinine advice I'd ever seen. *"A woman's duty is always to her home and husband. She must ever be neat, industrious, and cheerful. Save your tears and complaints, for they are unwanted and disagreeable. Keep your conversation to pleasant, light topics."* He set his elbows on the table. "That's not advice you'd follow. That's not advice I'd want any woman to follow."

Abashed, she slid her gaze away. "Well I . . . never really read the articles. Just looked at the fashion plates." Her eyes returned to his. "Did it *really* say that?"

He picked up his spoon and ate. "And more. I've got a good head for remembering the written word. Want me to recite *The Proper Conduct for Unmarried Ladies*?"

She made a face. "I'd like to keep eating." And so she did, until a moment later, when she muttered, "Sorry."

He'd heard her, but pressed, "What's that?"

"I'm sorry for leaping down your throat." She prodded at her stew. "It wasn't really called for."

"You're right," he said. "About the advancements we've made. But there's still a far way to go. I don't imagine your skin color makes it easier, either."

She looked surprised, but not angry, by his candor. "It seems as though we've both had battles to fight during our lives," she said. "Some quieter than others."

They fell silent again, returning to their meal. As they ate, he glanced around the cottage. Something was missing. But he didn't know what. All the necessary furniture was there, and God knew an engineer might squeal in delight at the masses of tools, equipment, and semi-assembled devices. The large cooking and heating apparatus took up a goodly amount of room. Flour, and sugar occupied an open cupboard, as well as a few weeks' worth of butter and eggs. A skirt and petticoat peeped out from a partially opened trunk in the corner, reminding him of the shy girls peering around corners at Admiralty balls.

Everything a person needed for survival was here. But there was a subtle absence.

"No photographs," he said.

She glanced up, puzzled.

"Pictures of your family," he explained. "The way you talk about them, I'd have thought you would have brought at least a photo of them." He leaned back in his chair, which creaked beneath his weight, and contemplated her. "Or maybe you don't want them around here. Maybe you've pulled anchor on your past."

"The boarding house where I lived was destroyed in the

battle. Nothing was left." She said this flatly, a fact she'd grown used to. "Everything I owned—clothing, books, photographs—all gone."

"I'm . . . sorry," was all he could think to say. Jesus, was every word out of his mouth going to be the verbal equivalent of a rampaging elephant?

She shrugged, unconcerned. "Ever heard of Buddhism?"

"It's some kind of Eastern religion or philosophy." In Chinese ports, he'd seen monks in their saffron robes, and statues of a serene man.

"Buddhism started in India, but most of its practitioners now are farther north and east. Part of its teachings are the Four Noble truths. The first is that life is suffering."

"Cheerful."

"As opposed to giddy Anglicanism."

He leaned farther back in his chair, and it made another complaining groan. "I was the captain, not the chaplain. How a man prays—or who he prays to—doesn't matter to me."

"Well, Buddhists accept the fact that in this life, we're all going to suffer. Sadness, anger, fear. Sickness, age." She glanced down at her leg. "Injury. It's part of human existence, and pretending otherwise just leads to more suffering."

"A grim view, but truthful." Even before he'd joined the navy and been witness to countless battles, growing up in Wycombe had shown him the harshness of the world. A worker got injured on the job, they didn't work. No work meant no pay. The other workers tried to pool their wages to buy food and medicine, but there was only so much they could do. And there were workers who lost their jobs, replaced by automatons. People starved, lost their homes.

Even the factory's owner—his son couldn't walk, struck down as a babe by infantile paralysis. The boy used a tetrol-powered chair to move around. Rich or poor, it didn't matter. Pain had a way of finding everyone.

"It's not all dark forecasts, though," Kali continued. "Suffering can be avoided. There *can* be happiness. That's the second noble truth."

Seeing that she'd finished her meal, and he'd cleaned his own pot, he cleared the table. He couldn't remember ever having a mealtime conversation like this before, not even with his officers on the *Persephone*. Or even with Emily. Emily had also been insistent on propriety, so the most he'd coaxed from her were kisses and a few touches—which always left him aching with frustrated desire. Eating with Kali in her home, rather than the picnic meals that they'd been sharing over the weeks, felt more intimate than anything Emily had been willing to give. And there was more closeness merely talking with Kali than he'd ever had in a paid woman's arms.

"I'm wagering whisky doesn't have anything to do with avoiding suffering," he said, returning to the table.

"No," she answered with a smile, "but a good whisky can certainly make a rainy, chilly day more pleasant."

He patted his pockets. "Didn't bring any with me."

Glancing at her cupboard, she sighed. "I didn't, either."

"Next time, I'll bring a bottle." Airships stocked a fair amount of spirits for the crew, though it was always doled out with discretion. Many of the finer bottles of whisky and brandy had broken in the crash, but some remained—which he portioned out to himself in small increments—and the crew's store of gin had survived. Unfortunately, his implants meant it took nearly an entire jug of spirits for him to feel any of its effects, yet he liked the taste. He used a spent shotgun shell to dole out his daily drink.

"You'd better not," she said. "I can't hold my liquor. It takes just a few sips to get me stewed."

He grinned. "Good to know."

She scowled without heat. "No shenanigans, Fletcher."

"An angel, that's what I am. A perfect angel."

Laughing, she rose smoothly from the table and began to prepare tea. Her motions had grown much more fluid over the past few weeks, her strength and confidence growing. Maybe their walks had something to do with it. He'd like to think so, that he contributed something, however small, to her progress.

Even without the change in her movement, warmth spread in his chest as he watched her move through her cottage. The straight line of her back. The small but unmistakable sway of her hips, hinting at the sensuality she hid beneath her staid wool dresses. As she set the kettle on to boil, his eyes followed the curve of her neck, and the soft wisps of black hair curled at her nape, like shy invitations to be touched. Invitations he desperately wanted to accept.

Unaware of his thoughts, she measured out tea leaves. "One of the origins of suffering is desire."

He sat up straight. *She can't bloody read minds, can she?*

"Desire for sensory pleasures," she went on, continuing to make the tea, "food . . . sex. And things. Material possessions. We always want what we don't have. We feel anger or envy if someone has more than we do. So we're supposed to let go of our attachment to the corporeal world—including objects.

Things. All they do is provoke craving, and that robs of us happiness, contentment."

She set two cups down on the table, the same two she'd provided when he'd first come to her cottage. He had no real measure of time on the island, but it felt as though only days had passed since then—and that she'd always been a part of his life here. But it didn't make him comfortable. The more time he spent with her, the more his heart beat thunderously in his chest when he saw her. The more her husky voice, with its mosaic of accents, throbbed through him and teased his dreams.

"So you're not sorry that you lost your belongings," he said as she sat down again.

Her smile was wry. "I miss them every day. Especially the photographs of my family. And my dog, Chaaya. I had to leave her behind when I came to England." A look of pure longing and love crossed her face when she spoke her pet's name, and he felt small and foolish for envying a dog.

She'd never talked of a sweetheart or a lover. Possible that she didn't have one, but she seemed like a woman in full command of herself. Maybe the bloke had died in the devastation of Liverpool. If she grieved, she kept that specific sorrow to herself. Fletcher did and didn't want to know, selfish bastard that he was.

"But I've got memories of them," she continued. "Unlike photographs, those can't be destroyed."

He sipped at his tea. It nearly brought tears to his eyes with its perfection. "You're very wise."

This time, her laugh was full-throated, rich. "Words mean nothing. I've got plenty of words. In here and here," she tapped her temple, then the space between her breasts, "I'm a damned muddle."

He raised his mug. "Here's to muddles, then, because I'm more tangled than those wires on your desk."

After clinking her cup against his, she glanced over her shoulder and sighed. The knot of wires crouched at the corner of her worktable, as if slyly challenging someone to unravel it. "They got that way in transport, and now I can't seem to unsort them. More's the pity, because I could use them."

"I'll give it a go."

Her brows lifted.

"Think I can't?"

"Well, your hands . . ." She blushed. "They're rather . . . enormous."

Enticing, that blush of hers. "But nimble. Come on, hand it over."

Reluctantly, she rose and retrieved the clump of wires. Then set it down in the middle of the table. "And no cutting them, either. That's cheating."

"Woman, you impugn the honor of Her Majesty's Aerial Navy." He picked up the wires and began slowly, slowly picking them apart. It was a careful, arduous process, made all the more complicated by the fact that the wires were almost all copper, so it was difficult to determine what belonged to what.

He glanced up. She had her elbows on the table and watched him like he was a performing animal or wonder automaton.

"Don't you have something to do?" he asked.

She waved her hand toward her workbench. "Dozens of projects."

"Go do one of them. I can't work if you're gawking at me."

She batted her long, dusky lashes as him. "I'm making the big, strong Man O' War nervous?"

"Not nervous," he grumbled. "Distracted."

After heaving another sigh, she rose from the table. "As you like." She moved to seat herself at her workbench, but stopped. "I distract you?"

He refused to look up from his work, or even speak. Just grunted.

She muttered something in Hindi, then settled down to her own work. More silence fell as they both worked, with the only sounds the rain upon the roof and the clink of her tools as she worked on a device whose purpose he couldn't yet figure out. As he untangled the wires, his mind fell into a pleasant state of nonbeing, anchored to nothing, concerned only with separating the filaments. He drifted, quiet in himself, peaceful. Yet he was always aware of her, the curve of her back as she bent over her project.

Only once did he glance at her bed, close enough to where he sat that he could stretch out one leg and brush against the blanket spread across it. He didn't consider himself an imaginative man—he had a skill for planning battles and thinking well under pressure—but when it came to flights of fancy, he wasn't particularly adept. Yet he could easily imagine her laying there at night. The shape of her body beneath the blanket. He decided she left her hair unbound at night, and that it spread fragrantly across her pillow. And maybe, just maybe, she thought of him.

God, she didn't—she didn't *touch* herself, did she? As he had been lately when he lay in bed and thought about her.

The idea—her touching herself as she pictured him—had him iron hard in an instant. His hands seemed to swell, and the knot of wires became impossible to untangle. With a muttered curse, he pushed it away.

She grinned at him over her shoulder. Which didn't help the situation with his aching erection. He edged closer to the table so she couldn't see his groin.

"Are you giving up?" she teased.

"Just need a break," he growled.

"Ah, where's that fighting spirit I've come to rely on?"

Blood returned marginally to his brain. "You rely on me?"

"No!" she said at once, blushing. "Perhaps a little. I'd, ah, rather not have to hunt if I don't have to."

He smiled to himself as she busied herself with a pair of pliers. Good to know that they were both fumbling their way through this indefinable thing between them. He took another sip of tea, and an idea suddenly struck him.

"When's the ferryman scheduled to make his next delivery?"

She half turned in her seat. "I'd almost forgotten. Two days, I think." She shook her head. "I can't believe I've been here nearly a month."

He wanted to ask her if it had been a good month, or if she regretted coming to the island. Instead, he said, "Don't tell him about me."

She frowned. "Why would I?"

"Say nothing. If he knows I'm here—"

"He'll telegraph the navy, and they'll come for you."

"You know I don't want to leave." He wouldn't rejoin the fight to become another instrument of death. But slowly, over the month, he'd begun to see this island less as a self-imposed exile and more of a private refuge for himself and Kali. Even if they never became lovers, he could happily stay in this place for the rest of his days.

"Good," she said, turning around to her workbench. "Because I want to stay, too."

He pictured what it could be like, with her on his lap, her head resting on his shoulder as they sat by the fire, arms around each other. Thank God she had her back to him, since he was certain his gaze was full of naked yearning.

CHAPTER NINE

The ferryman Campbell arrived on the appointed day. He seemed shocked that she was still alive, and more surprised that she was sane. But she'd carried on a perfectly banal conversation with him as he'd unloaded her supplies, asking after the health of his wife and children and the quality of his journey from South Uist. She didn't inquire about the state of the world beyond the Outer Hebrides—whether there'd been any significant progress in the Mechanical War, or if he knew anything about the status of Liverpool.

Life was orderly. It was contained. She'd achieved a kind of comfort and surety she'd never known. Hard to think that a Man O' War needed any further strengthening, but he smiled more now, and that gruff wall he'd put up between himself and the world seemed to be slowly eroding.

As Campbell carried her supplies up the slope to her cottage, she considered increasing her order for next time. There were sheets of metal, spools of wiring, fresh paper for drawing up diagrams. All sufficient to keep working. Yet she'd only planned on feeding herself. And though Fletcher tried to rein in his appetite, she knew he was hungry. It was hard to tell because of his thick beard, but his cheeks seemed more hollow. More eggs, butter, and meat could help put food in his flattening belly. Not that she'd looked at his stomach, hidden as it was behind a waistcoat he'd begun to wear. But she had noticed it seemed flatter than before.

Yet if she asked Campbell to bring her more supplies, he'd grow suspicious and wonder why one woman could need so much food. She had to make a choice. Give Fletcher more to eat, or protect his privacy.

So when Campbell asked, "Is there anything else you'll be wanting for the next time?" she answered, "Just a few pounds more of beef. I'm trying to tame some of the owls here and they want an incentive." Thirty pounds of beef would've been a better request, but she doubted an island-full of owls could finish that off before it spoiled—unlike Fletcher, who'd eat the whole of it in three days. And she had no plans on taming him.

The ferryman only shrugged at this request. He tramped back along the beach, where his boat bobbed at anchor. "And you're sure you're well, Miss MacNeil?"

"Very well, indeed." This wasn't a prevarication. She meant it. Her dreams troubled her less and less, her leg felt stronger, and she was getting exceptional amounts of work done.

There was Fletcher, too. Who'd come to her cottage again yesterday when the rains hadn't stopped. She didn't think she'd like sharing the small space with anyone, but it felt natural, comfortable, to have him there, despite his size. He'd even brought a book to occupy himself—a treatise on the potential of civilian aerial travel—and they'd spent the afternoon in companionable quiet.

It had been so companionable, in fact, that her heart had sunk when he'd left just before supper, insisting that she didn't have to feed him twice.

And there'd been a moment—a breathless, moment—when they'd stood at the front door, face-to-face, after he pulled on his coat to head out. His gaze had slid down to her mouth, and she'd stared at his, and time and space dissolved. She'd known only the heat radiating from his body—he gave off a pleasant smell of warm metal—and the ache within her own, wanting, *needing* to touch him.

She'd thought for certain he'd kiss her. Or, if he didn't, then she'd kiss him. But he didn't move, and before she could rise up on her toes and link her fingers behind his neck, he'd nodded and wordlessly hurried off into the rain.

She'd wanted to kick something. Preferably him.

Now she just waved Campbell off as he hoisted anchor and chugged away from the island.

Almost as soon as she returned to her cottage to put away her supplies, there was a boom of thunder and the rains started again. Kali's heart sank. She and Fletcher had agreed that he'd stay away from her side of the island today, since they'd no idea when Campbell would arrive. They'd decided that if there was enough of the day left afterward, she'd go to the *Persephone*. Now that was impossible. True, she'd gained strength and confidence with her walks and hikes, but she still wasn't comfortable with the idea of trekking over the island in the rain.

It wasn't a gentle drizzle, either. Like a released magic

curse, the rain quickly turned into a storm. Her cottage nearly shuddered from its force. Wind rattled the windows. It sounded as though a whole unit of soldiers in heavy boots was stomping on her roof. Thunder shook her right down to her bones, and lightning bathed the inside of her cottage with shocks of light. The temperature plummeted, and she threw more peat into the fire.

At least Campbell would've have reached home by now. He was safe.

But it looked like it was going to be a long, lonely, and storm-wracked day. She settled in to work. But her concentration kept shattering with each clap of thunder. The bombs had sounded much the same, deafening with each impact, the earth itself unstable.

It's only a storm. No Hapsburg or Russian airships. Just masses of warm, damp air moving upward and cooling and condensing. Clouds form and rain falls. Lightning's just an electrostatic discharge. Thunder is merely air's expansion from the lightning that makes a shock wave. All perfectly explainable. Nothing dangerous.

If lightning were going to strike anything on the island, it wouldn't be her cottage. What about the metal tanks on the *Persephone*? She had to hope that Fletcher would be all right. There wasn't much she could do to help him.

But the cottage still shuddered with each clap of thunder, and the wind tore at the roof. It felt as if the ghosts of her past were attacking her haven.

Dusk crept in, though she could barely tell in the darkness, and the storm worsened. As she sat down to a supper she didn't want, she thought, *Storms rage, but they pass. A day or two more.*

Hadn't she endured monsoon season in Nagpur? The Nag would overflow, though they lived far enough away from the river to avoid the worst of the flooding. But her worst enemy during June and September had been boredom. This shouldn't be any different.

Except she'd survived a bombing, and the sky wasn't nearly as benign as it had been before. And monsoons didn't shake the house like a horde of demons.

She now heard the unmistakable sound of shingles torn from the roof. Then a dreadful creaking sound. She looked up just in time to see the ceiling collapse.

How long she lay beneath the fallen roof, she couldn't tell. Maybe hours. Maybe minutes. But then everything around her shook, and she feared that what was left of the house would break apart and bury her even more.

Suddenly, the roof pinning her disappeared. It flew away, tossed aside by a wild-eyed Fletcher. He loomed over her, rain splashing against his wide shoulders. Shoulders that seemed to shield her from the worst of the storm. More water beaded in his wild hair and thick beard.

"Fletcher?" She knew he was strong, but she'd no idea that he could take a slate-shingled roof and fling it like a book.

His shoulders eased slightly, though he didn't lose his ferocious expression. "Wiggle your fingers and toes for me."

Though they were numb from cold, she did move her fingers and toes. "They're fine."

"And your arms? Legs?" There was that commanding tone again as he glowered down at her.

She tested them. "Also fine. Help me up."

His arm curved around her shoulders and gently raised her to sitting. The storm continued to pour around them, but through the cascades of rain, she saw her cottage. What remained of her cottage. Only three walls still stood, and the roof was halfway across the field.

Dear God—the power he had. "What are you doing here?"

He glared up as another bolt of lightning shot across the sky. She couldn't stop her flinch. "Got worried when the storm started. This place is as safe as a house of paper. I headed over here to check that you were all right."

"But if the ferryman was still here—"

"Didn't give a damn."

"But—"

"No more questions. Not until we've got you out of the rain. Now put your arms around my neck."

As she did, his own arms came up to cradle her against his chest. They were both soaked through, but he still radiated heat, and she pressed close against the broad expanse of his chest to gather that warmth. He stood, then ran, still holding her close.

Perhaps under different circumstances she might be more scientifically curious about the speed of a running Man O' War. But not now. All she felt was his strength, his swiftness. The world turned into a blur of darkness and rain. She could barely make out shapes of trees or familiar landmarks. It was only Fletcher, holding her, racing against the storm as he held her as gently as one might hold a clockwork butterfly.

The *Persephone* finally loomed into view. A few lights

glowed in the portholes. The sight nearly brought tears to her eyes. Shelter. At last.

Fletcher hurried around to the back of the ship, to his quarters and the bank of windows that lined them. He held her with one arm, and she felt the power gathering in him before he leapt up, catching hold of an open window's sill. He hauled them both up and over, until they were in his cabin. He slammed the window shut, the rain continuing to hammer against the glass. His boots pounded against the floor as he strode to a chair. Carefully, he set her down in it. He stalked to his bed. The frame groaned and twisted slightly as he pulled it up from where it had been bolted to the floor. He dragged the whole piece of furniture over to the stove, then gathered her up again. Gently, he set her down on the bed.

"Take off your clothes." He knelt in front of the stove and stoked its flames higher.

Her fingers shook too much from the cold to undo the buttons lining the front of her dress. "C-can't."

He tried his hand at the task, but either the cold or something else made him clumsy, and he couldn't slip the buttons through their holes. Cursing, he pulled something from his boot. Light gleamed on a knife's blade.

"Hold still." There was a damp ripping sound, and suddenly the front of her dress gaped open. Beneath, her wet chemise was as transparent as glass.

She was undecided between modestly pulling her dress closed, and getting the damned sodden thing off her. Concern for health won out. She pulled off her wet and ruined gown, shimmying out of it and her sopping petticoat.

He grabbed the mass of it from her and threw it into a

corner. The only light in his quarters came from the stove, and with his back to it, he formed a massive, dark shape of unforgiving, hard angles and thick muscles.

"Everything," he said.

"I'm . . . n-not getting *naked*—"

"All of it," he commanded. "If you get lung fever and die because you're *shy*, I'll strangle you."

"Excellent . . . b-bedside manner." But she continued to shake with cold, so after making him turn around, she did as he ordered, peeling off her chemise, drawers and stockings. Covering herself with the blanket draped across his bed, she threw her remaining wet clothing into the corner, though her aim wasn't as good nor her arm as strong, and her underwear wound up lying in the middle of his quarters.

Now she was naked, save for a blanket, sitting on Fletcher's bed.

"Your clothes all off?" he asked without turning around.

"Yes—don't turn around, yet." She had to get her prosthetic leg off. He might have seen part of it before, but he'd never seen the straps fastening it to her thigh—or her stump. Quickly, she undid the buckles. She shoved the artificial limb beneath the bed, then threw the blanket back over her legs.

"You're c-clear," she said.

He turned around. She followed his gaze as it caught on a sliver of her exposed shoulder, and heard him suck in his breath. Sudden heat pulsed through her, chasing away the cold.

"Now you," she said.

"Man O' Wars don't feel the cold the same way. We don't get sick as easy."

"But you're not immortal." When he hesitated, she pressed, "The nearest doctor is miles away, and I don't have any way to fetch her. So disrobe. That's an order."

"We're not in the navy." But she continued to glare at him until, swearing under his breath, he began to pull his clothing off. Coat first. He wore no waistcoat, and his white shirt had turned as transparent as her chemise, clinging to his skin. She watched avidly as he pulled down his braces then stripped away the fabric and let it fall to the ground.

She gasped. It was impossible to keep silent. She'd seen shirtless men before, but never a Man O' War, and never Fletcher—whose body she'd tried to imagine many, many times. But imagination hardly did justice to fact.

She knew, for example, that he'd have exceptional musculature. Yet that was nothing compared to seeing those muscles with her own eyes. He'd said he'd lost weight over the course of his time on the island, but he was a hewn wonder, sleek and strapping. Every muscle was sharply defined. She could hardly imagine what he'd look like when at his peak. But this . . . this was astonishing.

Steam literally rose from his body.

Her gaze moved to the telumium implanted into his left shoulder. It curved along the shape of his body, like Roman armor, yet it flexed and moved as smoothly as flesh. A scientific and engineering marvel. But not nearly as fascinating as the man standing before her.

He caught her staring at him. His expression turned guarded, though he continued to face her. As if he expected revulsion. Had Emily seen him this way and been repulsed? For many reasons, Kali hated that woman.

"Those are quite intriguing," she said, pointing to his right arm and his right pectoral.

He glanced down at the tattoos—a tangle of thorn-covered roses and serpents interwoven amongst the vines. There was an Eye of Horus, too, and a bladed weapon of some kind. Some were more faded than others, but they all highlighted his striking physique. He said nothing.

"They must have a special meaning," she prompted.

"Only that I was young when I enlisted."

"They're beautiful," she murmured. Holding his gaze, she added, "*All* of it's beautiful."

Tension eased from him. Yet not from her. Here he was, half-dressed, with those exquisite lines of muscle running along his hips and vanishing beneath the waistband of his trousers. Here she was, naked but for a blanket. She wanted so badly to walk to him, press herself against him.

She couldn't. She had to stay exactly where she was, trapped by her injury.

"I think everything needs to come off." Not even a tiny quiver in her voice—very good, she thought. "You can't be too careful with your health."

"Look somewhere else, damn it," he growled after a moment.

She placed her hands over her eyes. "Here they'll stay until you tell me otherwise."

He muttered something, but judging by the sounds, he was pulling off his boots. And then his trousers and drawers.

Kali did what any sane and sensible woman would do in her place. She peeked.

It took every bit of will she possessed not to gasp again.

The muscles of his thighs and calves were thick. He had long feet. And his cock . . .

It stood at half mast, and even in its semi-hard state, she could barely believe its length and girth. Either he'd always been a big man, or the telumium implants had made him so. It didn't much matter how he'd gotten that way. This was who he was now. A confusing mixture of apprehension and desire filled her. A woman would have to be capacious indeed—or very aroused—to accommodate him. Capacious she wasn't, but she could be aroused. Quite aroused.

The view of his buttocks as he turned to fetch a pair of dry trousers made her salivate. Every flex and contraction of muscle showed, and he was nicely curved, unlike some of the men she'd known, with their flat behinds. She watched his glorious muscles work as he tugged on trousers—but no drawers—then quickly covered her eyes again when he faced her.

"I'm decent enough," he rumbled.

She took her hands away from her face. *I'm not going to tell him that I can plainly see the shape of his cock through his pants. I won't say a bloody thing.*

"Warm now?" he asked.

"Getting there."

He stood with his hands on his hips, as if deliberating. Finally, he crossed the cabin and sat beside her on the bed.

"Not trying to be forward," he muttered. "I give off a lot of heat."

"I know," she said.

They sat close but did not touch. Her whole body felt tight and sensitive, aware of everything, almost painfully so. She shuddered.

He looked concerned. "Still cold?"

"No. But . . . when the ceiling collapsed . . . I thought . . ." She shivered again. "I thought if I did survive, I'd be missing another leg."

He cursed, then wrapped an arm around her shoulder. She wanted so badly to lean into him, to surrender her fear, to let herself, for a moment, be vulnerable. But she wouldn't allow it. She sat straight. The heat of his body wove into hers—the only concession she'd allow.

"You're safe now," he murmured.

"There's no such thing as safety. Just avoiding catastrophe."

He moved so that he looked directly into her eyes. "Listen to me, damn it. I'll keep you safe. I promise you."

She smiled sadly. "Nobody can make that promise. Not even a Man O' War."

"I accept your challenge."

"It's not a challenge, Fletcher. It's the truth. I'm nobody's responsibility. Despite this"—she gazed down at the abbreviated shape her missing leg made beneath the blanket—"I won't be cosseted like a newly-hatched egg."

His expression darkened. "Who the hell said anything about cosseting?"

"It's—"

"A ship can't run on its own," he said, his voice rough. "Not even the biggest ironclad or most heavily armed airship. Without a crew, it just drifts. Maybe . . ." He seemed to struggle to find the words. "Maybe people are the same way. Maybe they need each other to keep from foundering. And maybe . . . maybe there's no shame in that. In . . . needing."

She opened her mouth to speak. But no words came. Because he kissed her.

The first touch of his lips to hers verged on tentative. But the kiss turned fevered, hungry, in an instant. He brought up his hands and cradled her head, his mouth against hers, both demanding and giving. He tasted of rainwater and burning need. She answered his need with her own, a floodgate of desire opening.

Her hands clutched at his shoulders. Beneath her palms, his skin was hot, so hot—tight and satiny where he was flesh, sleek and burnished where he was metal. He resonated with energy barely restrained. She'd seen the feats of strength and speed he was capable of, but nothing truly revealed his power until now. Her belly clutched in excitement, and her pulse roared in her ears louder than the storm outside.

She dug her nails into his flesh. He growled in approval, deepening the kiss. One of his hands wrapped around her waist. He pulled her hard against him, her breasts pressed to his unyielding chest. Sensation shot through her, the tight tips of her nipples sensitive, radiating pleasure from the rub of the blanket's coarse fabric and the feel of him, solid, male.

God, it had been so long since she felt anything like this. Even before the attack at Liverpool, she'd not had this kind of want. No one she needed this badly, or who wanted her with the same demand.

She jolted as his hand dipped beneath the blanket and cupped her breast, then moaned as he stroked her. His large palm easily held the fullness of her breast, caressing her, teasing her. His teeth scraped along her neck, then he kissed her throat as if to soothe the blaze he'd roused in her—she wasn't soothed. Only inflamed.

He bent his head, and when his tongue found her nipple, circling it, she gasped. The brush of his beard, the feel of his lips and tongue—it was too much, and hardly enough.

Her hands went exploring. Feeling the solidity and contours of his torso, and lower, along the ridges of his abdomen.

Before her hand could travel lower, something skittered across her whole leg.

Hazed with pleasure, she glanced down. And yelped.

A rat perched on her leg. Sitting back on his hindquarters, its little pink hands held in front of its gray body, black eyes staring up at her inquisitively.

She wasn't afraid of rodents, exactly. But she hadn't anticipated hungrily kissing Fletcher and then finding a rat on her leg.

Fletcher pulled back. He sighed as he looked at the rodent. But instead of flinging the rat across the room, he scooped it up in his hand and held it up to eye level.

"Bloody bad timing, old man," he growled.

The rat's whiskers twitched, and it crept forward and nuzzled Fletcher's nose.

"That's your *pet?*" Kali pulled the blanket close around her.

"Saved him from an owl. Then made the mistake of feeding him. Now he won't leave." He glanced at Kali. "I suppose he's curious about visitors."

"I . . ." She didn't know what to say. Her body still hummed from his kiss, his touch, and now they were talking about his pet rat. The story would've charmed her, if she hadn't been so muzzy-headed with thwarted desire.

"Shove off, Four." He set the rat onto the floor, and it scurried away, but not before casting another inquisitive glance at her.

"Four?"

"Short for four-pound shot. The smallest cannon shot."

"Of course." She took several deep breaths, steadying herself. "But I'm not finished with you. Not at all." But when she reached for him again, he captured her hands with one of his.

"Kali, listen—"

She tugged her hands away and crossed her arms over her chest. "No good conversations ever begin with *Listen*." If only she could get up and storm off.

"Too bad," he countered. His face looked carved of granite. "You'll hear what I have to say."

She didn't know if she wanted to, but she couldn't very well get up and leave.

"You have a man?" he demanded. "Some lover or sweetheart you left behind in Liverpool?

"No," she said quietly.

He looked stricken. "Hell—he wasn't killed, was he?"

"I didn't have anyone when the battle happened. A lover, a few months before, but he wasn't . . . we couldn't make it work. And he survived the attack. Moved back to his hometown of Barnsley and married his childhood sweetheart." She couldn't blame Wallace for hurrying into the shelter of normal life, but she did wonder if he'd found the safety he had sought.

But none of that mattered now. Not after that kiss with Fletcher.

"I want you, Kali. So damn much." Hot as a furnace, his gaze raked her. She could see in his eyes what he wanted to do to her. To do *with* her.

Every part of her body seemed to burst into flame. She could picture all the things he wanted, picture them as vividly as images projected from a cinemagraph.

"I want you, too," she rasped. "But I sense a reason we're not going to have each other."

There was a long, agonizing pause. Then, "I *care* about you, Kali." His voice was rough, as though he had to pull the words from deep within himself and present them to her, bloody and beating.

He stood from the bed and strode to the windows. His trousers hung low on his hips, and the fabric barely hid the shape of his cock beneath. Pure sexual frustration threatened to strangle her.

His back to her, he braced his hands on the windowsill. Firelight carved his back into an intricate topography of dark and gold, including the scars from his lashing.

"Damn it," he growled without looking at her, "I want to take you to bed, so damned much. But I won't lose this . . . this friendship we have."

"We won't—"

But he didn't, or wouldn't, hear her. "Becoming a captain lost me friends. I couldn't have them. I was in command. Can't command men to fight and possibly go to their deaths if you're also their friend."

She'd never thought of it in those terms. The island itself was remote, but he'd been isolated before, even surrounded by a hundred crewmen.

"And with . . . Emily . . ." He seemed to not want to speak her name. "We liked each other. Maybe loved each other."

Gods and goddesses, Kali did *not* want to hear this.

"But I don't think she ever really knew me," he continued. "Not the way you do. Don't take that from me," he said, low and rough. He spun to face her. "Don't take this"—he gestured to the space between them—"away from me."

"I . . . won't." This had to be the oddest conversation she'd ever had, with a man begging her not to have sex with him. Odd, and wonderful. She desired him, so much that she ached with it—but a person to care about and who cared for her, who respected her and she respected in kind . . . that was far more rare than desire. It had taken careful, slow navigation to get them where they were now. And she wouldn't throw any of that away.

"Look," she added. She stuck her hands under her thighs, pinning them to the mattress. "I can't even pinch your bottom."

He laughed, a rueful sound. But grateful, too. Finally, he said, "I'd say I'm sorry about your cottage, but it makes me happy to have you here."

"I'm glad to be here," she said, and meant it. But she'd never sleep easy aboard the *Persephone*. Not with him so close, and so impossible.

CHAPTER TEN

Fletcher refused to look at her arse. In theory, anyway. But if Kali was going to wear trousers, trousers that *he'd* supplied, staring at her ripe peach of a behind was unavoidable. If a mermaid swam past a seagoing vessel, or a winged horse soared alongside an airship, he'd look. Yet he wouldn't feel like such a damned hypocrite.

No, not a hypocrite. He'd been plain last night. He hungered for her. They'd struck a delicate balance, though. One he wouldn't spoil.

But—*God*. Did she have to have such a pretty arse? Round and pert, perfect to grip. He'd grab hold of her bottom and pull her to him, and they'd . . .

"Find anything more?"

Her voice snapped him out of his trance. Tearing his gaze away from her as she picked over the remains of her cottage, he kicked aside a heap of rubble, revealing the gleam of brass and wood.

"Tools," he said.

Face alight, she hurried through the wreckage. She bent

over to examine his findings, and this time, he made himself stare at the pile of her salvaged belongings. The rain had stopped early that morning, leaving everything slick and muddy. Some of her projects—things he couldn't begin to understand their function—were beyond recovering, smashed to tiny bits by the fallen roof. Her cooking apparatus now resembled a large crumpled rubbish bin. A few items had managed to survive in decent condition, and she'd greeted them like lost friends.

Her food supplies had been thoroughly spoiled by the rain. And her trunk of clothing had been partially crushed by the roof. The contents had survived, thank God. That morning, he'd given her a midshipman's uniform, and though she'd expressed some worry about her prosthetic leg and the trousers, her movement hadn't been compromised at all.

His moral fortitude, however, was being battered against an anvil.

"My rasps and pliers!" She sounded like a child visiting their first Mechanical Twelfth fair. He heard the clink of metal as she placed the tools in her satchel. "That's nearly everything. Keep an eye out for my hammer."

"We already found three hammers." He'd discovered them and the majority of her tools beneath her destroyed workbench.

"Not my repoussé hammer," she said. "Ah, wait—here it is!" Grinning, she held up a hammer with a wide, flat face and a rounded end.

"Ruddy fantastic," he muttered.

Placing the hammer into her satchel, she stood. "What's got your rigging in a knot?" She smirked at her own nautical reference.

"Didn't sleep well." As a Man O' War, he didn't need much sleep to function, only a few hours, but even that had been tough to come by last night. He'd given his quarters—and bed—to Kali, and slept in what had been the first mate's cabin. The mattress lay on the floor because the bed frame had been destroyed in the crash, but that hadn't been the source of his restlessness.

No, he was looking at the reason why sleep was going to be scarce, and she was surprisingly cheerful considering that her family's cottage had been practically flattened. He would've thought that facing more wrecked buildings would trigger memories of Liverpool. But at least here, she'd been able to recoup some of her losses, and that seemed to be the difference.

Her cheerfulness dimmed slightly. "I couldn't sleep much, either."

Damn, he'd been so fuddled with Kali in trousers and having her aboard the *Persephone*, he hadn't noticed the shadows beneath her eyes.

"Are my quarters too cold? Is the bed uncomfortable? There are more mattresses in the ship. I can move them in, and I'll find something to seal up the windows so no breezes get in. Or was it Four? He likes to sleep on my chest, but if he bothered you—"

She held up a hand. "At ease. Or stand down, or whatever you call it. I had . . . other things on my mind."

Their gazes locked. Her cheeks darkened, and he realized something—she'd been thinking about him, about their kiss. Just as he had.

"I'll acclimatize," she said. "A few days, and it'll be just like sharing a house with my brother—if I had one." Then she shook her head. "What a bunch of delusional codswallop. I'll *never* think of you like a brother."

Thank God for that. Because if brothers felt for their sisters anything like what he felt for her, the world would be populated by people with single eyes or extra fingers.

"We'll work on fixing this place up," he said instead.

She glanced around critically at the wreckage. One of the walls had caved in, half the roof lay across the field, and the rest of the place was covered in mud and debris. "It seems like a forlorn hope."

"We've got a Man O' War's strength and an engineer's brains," he insisted. "It'll come together before you can say . . ." He couldn't think of a single appropriate engineering term.

"Hydrometer," she offered. "And I believe I just said it, but my cottage is still a shambles."

He rubbed his forehead. "I think you were placed on this island to be my personal torment."

Instead of scowling or taking offense, she only smiled. "Examine your karma."

"What's karma?"

"Bringing certain consequences on yourself, good or bad, because of past actions. Could be in this life, or from a previous one, but the result's the same."

Fletcher sighed. "I'm doomed."

They'd brought lengths of rope and planks of wood from the *Persephone*, and from this Fletcher and Kali fashioned a pallet. Apparently, she had used a special device to carry all her belongings from the ferry to the cottage, but this had been destroyed, including the ether tanks the mechanism used. He hadn't thought to bring ether canisters from his ship, so they were left with a four-by-four foot pallet loaded down with her surviving possessions, ropes lashing them to the wood.

"If you bring me some ether," she said, "I can jury-rig an apparatus to help us carry all this across the island."

"Not necessary." He grabbed the ropes that held her possessions onto the pallet, and began to drag the whole heavy mass behind him.

"Now you're just bragging," she said.

"Tighten your screws, madam. This is the fastest way to get your kit to the *Persephone*."

She didn't look convinced, and he didn't blame her. It would have been a quick matter for him to run back to the ship and grab some extra ether. But he wasn't above a bit of flaunting. The key word in Man O' War was *Man*. And he was no better than any ordinary man, wanting to show off for a woman.

Moron. He didn't have anything to gain with this display. Except that he wanted it.

After a last, resigned look at her ruined cottage, she turned away and together they made their way back across the island to the ship. The pallet did slow him some, and even with her leg, she'd manage to get ahead of him a little, treating—or tormenting—him with the vision of her hips and arse in trousers.

He'd seen many women in trousers. They still weren't preferred over dresses, but a woman couldn't be a shipbuilder or navvy or stevedore if her legs kept tangling in skirts. And he'd be a liar if he said he didn't sometimes look, but he was always careful not to leer or let his gaze dawdle too long. Nobody wanted to be treated like a thing and not a human.

But, damn and curse him again, because he was mesmerized by the sway and curve of Kali's hips, the length of her legs, and that delectable bum.

You made your bunk. Lie in it.

Yet how could he learn the feel of her skin if he didn't know himself? Each day with her, the deadness inside him broke apart, bit by bit. But he was still coming to understand what it was to have her as a friend. What it was to be a man again, not a ghost.

Finally, his torment ended when they reached the *Persephone* and hauled her belongings aboard. She tried to refuse when he ceded his quarters to her, but he wouldn't be gainsaid. His own possessions had always been minimal, and in less than five minutes, he'd taken up semipermanent residence in the first mate's cabin. It was smaller, dusty, and littered with broken furniture and papers, but the mattress and blanket were clean. He carried an intact desk into the cabin—someplace for him to read—and with a lantern, all his needs were met.

He'd avoided the other crewmen's cabins until now. It felt like . . . an invasion of privacy. Some of the men had taken a few things with them when abandoning ship, but there hadn't been time for much. So Fletcher never looked at their personal letters and telegrams, their framed photographs, their journals.

Now he was living in First Lieutenant Walters's quarters. Fletcher had seen Walters safely piloting the jollyboat away from the crashing ship, so he didn't feel quite like a grave robber.

As Fletcher pushed Walters's belongings into a corner, he wondered. How was the first lieutenant now? He would've been assigned to a new airship. They wouldn't waste a man of his skill and experience on a seafaring ship. Crewmen and officers trained in aerial warfare were tough to come by. A good man, Walters. Young, and eager to learn, but cool in battle. It wouldn't surprise Fletcher in the slightest if the first lieutenant was promoted after what happened at Liverpool, with the possibility of becoming a Man O' War.

But no, Walters had had a fiancée. He'd spoken of starting a family. All impossible after the transformation. Though Walters's fiancée might be willing to accept his metamorphosis and the loss of having children.

A furious banging pulled him from his thoughts. It was coming from his quarters. He hurried down the passageway, but his cabin was empty.

He found her in his washroom, on her back, a wrench in her hands as she worked on some pipes.

"I can't believe you've gone four months without indoor plumbing," she said without looking at him.

"Captains don't learn how to fix their washroom pipes." He crossed his arms over his chest and leaned against the jamb. "There are woods nearby for . . . needs. And I bathe in the stream every day." Since she'd arrived at the island, he actually bathed twice a day—once before seeing her, and once after.

She eyed him. "You really have been living like an animal, haven't you?" Shaking her head, she resumed working on the plumbing.

"A healthy, clean animal."

"This whole ship needs a good fixing up." She sighed. "All the mechanical and engineering systems are in shambles. I suppose I'll just have to tackle it piecemeal, or I'll tear my hair out at the enormity of my task."

At the mention of hair, he pulled one hand through his own wild mane. "And these fixing-up efforts will extend to the ship's occupant, too, I wager. Cut my hair, give me a shave. Civilize me."

She shot him another glance. "I'm not playing Beauty to your Beast. Clean yourself up or don't. It's your choice."

Oddly, he felt a sting of offense that she didn't care about his appearance. "I thought all women couldn't wait to get their hands on a man and change him."

Though she returned to her labors with the pipes, her voice was tight when she said, "Whatever woman tried to alter you was an imbecile."

"It was my alterations that she couldn't stomach. And didn't think I was worth the effort to try."

She set her wrench down and sat up. Her gaze steady on his, she said, "Then she truly was a dolt. It's the man himself that matters, and you're worth every effort."

The toes of his boots became unreasonably fascinating. He couldn't tear his eyes from them.

The subject seemed to exhaust itself, because she didn't say anything else, but lay back down and continued working on the plumbing. They only spoke when she gave him instructions—it still jarred to have someone on his ship telling *him* what to do, but he'd have to adjust to this new paradigm. And, truthfully, he didn't mind it. They worked well

together. Over the course of the rest of the afternoon, he assisted her in getting the *Persephone*'s plumbing back in order.
Water was taken from the nearby stream to fill the surviving tanks, and she scavenged from the ship to build pipes and
whatever else she needed to make the *Persephone* more of a
place one could live in, and less of a temporary shelter.

Watching her work was a pleasure—the intensity of her
concentration, the confidence she used to make decisions,
even the moments when she stared off into nothingness,
thinking. He'd seen his ship's engineers at work, but those
men operated within confined roles, knowing exactly how
each part of the airship functioned and what was necessary
to keep them running.

Kali knew nothing about how an airship operated, but he
saw her learn it, witnessed her encounter problems and pro-
pose solutions. And she never questioned herself. She simply
thought the issue through and then resolved it.

"Don't know if my presence here is really necessary," he
murmured as she put the finishing touches on the washroom
in his new quarters. Dust and grime covered her, the finest
cosmetic he'd ever seen.

"I'd never get the actual heavy lifting done without you,"
she answered. "You filled the ship's water supply tanks, which
I never could have done on my own." Then she grinned. "And
the company isn't bad, either."

Company? They'd barely spoken all afternoon, except
when she asked him to hand her the soldering iron or hold a
piece of metal in place.

She didn't demand a constant stream of chatter—which
he couldn't have provided if he wanted—and though the sight

of her in trousers provided a continual distraction, he'd been just as comfortable here as he'd been at her cottage. Strange, when the *Persephone* had been his solitary home for nearly four months. But she fit in well here.

"You might've made a good engineer on an airship," he noted.

Tightening a valve, she smiled wryly. "Except the British Navy isn't keen on women in its ranks."

"That might change." He leaned against the bulkhead, feeling oddly useless as she continued to work.

"I hope so. For there are many women who'd serve their country, if given the chance."

His brows rose. "You?"

"I don't think I'd pass the physical."

"But if you *could*—"

She scooted out from beneath the washbasin and dusted off her hands. "I remember crying in my father's arms . . . I couldn't have been more than six or seven . . . angry and sad that I'd never get the chance to do what he did. Be of service to my nation."

"What'd he think?"

She used a rag to clean off her wrench. "He was sorry, but not sorry I wouldn't get the chance to get shot at. But it's my decision to make, not his. Not anyone's."

The thought of Kali in battle—the target of ether-powered cannon shot and bullets—made his gut clench. If anything were to happen to her . . . Cold fear scraped down his neck and back as he remembered seeing her half-buried beneath the ruins of her cottage, the visceral punch of terror that stole thought. But she hadn't been hurt beyond a bruise or two.

And he'd never have to worry about her being in battle. So long as they stayed on this island, she was safe.

"You must miss it," she said now. "The navy. Being captain of a ship. Having more than just this." She waved at the floorboards, slightly buckled from the crash, and the listing bulkheads.

"I liked being a captain at sea," he answered, watching her get to her feet. She'd only refuse his help to stand, so he tucked his hands beneath his biceps. "And those first years as a Man O' War gave me purpose. I don't miss war. But when I first crashed here, I didn't know what the hell to make of myself. How to act. What to feel. I was dead in a way. Now . . ." Now each breath felt like an education in what it meant to be alive.

She didn't press him for more. Instead, she turned the knob on the faucet. Something groaned and shuddered. But then, after a minute, water sputtered out of the tap. It was brown and filled with bugs.

Four, who'd been watching the proceedings with interest, squeaked and darted away.

"We'll have to let it run for a few minutes to clear the pipes out. I'd imagine a whole host of insects are irritated at receiving such a rude eviction notice." She slanted him a grin. "But if it means vexing a millipede in order to have a hot shower bath, I'll do so, gladly."

True to her word, after fifteen minutes, the water ran clear, free of insect life. He turned the hot water knob on the shower bath, and after more groaning, actual hot water came out of the shower nozzle. Man O' Wars didn't have the same sensitivity to temperature as normal humans, so he hadn't minded his ice-cold baths in the forest stream. Yet the feel of hot water on his hand nearly brought tears to his eyes.

He quickly shut off the faucet.

"I've set it up so that we'll be recycling some water," she said, "given that we've a limited supply and I don't want to tax the island's resources." She offered him an apologetic smile. "Not opulent living, washing in each other's bathwater."

"Ah, damn, here I'd been thinking we'd transform the *Persephone* into a Cunard luxury liner." But as he teased, the image of her in a shower bath—naked, water running all over her sleek and curved body—leapt into his mind, as if projected by a cinemagraph.

Hell. He really had to be demented if he looked forward to bathing in the same water that had touched her skin.

He cleared his throat. "You've worked miracles on this broken-down old ship. So . . . thank you."

She brushed past him as she left the washroom. "No thanks yet. There's still much to be done. My work's just beginning."

"Should I be excited, or terrified?"

Over her shoulder, she threw him a grin. "A little of both would be the safest option."

Fletcher had never known time to move more quickly than it did over the next week. Without discussing it, he and Kali fell into a schedule. The mornings were for gathering supplies to eat—hunting, fishing, collecting edible plants—as well as gathering peat. The afternoons were spent putting the ship back in working order. She was a single-minded whirlwind, whose energy nearly surpassed his own. They cleared out the passageways, putting all the debris he'd never touched into the former gunnery deck, and repaired the floors and bulkheads. She spent days studying the batteries, and the complex system that transformed his *aurora vires* into energy for the ship, and the ether that resulted from the process. As she did, she worked to get the electricity running on the ship.

"I'd wager lots of sailors want to be Man O' Wars," she said, her fingers buried within a web of wires.

Making himself useful, he spliced rope. He wasn't sure entirely what he'd do with hundreds of feet of rope, but when the complicated work on the ship needed doing, he was as helpful as a bear trying to carry an egg in its paws.

"New recruits are examined through spectral goggles to see their *aurora vires* rating," he said. "Barely five percent rate Gimmel or higher. Some are relieved. Others get angry." He shrugged. "Nothing changes your rating, though. You can train and face as many battles as you want. But the *aurora vires* is part of us when we're born—at least, I think so. They taught us the history of Dr. Rossini and her discovery, but I was more interested in whether I'd qualify or not."

"So you were an Aleph," she said. The top rating.

"Bet," he said instead, the second highest rating. It hadn't disappointed him that he wasn't the highest. He hadn't felt the need to be at the top. All he'd needed was to do his duty, and do it well.

Emily hadn't wanted any of it, whether he was the highest ranking or not. He'd heard that there were some ladies who actually tried to take Man O' Wars as lovers, and that they preferred Alephs, thinking them the most superior. Not wanting to be anyone's trophy, he'd avoided those women and their expectations as to what he should be. Including their disappointment that he wasn't the top grade. Courtesans catering to Man O' Wars weren't as particular. But then, they weren't paid to be selective.

To his surprise, though, Kali only smiled. "I would've guessed Bet. Alephs are overbearing brutes, I'm sure. Bullies and chest pounders."

"Not all of them." But *she* didn't think of him that way.

They hadn't any tetrol to make the galley function as it had before, but she built a device that allowed peat to fuel the stove as well as the clockwork spit. That night, they dined on roast rabbit and fish, and the following morning, she made them eggs. All her flour and butter had been ruined in the storm, but he'd done without bread and pies before her arrival. He only worried that she'd grow too lean on the island's Spartan diet. At least the ferryman would arrive in a few weeks to resupply her.

They both agreed that they needed to rebuild her cottage. Not only should the ferryman want to see it when he returned, but because she had her own home, just as he had his.

Yet day after day passed. They never went to her cottage. "Too damp today," she'd say, or he'd insist that the partridges would by migrating and they couldn't lose the chance to bag some more game. Neither of them objected to the objections.

Each day wasn't spent entirely in each other's company. When it rained, he went out on his own to hunt and forage. And sometimes, she shut herself off in the wardroom, which she'd commandeered as a workshop. She might emerge to bolt down some food, then hasten back to whatever it was she was working on. He didn't mind these absences. Gave him time to clear his head, time with his own thoughts.

At least she'd gone back to wearing dresses.

It troubled him, how easily they'd fallen into this arrangement. He wanted to be disturbed by her presence, to think his peace ruined, to resent her.

None of those feelings came. He woke eager to see Kali, though his sleep was restless and full of her. Often, he had to tear his gaze from her mouth and redirect his thoughts from unpinning her glossy black hair. It was too fragile, this thing between them. And he was still learning what it was to think of himself as a man and not a means of destruction again. To breach the distance he'd imposed around himself.

Though he did shave. A little. And trim his hair. Just a bit. Nothing drastic. Only the minor application of a pair of grooming scissors as, shirtless, he studied his reflection in a broken mirror. He hadn't looked at himself in months. It was a wonder she hadn't thought him truly some kind of animal, with his beard as thick as it was, and his hair like a mane. But with the newly-restored water running, and some scavenged shaving soap, mug, and brush, he took the uncultivated mass of his beard down to something slightly more tame—a jungle into a botanic garden. He wasn't much of a barber, so he trimmed off only an inch of his hair, lest he look like some kind of escaped lunatic asylum patient.

When he was done, he studied himself again. He'd never be a handsome man, with his large nose and heavy brow, but he'd lived nearly forty years with his face and they were on amicable terms. He could've shaved the beard entirely. The deck of an airship could be a damned cold place, and all the crew grew beards to keep warm. Man O' Wars didn't need the extra warmth. But after four months with it, he'd grown used to his facial hair. Liked it, actually.

Still, when he came into the galley for supper that night and Kali's mouth literally hung open when she saw him, heat flooded his face.

God, did I make a huge bloody mistake?

They both cleared their throats at the same time.

"You didn't do that on my account, I hope," she said.

"I did it on my account." He took his seat at the table. "You disapprove?"

"No," she answered with gratifying quickness. "Only . . . I never realized . . . you've got a dimple . . . just here."

He jumped when she leaned closer and her fingertip brushed his cheek.

"Damn thing," he muttered, composing himself. "Makes me look like a sodding baby."

Her gaze continued to linger on him, dark and bright as a midsummer sky. "Of all the things I'd confuse you for," she said, "a baby isn't one of them."

He'd once felt an earthquake when he was a young seaman on leave in the East Indies. The ground had shuddered and shook, and he'd thought the world was ending. It hadn't, of course. But it had scared the hell out of him. He'd learned later from a geologist that the violent shaking was the result of plates beneath the earth's surface shifting against each other. Breaching distances.

He felt it now, that shifting and shaking. But the earthquake was inside him. He didn't fear the distance between him and Kali, not as he had before.

There was a new danger, and though he'd faced every variety of peril, this one held the most uncertainty.

He needed her.

CHAPTER ELEVEN

K ali came instantly awake the moment someone's hand touched her shoulder.

"Easy." Fletcher's voice, low in the darkness.

She shoved herself upright, heedless of the blanket pooling at her waist. "What's going on? Are we under attack?" She fumbled with her prosthetic leg, kept just beneath her bed.

"No attack. We're safe."

She rubbed the heels of her palms into her eyes. "What time is it?"

Shadows still veiled the cabin, and she could just make out Fletcher's tall, broad outline as he paced to the window. "Almost time," he said cryptically.

"For what?"

He turned back to her. She felt more than saw his gaze linger on her, particularly where the blanket revealed she was wearing only a chemise.

"Get dressed," he rasped. "Meet me topside in ten minutes."

"But—"

Then he was gone.

She'd half a mind to go back to sleep. The dream had been so blessedly pleasant. Well, *pleasant* didn't quite cover it. She and Fletcher had been lying in a grove of mango trees, feeding each other dripping slices of fruit and licking the juice off their skin. They'd been growing quite sticky, and all around them had been not birdsong but a *raga yaman*, the lush, lilting music of the evening.

She'd just been sucking mango juice off of Fletcher's stomach when the real Fletcher had awakened her. Likely for something far less enjoyable than her dream. Perhaps one of the battery relays she'd rigged up had broken and needed repair. Though why it couldn't wait until morning, she had no idea. And none of the relays were on the top deck. The whole thing was an irritating mystery.

If she lingered in bed, he'd certainly come back to fetch her. And not to recreate her dream. Muttering, she lit a lamp and pulled on her clothes. Checking her timepiece, she saw it was just past six in the morning.

It was damned chilly in the cabin, her breath misting in front of her as she fastened on her prosthesis. After slipping on her boots, throwing on her cloak, and grabbing her tool belt, she left the cabin. She carried a lamp with her, since none in the passageways had been lit. At least the corridors were cleaner and straighter now than when she'd first arrived, and she had less risk of tripping and snapping her neck.

She climbed the companionway stairs leading to the top deck. Despite her cloak, it was bitter cold. The sky was still full black, except for the pale edge of ash on the eastern horizon. She scanned the deck, looking for Fletcher. Beyond the circle of light thrown by the lantern, she just made out his silhouette standing near what had been the central support column for the ship's main ether tank. Some other objects stood near him, but it was too dark to make out what they were.

Still muttering to herself, she crossed the deck to him. "All right, what needs fixing?" she grumbled.

He frowned at her. "Nothing."

"Then why drag me out of bed at an hour fit only for bakers and dipsomaniacs?"

He glanced at the object beside him. Several objects, actually. One was a barrel with the top part removed. Beside it stood the biggest coil of rope she'd ever seen. When unrolled, it had to be at least two hundred and fifty feet long. One end of the rope looped through several iron rings that had been riveted around the barrel. The other end of the rope had been tied with a massive knot to one of the ship's cleats.

None of it made sense, until she saw the dozen small ether tanks also mounted around the barrel. Each the size of a man's arm and encased in brass, they looked like they'd been taken from the ether cannons.

She looked at him. He appeared to be trying very hard not to smile.

"When did you do all this?" she demanded.

"We're not constantly in each other's pockets," he answered. He gazed at the eastern horizon. "And we're losing time. Get in."

She eyed the barrel. "Into *that*? It looks as safe as a raft made from biscuits."

The humor vanished from his eyes. "Ask yourself this: would I ever tell you to get into something dangerous?"

"I'll need a little help climbing in," she answered after a moment.

Suddenly, his hands clasped her waist, and she briefly flew as he lifted her and set her gently into the barrel. He climbed in after her. The barrel didn't boast a particularly large circumference. She and Fletcher pressed very close, his heat chasing away the cold.

"I suppose I shouldn't ask what the hell is going on," she said, slightly out of breath from his nearness.

"You engineers are all about predicting outcomes," he said with fond exasperation. He edged around the barrel, bending over the rim to adjust a small dial on the ether tanks, activating the gas stored in them. "A little surprise every now and then should be welcome."

As he activated the tanks, the barrel slowly rose. She gripped the rim with enough force to make her knuckles ache.

"Have you ever flown before?" he asked casually, continuing to trigger the ether tanks.

Tightly, she answered, "Civilians aren't allowed on airships."

"Not government airships, no, but there are Sky Trains in America, and rogue Man O' Wars who'll take passengers." The barrel continued to rise: a few feet, then five, then ten. The lantern on the deck of the ship grew smaller and smaller.

"I've never been to America, and as for booking passage with a rogue Man O' War, I don't want to wake up in my bunk with a slit throat." She shook her head slightly, her whole body tight as an overwound clock. "Just the usual earth and water-bound transport for me, thank you."

Finally, he activated the last ether tank, and the barrel

lifted higher and higher. Thank God it was so dark, so she couldn't get a true sense of how high they were.

"Afraid of heights?"

She managed a snort. "I've climbed the tower at Toxeth Cathedral."

"Yet you're stiff as a beardless midshipman at his first brothel."

His candor robbed her of words. But she recovered enough to say, "It's only ... there's nothing around me. No tower. Just ... open air."

His arms wrapped around her, pulling her closer, her back to his front. "Not true," he murmured. "You've got me."

And, saints and devas help her, she *did* feel safer with his arms encircling her, the broad and solid muscle of his chest and body behind her. She felt engulfed in the scent of warm metal. He'd never let her fall. Suddenly, the ascent wasn't terrifying but ... exciting.

It was still too dark to see much, but she could sense the growing expanse between herself and the ground. A wide openness, an absolute freedom—both terrifying and exhilarating. The ground formed a darker shape beneath them, wide and undulating, with the sky the color of spilled ink, dotted with charcoal-hued clouds. The lantern on the *Persephone's* deck became as small as a star.

"First time I ever flew," he said, his breath warm against her neck, "I couldn't decide if I was going to piss myself or never stop laughing."

She'd never heard him laugh, truly laugh, and suddenly craved the sound. "I can't imagine you being scared of anything."

"Well, I was, that first flight." Then he added, in a voice so low she barely heard him, "Scared the hell out of me when your roof fell down."

This impossibly strong man, this *Man O' War*, had feared for her, cared for her. And now he was taking her up into the sky. He might've been a good ship's captain, and at one time, he'd turned chairs, but it'd had been a considerable effort for him to put this strange flying contraption together.

They continued to rise higher and higher, and she finally saw the sea, black and glittering. Then the barrel jolted, stopping its ascent. It swayed gently in the draughts of air.

"Now we wait," Fletcher said.

She would've been content to simply stay up here in the darkness, his arms encircling her. But then—

"There," he whispered, pointing toward the eastern horizon.

A golden filament appeared where the sky met the sea. Roses bloomed in the air around that line of gold, and within moments, the indigo sky transformed to amber. The clouds were purple watercolor streaks reflected back in the gilded sea. The stars faded as the sky lightened. And the island itself brightened with morning. It was much like the view from the top of the hills, and, indeed, she saw them off to her right, with the emerging sunlight painting their rocky surfaces. The sky turned to gold, and the gray island became a place of life, of color. She watched it all, consuming it as one might watch a dream unfold.

Yet she wasn't asleep. She was too aware of the chill on her cheeks, the salty, vegetal scent of the air, the heat of Fletcher. And her heart, beating with a wild, aching joy.

"Thank you," she breathed. "This is . . ." Her voice trailed off, words too cold and small and petty to describe her feelings.

"Aye," he said after a moment. "It is."

She shielded her eyes as the sun climbed. "We could've had the same view from the hilltops."

"Not the same. We'd still have the earth beneath our feet, and nothing's like the sunrise from the middle of the sky."

Even with her greater strength and agility, a climb up the hills in the darkness would've been a challenge for her. He knew that. But he'd found a way to give her the rising sun.

She turned in the circle of his arms to face him. In the first rays of dawn, his eyes were bright as aquamarines, the angles of his face unforgiving and beautiful in their harshness. She grasped his biceps, which flexed beneath her touch, as stone might flex. Had she not known him as well as she did, she might've mistaken his expression for disinterest. But he'd worn the same mask before. When desire had burned between them in his quarters. And she'd felt his reticence, his uncertainty.

But now he didn't move away. He was immobile as a myth when she stretched up on her toes and put her lips on his.

Not immobile. His mouth was supple and demanding against hers. Kissing her ravenously. She had her own hungers, needs, and swept her tongue into the hot slickness of his mouth. He groaned deeply, his tongue stroking hers. One of his hands remained at her waist. The other slid down to cup her behind, and he made another animal sound of pleasure. She panted into him. There were too many layers of clothing between them, but she could feel his hips press tight to hers, and she arched against him, craving more.

It was and it wasn't a surprise, this pleasure and desire they called forth so quickly. Weeks had passed since that kiss in his quarters, the night he'd pulled her from the cottage's rubble and brought her to his home, the grounded airship. And in those intervening weeks, they'd grown more certain. Of each other. And themselves.

He moved from her mouth, trailing his lips along her jaw, down her throat. His beard rasped deliciously against her skin, and she moaned. Oh, God, what would that beard feel like on her stomach? On the inside of her thighs?

But then the sensation stopped, and she blinked to hazy awareness. He'd pulled back, his chest rising and falling, his pupils wide and jaw tight.

"Can't make love to you—"

She gasped, "If this is more nonsense about sex complicating things—"

"I can't make love to you *up here*," he growled.

He pulled her hands off his arms and made her grip the edge of the barrel. He moved around their small vessel, adjusting the activators on the ether tanks. Gradually, they sank lower and lower, and the earth and the *Persephone* grew closer.

"But when we get on the ground . . ." she supplied.

He was everything wild, held back by the tiniest link of silver in the chain of his self-control. "When we're on the ground," he rumbled, "I have plans for you. Plans I've thought about for a long time. But I prefer action to planning."

The moment they returned to the ship she found herself swept up into his arms. He strode down the passageway toward her quarters. She didn't bother complaining that she could easily walk the distance herself. All she wanted was to get to the cabin quickly. As he walked, she pressed her face into the crook of his neck, nuzzling against the column of his throat, breathing him in deeply. His steps faltered. He muttered a curse. But kept walking.

"We could use any cabin in the ship," she noted. "Nobody's going to complain."

"The captain's quarters has the biggest bed."

She liked the sound of that.

They reached the cabin and he gently set her down beside the bed. At once, they were in each other's arms, mouths searching, tasting. Uncertainty burned away. She tangled her fingers into his thick hair, tugging his head down so she could kiss him more deeply. He stroked a hand down her back, and his other hand wasted no time in cradling her breast. Her breath caught at the feel of him, a glorious heat that soaked into her clothes, her flesh. And when he circled his fingers around her tightening nipple, she moaned.

Impatiently, she tugged at his clothing. Layer by layer, they fell away—his coat, his shirt—until his torso was bare. Bright morning light gleamed on his telumium implants, across the hard contours of his chest, scars made from blade and bullet, the intricate designs of ink illuminating his skin as if he were a prayer book. She'd gladly sing from this hymnal.

She looked up to see him watching her carefully. As if in suspense, guarded.

Understanding came. She'd seen him bare-chested before, but not in the bright daylight, his every difference from a normal man emphasized in unforgiving sunshine. He feared her reaction. He'd been hurt by someone so badly before. And that fractured her heart, that of all the dangers he'd ever faced, her response to him made him afraid, even if only a bit. She realized she had the power to hurt him—a power she'd never use, but it stunned and humbled her.

In answer, she stroked her hands up his chest. He sucked in his breath at her touch. She stepped closer to him, pressing herself against the solidity of his torso, her palms flat against his pectorals. One was hot metal, the other, hot flesh. Beneath her hand, beneath the telumium, his heart beat wild like a cornered tiger.

She pressed her lips to him, first upon his skin, then upon the metal implants.

"Can you feel that?" she whispered.

Jaw tight, he answered, "Only a little."

"Then I'll just have to touch you where I know you can feel it."

He rasped a curse. "You're not the only one with that privilege." Within moments, he had helped her out of her dress, until she stood only in her chemise and petticoat. Then they touched each other everywhere, their hands as greedy to explore. She learned all the hard and lean surfaces of his body, the dusting of hair along his forearms, and the intriguing line of more hair leading from his navel down the flat of his stomach. Veteran he might be, but at her every caress and stroke, he shuddered and muttered invocations.

His hands weren't idle, either. He slid the pins from her hair, so it fell about her shoulders, and he stroked it, making her purr. He traced callused fingertips down her throat, across her collarbones, along her arms. Through her chemise, he stroked her breasts—her dark nipples plainly visible through the sheer cotton—his touch both reverential and confident. He had an instinct for what she liked, what she needed, reading her like a celestial chart. When she moaned and leaned into him, he knew what she wanted, and pinched her nipples lightly, making her cry out in pleasure.

She felt the strength in him, a man more powerful than she could ever truly fathom, and his gentleness, too. But he growled when she stroked down the front of his trousers, finding the thickness of his straining cock. She was never raised with any particular religion, but she prayed to the goddess Rati that she'd be able to take him inside of her. Then again, she was so wet, she'd need no divine intervention.

Fumbling with the buttons of his trousers, she finally got them open enough to reach inside and take him in her hand. Kali smiled to herself. It was true, that sailors had the foulest language imaginable, because Fletcher swore ornately as she stroked him, words that even she—a soldier's daughter—had never heard before.

Then his hand pressed against hers, stopping her. "Can't take more of that," he panted. "Or the trip will be over before we've even left the harbor."

"We can take as many trips as we like."

"But we only have one first time together." He tugged off his boots and peeled away his trousers, until he stood before her completely naked. This time, there was no hesitation or concern in his gaze. He trusted her in his moment of exposure, and it was a sweet suffering to be given that trust, when they were both so damaged.

"Your turn," he murmured, stepping close.

But she clasped his wrists when they went to untie her petticoat. Once that layer was gone, she'd be in nothing but her chemise and drawers. Her prosthetic leg would be plainly visible.

"I want to see you," he whispered.

She pressed her lips tightly together. He'd seen her artificial limb before, but the circumstances had been different. Not a precursor to making love.

"Fletcher—"

"You are so beautiful, Kali. So damned beautiful. Every part of you."

She seemed incapable of breath when she finally nodded, and he undid the ribbons of her petticoat. It slid to the floor. He knelt down and helped her step out of it, her hands on his shoulders for balance. And there she stood, one whole leg of flesh, one leg made of brass and wood.

"These, too." He looked up at her, his fingers hovering over the drawstring of her drawers.

Her chemise only reached the top of her thighs. With her drawers gone, he'd plainly see the straps fastening the leg to her.

God—could she do this? Expose herself to him this way? Part of her shriveled in fear. The other part wanted to dare him to look upon her, to test him. Test herself.

She couldn't speak, but she gave another nod. His long, thick fingers trembled as he tried to undo the fastening of her drawers, but he seemed to have trouble with the knot. So she gently pushed his hands away and untied the ribbon herself. These, too, loosened and her drawers slid to the floor, and once more, he helped her to step out of them.

There was no hiding now. It wasn't a smooth joining of metal and flesh like his telumium implants. This was much more crude, despite all her technological skill. Most of her leg was gone. It had been so ruined by the collapsing building, saving it would've been impossible. At least she'd been unconscious when they'd amputated.

The straps against her skin were not erotic. They spoke of a terrible injury, and the limitations of human ingenuity—and kindness. It was ugly, and she knew it.

She waited for Fletcher to turn away, or a shadow of revulsion to pass across his face. Instead, his gaze slowly moved up over her prosthesis—it took everything she had not to run from his gaze—to her thigh. But he also looked at the dark triangle between her legs, barely hidden by her chemise, and she saw not disgust in his eyes but desire. His gaze continued upward, until their gazes locked.

"What a warrior you are," he breathed. "A beautiful warrior."

Something hot and damp filmed her eyes. She hated him at that moment for making her feel so much—hated, and adored him.

But she couldn't be certain, truly certain, until he'd seen everything.

As he continued to kneel, she sat on the bed. Pulled off her chemise. His eyes darkened; she was nude now, without a single scrap of clothing. But not completely uncovered.

She didn't look at him as she unbuckled the straps, only focused on her task. One by one, she released the buckles, feeling the slide of the leather, hearing the clink of the metal. She sighed as the last buckle came loose. And then she set her prosthetic leg on the floor.

Now she was utterly naked. The most bare she'd ever been in her life.

She stared at the remainder of her leg. The doctors had done good work. The stump was smooth, with minimal scarring puckering her flesh. And she'd been careful to rub cocoa butter and honey into the healing wound. For all intents and purposes, she'd healed well.

No shame rose up when she looked at her stump. No disgust. It showed she'd come through an ordeal and survived. She saw her incomplete leg and felt . . . pride.

But what would another person think? A man? She'd never tested it before. Never wanted to see her pride in herself reflected back as someone else's disgust. Or, worse, pity. If she saw any of that in Fletcher's eyes . . . it would be like a second bombing. She'd scurry into a hiding place so deep, so concealed, she might never be found again.

As she continued to stare down at her legs—one complete, one only partly there—she started as Fletcher's broad hands stroked up her thighs. She looked up.

His face was sharp with desire, and his eyes . . . his eyes held so much admiration, she thought her heart would burst.

"You put me to shame," he murmured.

"I don't want shame." She sounded breathless. "I only want us."

He rose up and then stretched out on the bed with all his acres of delicious muscle. "I want everything." He gently pulled her down to lie partially beneath him, his hands in her hair, tilting her head back for a kiss.

"And that's exactly what you'll get," she answered. "Everything."

CHAPTER TWELVE

Fletcher was being given a gift. He understood that—from the filaments of telumium threaded around his heart, to his bones and blood. Kali wouldn't let merely anyone see her like this, but *he* had been granted the privilege of her trust. And he wouldn't waste it.

Her gasping response to his touch filled him with masculine pride. She needed pleasure, as much pleasure as she could bear. They both needed it, but he'd give her as much as his body could bestow.

He stroked down the curve of her stomach, then lower. Her hips bucked when he found her wet and already opening for him. Some animal snarled, and he realized it was him. He caressed her, lightly at first, learning her intimate geography, and then as he learned more—how to circle her bud just *so*, how to rub against her entrance in just this way—confidence grew. Especially as she moaned and writhed, her mouth open against his.

She always had a clever retort, a smart word, but now she made inarticulate sounds of pleasure as he palmed one of her breasts and stroked her pussy. Here, with him, she was free. They were free from the world together.

He felt her body tightening. "Not yet," he said, taking his hand away.

She made a sound of protest. "Don't turn away now. We've come so far together—"

"And we'll go farther." He loved her gasp of surprise and excitement as he kissed his' way down her body, stopping briefly to lick and suck her breasts, before continuing on downward.

He folded himself back, kneeling between her legs. He bit lightly along the flesh of her thighs, scraping his teeth there as she shivered and moaned. And then he licked her pussy—one long, slick stroke. Again. And again.

Goddamn me to a fiery hell, she's delicious.

He feasted. Discovered her every secret place. Took her clit between his lips and sucked. Her nails bit into his scalp as she held him in just the right spot, and the sting went straight to his cock.

With a cry, she arched up, her body taut. He stayed exactly where he was, her climax filling him with hot radiance. But he wanted more. And he brought her to release another time. And another. His gaze was riveted to her face, watching her pleasure, seeing her unguarded for him alone.

Pleasure was so much finer when it was shared.

Her strength surprised him as she pushed his head away. "I don't want to come again unless you're inside me."

His already aching cock became an agony of want. "Bloody hell, *yes*," he rasped.

She reached behind her to grab the headboard, her breasts

thrusting up with the movement. Climbing up her body, he was all shuddering need. When he'd positioned himself above her, his hands covering hers, their gazes met and held. They both kept their eyes open as he rubbed his cock along her folds, coating himself in her slickness. Neither looked away or closed their eyes as he placed himself at her entrance, and they stared into each other's eyes as he thrust into her.

They both cried out. She was tight and slick and everything perfect. All he wanted was to move, to thrust thick and deep, but it was a fact that Man O' Wars were bigger than normal men, and a few of his comrades had complained that they'd caused women pain during lovemaking. So he held himself still, letting her adapt, praying he wasn't hurting her too much.

She winced slightly, and he started to pull his hips back.

"Don't you . . . dare," she panted.

"Won't hurt you—"

"A moment. That's all I need." Even as she spoke, he felt her soften around him, and the tightness in her face eased away. "Yes."

He could only growl his agreement. This was exactly where he needed to be. "Going to move now."

"Yes," she breathed again.

Kali felt him draw back slightly, then slide forward. Pleasure shot through her, from the top of her to the base of her spine, and every place in between. God, he was everywhere in her. His was big, yes, but his presence filled her entirely.

His strokes went slowly at first, but as she gasped and

moaned her encouragement, his pace increased. She took him. Every thrust, every glide.

Sharp, exquisite sensation built, gathering force like a storm. And then it took her. She cried out once more in release. And then it was as if something within him broke free.

His speed increased—his enhanced body moving faster than an ordinary man. He plunged into her, the whole bed shaking with the force of his thrusts. She felt herself awash in wild pleasure.

Suddenly, there was a groaning sound. Something snapped. And then the bed frame broke, sending them crashing to the floor.

She gasped, but he seemed too far gone to stop. And she didn't want him to. A few more thrusts, and then his climax hit. She felt him pouring into her. He didn't make a sound, as if too deep in sensation. Until, at last, he sank down beside her. He turned them so that he was still within her, their damp bodies pressed tightly together.

For a long while, she couldn't speak. Couldn't think. All she knew was the aftermath of shared pleasure, and the feel of his body against hers, his breath warm against her face.

He nuzzled her throat, and she hummed her enjoyment.

"That was . . ." she murmured, ". . . worth the wait."

"Aye, it was."

"But let's not wait so long to do it again," she added.

He chuckled. "Ten minutes, and I'm your man." But there was no laughter in his voice when he said, "You've honored me."

She brushed damp strands of hair from his forehead. "We've honored each other."

They were quiet for a while, absorbing this. Then she said, "I'll have to reinforce the bed with a thicker metal frame."

"Scavenge whatever you need from the ship. Take every last piece of metal if you have to. It's a worthwhile sacrifice."

The only light in their quarters came from the clockwork cricket, its glass belly giving off a gentle glow. As Kali slept in his arms, her breathing warm and soft against his chest, he glanced over at the little automaton. A tiny North Star, that cricket. His guidance—or so he hoped.

Nothing was certain, except the continuing gleam of pleasure echoing through his body, and the fullness in his heart. He and Kali had spent the day in their wrecked bed, learning each other, discovering constellations of sensation. Images flashed through his mind: him lying on his back as she knelt between his legs, his cock in her hand and in her mouth; her above him, breasts swaying and her head bent forward as she rode him; the gloss of sweat along the curve of her back as she gripped the twisted headboard while he took her from behind.

It was as if they were trying to outrun something, their bodies pushing them on.

He could've gone all night, each time stoking the furnace of his needs higher. And he could tell from the fire in her eyes that she wanted the same. But she didn't have telumium implants feeding and fueling her strength. So when she fell into an exhausted slumber just before dusk, he let her sleep.

His stomach growled. Roared, in truth. A whole day in bed, and not a crumb to eat. He hadn't cared about or noticed his hunger when he and Kali had been tangled together. But in the peace that followed, his need for food was a beast that banged against its cage.

So I'll bloody starve. Better to stay in bed, with a soft and sated Kali wrapped around him, than rise and forage in the galley. As if even the smallest distance between them meant he'd return to what he had been before—removed, lifeless.

She stirred. Her eyes still closed, she murmured, "Didn't know there were wild dogs on the island."

"My stomach."

Her hand slid down to his belly, which twitched beneath her touch. "It's a wonder you haven't digested one of your internal organs. Poor ravenous Man O' War." Kali sat up, and pleasure warmed him when she didn't bother pulling the blankets up to cover her breasts. She pressed a hand to her own stomach. It grumbled, too. "Time to feed the animals."

She started to rise, but he gently lay a hand on her shoulder.

"I'll bring it."

For a moment, he thought she might complain. Argue that she could get food for herself. But instead, she sank back down into the bed. "Juicy roast chicken, creamed spinach, *pullao, matnacha rassa*—don't be gentle with the chilies—and a stack of *naan*. Oh, and a slice of chocolate tart."

He rose from the bed and stepped into a pair of loose trousers. He couldn't get used to walking around naked, even when he'd been alone on the ship. "Cold pheasant, wild bitter greens, and a handful of late bramble berries. They've gone a bit shriveled by this time in the season."

"It sounds like a feast." But no sarcasm edged her voice.

She seemed genuinely eager for whatever he brought. But he wished that he could bring her everything she asked for.

He headed for the galley. Before he left his quarters, he stopped in the doorway to have another glimpse of her in his bed. The cricket didn't provide much illumination. Still, his vision was strong, allowing him to see her, loose-limbed and comfortable, sprawled in the blankets. Warmth engulfed him—a woman waiting for him in his bed was a rare event. More than rare. It hadn't ever happened. And it was all the better that the woman waiting for him was Kali.

Yet he caught the slight frown between her brows as she stared out the window. Maybe her body had been sated, but her mind wasn't at ease. Something troubled her.

That specter of trouble followed him all the way down the passageway and into the galley, where he gathered up as much food as he could scrounge. Had he not been enough of a tender lover in the wake of their lovemaking? Should he have whispered poetry instead of telling her about their Spartan provisions? Damn it, he'd never really learned the way of women. Emily had found his clumsiness charming—until she didn't. And the idea of ruining what he and Kali shared twisted in his gut like a hot iron.

A broken plank served as a tray, which he carried back to his quarters, piled with all the food he'd been able to find. It almost surprised him to discover her still in bed. He lit a lamp as he entered the cabin.

She sat up at his approach. He seated himself on the bed and balanced the plank on his legs.

"Never been so glad to see dried up old berries," she said, and quickly popped a few of them into her mouth.

He took a bite of pheasant. Sailors were seldom fussy about what they ate, happy to have any edible food at all, and that hadn't changed for him when he became a Man O' War. The pheasant might be cold, and a little tough, but it tasted like manna. "The ferryman should be coming back soon with new provisions."

The frown returned between her brows. "Two weeks, I think. Time's gone all muddled since I've come to the *Persephone*." Her frown eased slightly. "I suppose I've been . . . occupied."

"There's a calendar in the navigator's room. We'll give that a study." He handed her a pheasant leg. "He'll be worried if you don't show. Might even have a look around the island." Which couldn't happen. "We should get back to fixing up your cottage."

She lifted an eyebrow. "So that's the way of it. Bed me then send me packing."

"If the ferryman sees your ruined cottage," Fletcher said through his teeth, "he'll know you don't live there. Then he'll wonder where you *do* live."

"And we can't have that," she murmured.

His unwavering gaze told her exactly what he thought of that idea. But then he glanced around his quarters. "*This* is where I want you. Not in your cottage."

"It's certainly more spacious here." Yet despite her words, she reached across the plank holding their food and took his hand. Though they'd spent the whole of the day making love, this simple touch made his heart pound. "The company's awfully pleasant, too," she added with a smile.

He snorted. "First time anyone's called me *pleasant*."

"Maddening, then," she corrected herself. Her mouth curved. "And marvelous."

They both leaned across the plank to meet for a kiss. She tasted of berries—both sweet and tart. Apt.

Silence fell as they continued eating. Both of them were too hungry to pause for caresses, or any of those things he imagined lovers did when sharing a meal in bed, like feeding each other. Did he miss it? He'd never known that kind of after-sex play. But this quiet and matter-of-fact sating of their hunger seemed right to him. They weren't typical, he and Kali. And he'd only feel clumsy and awkward if he'd tried to play the part of expert seducer. She didn't seem to expect it, either. She knew him.

A strange feeling crept over him. For half a moment, he'd wondered if the berries he'd picked had fermented, because his mind and body felt muted, quiet. He felt at ease in himself. Comfortable. He could taste all the flavors of the food. He saw the lamplight gleam on Kali's skin, in her hair and eyes.

Each breath in and out felt revelatory, as if he only just realized that he was alive.

Was this contentment? Happiness? He'd little experience with either to know. But he'd never felt as *right* as he did at that moment. Everything in alignment.

It was her. Kali the engineer.

They finished their meal too quickly. He set aside the plank. It wasn't enough food, and his stomach still complained when the last of the berries had been eaten. No one had ever tested if a Man O' War could starve to death, consumed from the inside out by his body's demands for fuel. Would he find out? And did it matter?

He glanced at Kali as she licked her fingers, trying to savor the smallest bit of their meal.

It does matter.

Kali watched his face, the shifting play of emotions that he no longer hid from her.

"You must miss it," she said. "Flying."

"Didn't think I would."

"But our jaunt changed your mind."

"It's ... nothing feels like it. Not the fastest train or riding high in the main course yard as a ship cuts through the water." He shook his head. "Can't describe it. That's for poets, not Man O' Wars."

She didn't need his words. Longing shone in his eyes, the kind of yearning one felt for a lost lover. Perhaps Fletcher had forgotten how much he loved her still—the skies—but their dawn outing was like catching a glimpse of that lover years later and finding her as beautiful as ever.

"I could make the *Persephone* airworthy again," she murmured.

He stared at her. "There's ether, but the turbines are cracked off so we couldn't move once we're airborne. She's wrecked."

"Not entirely. I've been studying the ship these past weeks. The things she needs to fly weren't completely ruined in the crash. Including the turbines. We'd lose the bottom decks, but it wouldn't take much—a few days at most—to get her operational."

"I'm staying," he said. "The moment I'm back in the sky, the navy will know. And I'll be back to destroying lives again."

"Fletcher," she said firmly, "I saw it. I was there in Liverpool. You don't bring destruction. You bring *safety*."

"I . . ." He scowled, looking away.

Her heart beat thickly in her chest. Here she was offering him a way off the island, and though the possibility had existed before, now he could leave on *his* terms—not as a means of death, but a protector of life.

He glanced back at her. For a moment, yearning gleamed brightly in his gaze, then dimmed. "No. This is where I'll stay."

Strangely, relief unknotted between her ribs. She could live on Eilean Comhachag without him—that had been the plan from the beginning—but even if they finished the repairs on her cottage, made it more efficient and modern than ever, the thought of not having him nearby, not hearing his voice and his bone-dry humor, not seeing him each day . . . The thought made her insides wither.

She only wished there was some way that he could learn to see himself as he truly was.

"I'll hunt rabbit tomorrow," he said. "I've been hunting mostly pheasants since you've been aboard, but I need to keep their population steady, so rabbits it is."

"I'll join you."

Fletcher's heart kicked. She'd never offered to accompany him before, always busy with her inventions and projects. "You wouldn't like it."

"A little blood doesn't scare me. I butchered those rabbits you brought me."

"Notice anything about the carcasses?"

She frowned. "They seemed like normal rabbits to me. I've never studied animal anatomy, but they appeared to have had the regular compliment of muscles, organs and bones. Although," she added thoughtfully, "the bones that comprised their necks seemed odd. They faced a different direction than the spine."

He held up his hands. "These are my weapons when I kill them. Even with the ether deactivated on the rifles, the bullets are too powerful. They'd shred the poor beast and leave us with nothing edible. I had to find another way to hunt them."

A little color drained from her face. "You break their necks."

"It's fast," he said quickly. "They don't suffer. But it's the only way. Don't think you want to watch me snapping rabbits' necks."

"Maybe I'll stay on the ship," she continued, "or we could fish."

"Fish don't stay fresh as long as rabbit or pheasant."

"I've been working on plans for a refrigeration unit," she said, "powered by the ship's batteries. Mind, it won't be small. Probably take up a third of the gunnery deck. But we'd have fresh food for a sight longer than we do now."

The mechanics that made him extraordinary had been someone else's invention, same with the construction of his ship. Yet Kali's intellect continued to astound him.

He liked her use of the word *we*, as well.

Unaware of his thoughts, she continued, "It'll take some doing to get the refrigeration apparatus functioning before Campbell returns to resupply me. And there's the cottage to fix up." Her gaze turned distant as she thought of all the tasks that lay before her.

A thought had been eating at him like a slow-acting acid. "Your arrangement with Campbell—it has a finite date."

Her gaze snapped back to his. "I never settled on one."

He exhaled.

"But, Fletcher," she reached across the distance between them, and interlaced their fingers, and her eyes were dark and too damned sad, "this isn't permanent. There will come a day when I go back with Campbell."

"Go back." He felt the gears of his own mind grind to a stop. The words she spoke sounded like another language. He tried to translate them into words that made sense, but even when they did make sense, they made no sense at all. "You're leaving."

"No," she said. But before he could feel any sense of relief, she added, "Not yet."

"But you will." Was that his voice, the noise that sounded like rusted machinery?

Quietly, she said, "At some point—yes."

"When?" He pulled his hand free from hers, even though he missed her touch, and stood. His skin felt tight, and his chest burned. The rat, Four, had come to investigate whether or not there were any bits of food after their meal, but the little animal scurried back into the walls to avoid Fletcher's pacing.

"When I'm ready," she answered.

"Got a date for that?" he demanded, turning to face her. She'd slipped on her chemise, a barrier between them, when she'd been so free and open only minutes earlier. "November? December? Back to civilization just in time for Christmas?"

She didn't flinch at the edge in his voice, even as he hated it, himself. He hated everything about it: that he could be so cruel to her, that she'd become so important to him that the thought of being without her on the island made the future months and years look like a world leached of color. But the words came, whether he wanted them to or not.

"I don't know when," she said, calm as the Atlantic doldrums.

"But you *will* go," he repeated, as much for himself as for her.

"One can't make a life here."

"I have."

Her eyes were full of shadows and understanding. "Have you?"

He felted riveted to the floor, breath pounding in and out of him. That goddamn engineer's mind of hers. She cut right to the heart of him, as if he'd been drawn up like some bloody blueprint and she could study all his parts, all his needs and hungers and fears.

Somehow, he managed to tear himself from the floor. Without another word, he slammed from the cabin.

CHAPTER THIRTEEN

Kali debated going after him. She'd hurt him, and perhaps that had been a surprise, perhaps it hadn't. Never had she planned on hurting Fletcher, yet as she sat up in bed and stared out the window, seeing mostly her own ghostly reflection, it seemed there'd been a terrible inevitability to it. They were both walking wounded. Something was bound to open the wounds again.

But what could she tell him? What would take his pain away? She wasn't Emily, rejecting him because he was a Man O' War. But he might not see it that way.

The glow of her pleasure—from the aftermath of their lovemaking, from the knowledge that he cared for her enough to want her with him—had cooled.

She'd never felt real emotion for any man until she met him. And that meant she'd hurt him, and herself. Was that the nature of caring? Did it mean inevitable suffering?

Sitting there in bed debating the nature of the human heart would solve nothing. She strapped on her prosthetic leg, then stood and threw on a robe. Taking a lantern with her, she moved down the passageway until she reached the closed door to his quarters. She tapped lightly on the door.

"Fletcher, please," she said, when there was no answer. She pressed her hand to the door. "It's got nothing to do with you. Or the fact that you're a Man O' War. I always knew I'd leave this island and rejoin the world. This place is . . . a temporary haven. Our time together has been some of the best of my life." She'd never spoken truer words. "Yet we both know that this place . . . it's not real. It's an in-between. Somewhere to learn how to live again. I *want* to live again. Don't you?"

More silence from the other side of the door. Frustration welled. She wasn't the sort of person who blathered on about things like *feelings*, not unless it truly mattered. The quiet between them had been just as valuable as the words. Yet here she was, trying to give him what she could, and he remained locked in stubborn, childish silence.

If he thought to hide from her, and that she wouldn't pursue him, he didn't know her very well.

"Damn it, Fletcher. Let me in." She tried the handle of the door. It turned easily in her hand, and the door swung open.

Holding up the lantern, she stepped inside. His cabin was empty.

A quiet, bitter laugh escaped her. She'd been pouring herself out to an unoccupied room.

Instead of returning to her quarters, she searched the ship. All the cabins, all the chambers. The gunnery. The magazine. The topside deck, where the ether-powered barrel they'd taken up into the sky still stood, tied to the airship. Aside from encountering a surprised Four in the galley, she was the only person aboard the *Persephone*.

He'd gone.

She stood topside, scanning the moor. Without his enhanced sight, she couldn't see much. Only the black sea of heath, and the dark shapes of the hills.

An engineering periodical had run an article about a scientist in Suriname making progress on goggles that would allow the wearer to see in utter darkness. If only Kali had those goggles, she could find Fletcher. But the goggles hadn't yet been perfected, and even if she had a pair, she wasn't certain she wanted to chase after him, when he'd run from her like a wounded animal.

He would return. Maybe not for her, but at least because he had to be back on his ship. Though she wondered if he was angry enough to stay away and let the energy and power build up within him, until it broke and caused a berserker rage.

Chill night air cut through her thin robe and chemise. She shivered, but waited a little longer, hoping he'd return. When her fingers and toes numbed, she headed down the companionway, into the ship that had only been her home when he'd been there. Without him, it was just an empty carcass on the moors.

In the morning, she dressed and entered the galley to scrounge for breakfast. She stopped abruptly in the doorway. Fletcher stood at the tall food preparation table, cleaning fish. He looked windblown but focused on his task, keeping his head bent as she slowly came into the galley. It felt like those first few times they'd encountered each other, that same uncertainty and caution she'd show around a feral creature.

She knew he was aware of her presence. He'd surely heard her stirring in her quarters not fifteen minutes ago, and her progress down the passageway, but he'd made no move to go to her, or even acknowledge that he'd returned after . . . well, she'd no idea what he'd done or where he had gone after abandoning ship last night.

Like a chophouse patron waiting for his meal, Four sat on one of the chairs in the galley, hoping that Fletcher would toss him a scrap of fish meat or guts. The rat barely paid her any notice. Just like the man.

Voice flat, Fletcher said, "Breakfast will be ready in twenty minutes."

"I can help clean the fish," she offered.

He shook his head. "It'll go faster if I do it."

She planted her hands on her hips. "So this is how it's to be, now."

"Don't know what you're talking about."

"We were partners. Friends." She stepped closer. "Lovers."

He gave the tiniest flinch, as though the word itself was an iron filing shoved under his fingernail. His knife slipped, and ran down the center of his palm. She darted forward, to help staunch what would surely be a bad cut, but he only held his hand away.

"No damage done," he said gruffly.

She glanced up and saw the unhurt expanse of his palm. So a Man O' War's flesh was tough to pierce, but his heart had its vulnerabilities.

He resumed his work, his knife fast and brutally efficient as he gutted the fish and dropped the entrails into a waiting bucket.

"I don't think that's so," she said.

"Don't know why you'd want to go back," he muttered. "Liverpool's gone."

"There's always Plymouth or Southampton, or even London."

"But you're safe here." *With me*, seemed to be the silent adjunct to his words, and her own heart ached.

"What if . . ." She struggled, half afraid of what she was about to say. "What if I didn't go back alone?"

His knife slowed, stopped. Letting go of the blade, he set his hands on the table, his wide shoulders forming a protective barrier. His eyes wouldn't meet hers. "I can't," he said hoarsely.

"They'd take you back in an instant, the navy." She spoke quickly, as if the speed of her words could somehow convince him, shut out any arguments. "I'm certain they could find some other role for you besides combat. A coastal patrol, perhaps. Even something on land that would keep you near batteries, so you wouldn't have to overload. It can be done, Fletcher." She gripped his forearm, feeling the heat of his skin and the tight, corded muscle. He'd rolled up his sleeves for the messy business of cleaning fish, so they touched, skin-to-skin, as they had yesterday. Except it had been more than her hand on his arm. It had been them touching each other everywhere, inside and out. The memory of it sent a thick pulse of need through her—need for sensation, need for *him*.

He lifted his gaze to hers. Her breath caught at the agony in his eyes. "Kali—"

Suddenly, he tensed. The pain in his eyes disappeared, replaced by alert wariness. He snapped upright. His hand went to his waist, and his fingers closed around the grip of his ether pistol.

"What is it?" she whispered, unease scraping along her back. She couldn't hear whatever it was that Fletcher heard, but that meant nothing. His senses were far sharper than hers.

He held up a hand, and she immediately went silent. Noiselessly, he slid from the galley, then edged up the companionway to the top deck. Kali deliberated for half a second, then ran to her quarters and grabbed her shotgun. As fast as she could, she joined him topside.

He stood at the rail, staring off toward the west. Whatever he saw, it made his jaw harden. She swore quietly, having forgotten her spyglass in her cabin, so she could only watch, and wait, to see what emerged from the low-lying morning fog.

Her chest tightened when she finally saw three figures appear on the moor. Heading right toward them. She tried to dismiss her fear: whoever those people were, they could just be fishermen who anchored their boat and decided to explore the deserted island. But Fletcher's caginess was infectious. In the months she'd been on Eilean Comhachag, no one had come to the island except Campbell, and only then because she paid him to.

Fletcher let out a florid oath as the figures drew nearer. They were still too far away for her to make out anything more than their shapes, but he'd seen something she hadn't. He held himself in suspension. She didn't know if he was going to vault over the side of the ship and meet the newcomers, ether pistol ready, or wait for them to come to the *Persephone*.

He glanced at her, his eyes bright and sharp and dangerous. "Damn it. I thought about this moment too many times—it wasn't ever going to happen like this."

"Fletcher, tell me what's going on. Who is that?"

His mouth flattened into a tight line. "You'll know in a moment."

Part of her wanted to end the suspense, and scale the rope ladder he'd made for her to get down from the ship, then run to face off against the outsiders. But it was a foolish impulse, and she stayed where she was beside Fletcher, though she double-checked that her firearm was loaded.

The people came closer, and she could finally make out details of their appearance. Two of the men seemed especially burly, though the third man of average build seemed to be the leader. All of them were dressed in ordinary seafaring clothing.

As they neared, the leader waved his arm overhead and let out a halloo. There wasn't anything threatening in his tone. If anything, he sounded happy to see them.

Fletcher returned the gesture, waving his arm, but giving no halloo.

At last, the three newcomers reached the downed airship. The man in the lead looked up at Fletcher with a wide grin. His gaze darted to her, but didn't linger. His two associates had no expressions.

"Captain Adams," the leader said, beaming, "words cannot express my pleasure in seeing you and the *Persephone* again."

Kali started. She'd never known Fletcher's surname until now.

"Lieutenant Mayhew," he answered. Though he spoke with caution, there was genuine pleasure in Fletcher's voice.

She said nothing, but her mind whirled. It was clear Mayhew had served under Fletcher aboard this airship.

"Permission to come aboard, sir?"

A moment passed. Then, "Permission granted. There's a ladder portside."

Giving Fletcher another grin, Mayhew and his companions hastened around the ship. As they did, Fletcher let out one long, exhausted exhale. He turned weary eyes to her.

"It seems I'm no longer dead," he murmured.

Kali set her shotgun down and waited beside Fletcher— Captain Fletcher *Adams*—as his former officer and the other men climbed the ladder. Her stomach was strangely knotted, encountering a living part of Fletcher's past. There was something else, something hot and possessive, that curled in her.

God, after all her talk of leaving the island, was she *jealous* of Mayhew? It couldn't be so. But the lieutenant—who looked perfectly pleasant, with his sandy hair and neatly-trimmed mustache—had shared something with Fletcher that she never could. They'd been colleagues, working together on this airship. They had been in combat together. War was a kind of solder that joined men together in an unbreakable bond.

She shook her head, trying to clear the maelstrom of thoughts. Gazing quickly at Fletcher, she could only imagine what he must be feeling. Pleasure at seeing his old comrade. Anger and sadness that he'd be forced to leave Eilean Comhachag, when he'd made it clear he didn't want to go.

"He doesn't have to tell anyone that you're here," Kali murmured quietly.

Fletcher's mouth tightened even more. "I can't do that to Mayhew—make him lie to the navy. It'd be a grave dereliction of duty."

Any further discussion was cut short by the arrival of the lieutenant on deck. His two companions followed shortly after. As soon as Mayhew's boots touched the deck, he strode forward, hand outstretched. "Captain, my heart has never known such joy in finding you."

Fletcher shook the lieutenant's hand. "It's good to see you again." He didn't sound entirely insincere, either. When Mayhew's curious gaze skimmed over to Kali, Fletcher said, "This is Miss . . . Miss . . ."

"MacNeil," Kali filled in for him. Just speaking her last name again felt like slipping into another self. She shook Lieutenant Mayhew's hand. "By sheer coincidence, Captain Adams and I happen to be neighbors on this island."

Mayhew frowned. "Does anyone else live here?"

"Only us." Before Mayhew could press for details, Fletcher glanced at the other two men standing impassively nearby and asked, "And your friends?"

Mayhew spoke for them. "These two gentlemen are Misters Grady and Robbins. Local men I've hired."

"Hired to do what?" Kali asked.

The lieutenant's face broke into another grin. "Why, find the captain, of course." He stared at Fletcher. "They searched for weeks, sir, trying to locate you. There had been hope that perhaps you'd managed to land the *Persephone* and survived. However, all their searches proved fruitless. Everyone thinks you dead, and the airship destroyed or lost beneath the waves. You've been declared dead, and the ship lost."

Fletcher held out his arms. "Here we are, sound as an iron bridge."

"But, sir, if you survived, why did you not notify anyone?"

Shuttering his expression even more, Fletcher answered, "My reasons are my own, Lieutenant."

Mayhew slid another glance at Kali, a knowing expression on his face. She barely resisted the impulse to roll her eyes or punch the man, or both.

"How is it that you're on our island, Lieutenant Mayhew?" she asked instead. "The navy believes Captain Fletcher dead and the *Persephone* permanently missing. You've no reason to be here."

A brief shadow crossed Mayhew's face. "Indeed, Miss MacNeil, I don't. I had to trust the Admiralty that they'd done all they could to rescue or recover the captain. But, as you see"—he gestured down at his clothing—"I'm not here in an official capacity. Most of us who've survived Liverpool were given commendations—oh, and you were given a posthumous Victoria Cross."

Fletcher didn't even blink at the mention of this, the highest honor that could be bestowed upon a man in service to his country.

Mayhew seemed taken aback that Fletcher seemed unconcerned about his medal. But he pressed on, "Everyone who served in the sea and air at Liverpool were given extended leave. With the Huns and Russians trounced so thoroughly, we all have a moment to catch our respective breaths."

"The other men," Fletcher said, his voice hard and urgent. "They all survived the evacuation?"

"Every one of them," Mayhew answered. "Some were injured, but nothing serious."

Fletcher let out a long exhalation, one that spoke of profound relief.

"So you've spent your leave looking for Captain Adams?" she asked. "That's an unusual amount of devotion to a commanding officer." She glanced at Fletcher. He'd never given any indications—certainly not yesterday—that he preferred the company of men, or that there was one man in particular who had held a special place in his heart. But then, there was still much about Fletcher she didn't know.

The lieutenant beamed. "Captain Adams was always so tolerant of my interest in inventions. How could I not try to find the one man who'd been so encouraging?"

She remembered Fletcher mentioning the tinkering Mayhew used to do. "The captain's very good about accepting people for who they are."

Fletcher said nothing, looking distinctly uncomfortable at hearing himself praised.

"But now that I'm here," Mayhew continued, "back on the *Persephone*, it makes me wonder . . ."

"Wonder what?" Fletcher asked.

The lieutenant cleared his throat. "There's something on the ship . . . an item of personal significance . . ." He looked slightly abashed.

Men on ships often kept with them little trinkets or things that reminded them of home, or held meaning. Something from their family, or a wife or sweetheart.

"If I might," Mayhew went on, "I'd like to search my cabin. The item is very important to me."

At last, the granite of Fletcher's expression softened. "I'm sorry, Lieutenant, but you won't find much left."

Confusion flickered across Mayhew's face. "But as we approached the ship, I saw that the deck with the officers' quarters was still intact."

"Come with me." Fletcher headed toward the companionway. Mayhew followed immediately, which seemed odd to Kali. As progressive as society had become these past decades, a man in the Queen's service would always show courtesy to a woman and allow her to proceed him. But Kali couldn't be affronted. She'd never liked those outmoded rules, and clearly, whatever Mayhew had been looking for meant a good deal to him. What was the point of useless courtesy when one's heart hung in the balance?

So she followed, too. But her neck chilled when she heard Mayhew's silent companions behind her. An irrational part of her wished they'd stayed topside. Though they couldn't compare to Fletcher in size and strength, for normal men, they were quite big, and brawny. A seafaring man's life must be a strenuous one, to build such muscles. But Campbell didn't look anything like these two. And she'd set her shotgun down.

Fletcher pushed open the door to the cabin that had been Mayhew's. The lieutenant let out an anguished groan.

Catching up with them, she peered over Mayhew's shoulder. Fletcher had shown her his cabin some time ago, but the destruction was new to Mayhew. Though most of the cabin's bulkheads were intact, the exterior wall was missing—a jagged wound in the side of the ship. Everything in the lieutenant's quarters that hadn't been bolted down must have flown out. Lost somewhere between Liverpool and the island.

"I'm sorry, Lieutenant," Fletcher said as the lieutenant frantically searched the cabin. "Your search is in vain. When I was going through the ship, looking for things to scavenge, I never uncovered anything in here. It was as you see it now. Empty."

But Mayhew's grief quickly shifted into a hard, wild urgency. He whirled to face both Kali and Fletcher in the doorway. "I remember the battle. This side of the ship hadn't taken this damage when you ordered us to evacuate."

"No," Fletcher murmured, "it hadn't. I recall how you wanted to return to your cabin to fetch something before the evacuation—and I had to get the master-at-arms to bodily throw you into the jollyboat. You disobeyed a direct order."

Yet the lieutenant didn't seem to care. He pointed at the gaping wall. "When did this happen?"

Kali's brows rose. Now Mayhew had stopped calling Fletcher *sir* or *Captain*.

Fletcher seemed to have noticed the change, too. He folded his arms across his chest. "When I was looking for a place to set the *Persephone* down. Her hull dragged across some mountains. Not that far from here." He squinted as he stared past Mayhew, contemplating the massive laceration in the side of his airship. "Then I saw this island, and that it had these moors. They'd make for a good landing spot. So I circled to get her into position. I saw some debris fall from the ship. Maybe something from your cabin." He shook his head. "Wasn't paying much attention to falling debris at that point. I just wanted to get her down without killing anyone on the ground."

Anyone, except himself, she thought. She and Fletcher had both faced death with eyes open, but he'd done so willingly.

"If any of those items managed to hit the ground on the island," Mayhew said urgently, stepping closer, "where might they land?"

"There are some cliffs southwest of the ship," he answered. "On the other side of the hills. That's the most likely location."

She turned to him with a frown. "You never took me there."

"It's a dangerous place. Didn't want you hurt."

"You've been there, though?" pressed Mayhew. "You must've seen something."

"Nothing to hunt on that cliff, and it's ready to fall into the sea at any minute. Somebody that weighs as much as I do could make the whole thing crumble away like rotten bread. Like I said, dangerous."

"Take me there," Mayhew demanded. At Fletcher's stony silence, the lieutenant seemed to collect himself. "If you'd be so kind, sir, I need to go to that cliff. See if what I lost is there." His gaze turned imploring. "You can understand that, Captain? Trying to recover what you miss?"

Fletcher glanced at her. A long moment passed. Then, "We'll find what you've lost."

CHAPTER FOURTEEN

This couldn't have happened at a bloody worse moment.

The thought bored into Fletcher like a tetrol-powered drill as he led Mayhew, Kali, and Mayhew's hired men toward the cliffs edging along the southwest of the island. He threw a quick glance over his shoulder. The terrain sloped sharply, but Kali kept pace, her strength and agility so vastly improved that no one would notice that she walked on an artificial leg. Not without looking up her skirts. And he'd plow his fist into the face of anyone who tried that.

She caught his gaze, and, like a ruddy coward, he turned away quickly, his eyes focusing on the incline instead of the unspoken words in her look.

Hell. It wasn't supposed to end this way. He didn't know how he'd planned on it ending, in truth. Maybe he'd been naïve, thinking they could just go on as they'd been doing forever. His mouth quirked into a humorless smile. *Naïve* was never a word he'd imagined to describe himself. But when it came to Kali, he found himself more altered than when he'd been transformed into a Man O' War.

And here was Mayhew, throwing another spanner in the works. Much as the lieutenant wanted . . . whatever it was he sought . . . he'd have to report finding Fletcher alive to the Admiralty. Fletcher's grim smile remained firmly in place. Here he'd been angry with Kali for wanting to leave the island, and now he was the one who'd depart first. He hated the idea of her alone here, but he couldn't force her to come with him, and it didn't seem likely that she planned on returning to the world within the next few days.

He'd fix up her cottage before he left. She could always stay aboard the *Persephone*, but she wouldn't want to. The cottage was *her* place. The wrecked airship wasn't much of a home. It hadn't been for him. Not until she'd lived there.

He had to push all those thoughts from his head. Just as he had to push away the ache that clutched at his chest when he thought about parting from her. And what he'd be forced to do when he returned to civilization.

Right now, he needed to concentrate on getting to the cliffs, and seeing if Mayhew's precious possession could be found. The next voyage would come soon enough, whether he wanted it to or not.

The cliffs were located in a notch just behind the hills. They were too narrow to approach from the north, so he had to take them up the hills first, and then they'd need to carefully negotiate their way down. He didn't want Kali anywhere near those cliffs, but she'd insisted on coming along, and he couldn't forbid her from doing anything. It was one of the things he loved about her.

He almost stumbled. *Jesus, where'd that come from?* He shook his head. No. He was wrong. He cared about her. Respected her. Desired her. But . . . love? He didn't know what *love* meant, only that it wasn't meant for men—or Man O' Wars—like him.

And Kali deserved to be loved—he knew that.

"How much farther?" Mayhew demanded, sounding breathless and agitated.

"Not much," he threw over his shoulder. The lieutenant had been acting more and more odd since he'd first set foot on the deck of the crashed airship. It didn't seem like him. Mayhew had been an even-tempered bloke, quick to obey an order, and generally liked by the crew. He did keep to himself, with his tinkering, yet was friendly enough. But maybe Liverpool had changed him. God knew Fletcher wasn't the same since the battle.

They reached the top of one of the hills, and everyone stopped to look down. The other side of the hill sloped down precipitously about thirty feet to a narrow cliff top. Rocks and shrubbery dotted the ground.

"There, you see!" Mayhew cried, pointing. "I see a bit of metal in the scrub." He hurried forward, sliding his way down the side of the hill.

"Easy, Lieutenant," Fletcher snapped. "You go bounding around down there and the whole cliff's likely to collapse beneath you."

But Mayhew wasn't listening. He staggered as he reached the rocky cliff top, then scurried toward a dull metallic gleam hidden within a shrub. But his face fell when he pulled out a wrench. "Damn and hell!" He threw the tool, and it went spinning, end over end, over the cliff's edge. A long moment passed before Fletcher heard the wrench's faint splash into the pounding waves below. The distance down had to be at least four hundred feet.

"It's not here," Mayhew snarled.

"Stand down, Lieutenant. I'll help you search."

"Me, too," Kali said.

He placed a cautioning hand on her wrist. "It won't hold all of our weight. Not for long. If the cliff did break, I'd survive the fall, but Mayhew wouldn't. And neither would you."

She looked as though she wanted to debate the subject, but she said nothing, only giving a small, clipped nod. "Be careful."

"Man O' Wars don't need to be careful," he answered.

"I don't care if you're a Man O' War," she replied, her voice tight. "Your safety—that's all that matters to me."

Her words sent a sweet pain knifing through him, and he wished to God that Mayhew's two men weren't standing nearby, looking bored, because he ached to kiss her. Having tasted that pleasure yesterday, each hour without it now was torment. One thing was certain: he'd kiss her again—and hopefully more—before he left the island. He needed her one last time. It wouldn't be enough, but he'd take whatever he could.

"Likewise," he answered. After giving her wrist a gentle squeeze, he made his way down to the cliff, moving with more caution than Mayhew had shown.

"What am I looking for?" he asked the lieutenant when he reached the top of the cliff.

"A steel strongbox, this big." Mayhew held his hands twelve inches apart. Despite the chill wind whipping up the side of the cliff, sweat glossed his forehead and stained the collar of his shirt.

They searched through the scrub. The cliff itself was only about forty feet long, but the brush grew densely, and more had likely grown in since the *Persephone* circled overhead, losing debris like a leper losing flesh. Mayhew frantically tore through the shrubbery, cursing whenever he discovered something that wasn't the object of his search.

It was like robbing someone's grave. They pulled out framed photographs, some articles of clothing—now rotting from exposure—more tools. Fletcher's consolation came in knowing that the men who'd owned these things had survived. Still, he couldn't lose the cold that crept up his arms as he searched.

Fletcher had little hope they'd find the strongbox. He kept looking, however. Whatever it held, the box must contain something vitally important to Mayhew. Letters, perhaps, from someone no longer living. A family trust. A keepsake from a better time. The damned thing about time was that it moved forward whether one wanted it to or not.

He cast a glance up at Kali, who was watching him, her hands knotted into fists as they held her skirt in place from the gusting wind. Her face was tight and drawn, but her eyes were bright as she followed his progress.

He'd want some object—a token, the smallest scrap of anything at all—to remind him of her when he left and all that remained of their time on the island was memory. The idea of not having something of her with him struck him as a physical pain. So he understood Mayhew's desperate, if fruitless, efforts.

As Fletcher continued to search through the brush, the ground beneath him shifted. It moved just a little, but enough to remind him how precarious the situation was. He'd have a long fall, and the landing wouldn't be pleasant.

"I'm not finding anything, Lieutenant," he said over his shoulder, "and this cliff won't hold us much longer."

Mayhew looked frenzied. "No! It *has* to be here." He picked up an object, a dented case for a pocket watch. "This is mine. So whatever was in my cabin has to be here."

"What *are* we looking for, Lieutenant? What's in that strongbox?"

Mayhew was silent for a moment. "Something ..." He glanced off toward the horizon. "Something that makes me a better man."

Fletcher gazed up at Kali, watching them as they searched. "Then we keep looking."

He decided to give the lieutenant ten more minutes. Then he'd drag Mayhew back up the hill and tell him it was over. The lieutenant wasn't in uniform, but Fletcher still outranked him, and he wouldn't let Mayhew survive the battle at Liverpool only to die here, on this tiny island in the Outer Hebrides, for sentiment.

Tokens and keepsakes were only things. What mattered was the heart's own memory. If something truly mattered, it wouldn't suffer the fate of decay or loss. He'd have Kali with him always, even if her presence was a sweet pain lodged between his ribs forever.

A gleam of metal, covered with mud and scrub, caught his eye. It lay very close to the edge, so he picked his way toward it. It'd be a sodding shame if he found the strongbox, only to have the rocks and earth crumble away beneath him and send them both tumbling into the sea. He'd live, but finding the box beneath the pounding waves would be impossible.

"What is it?" Mayhew demanded, as Fletcher sidled closer to the bit of metal. The lieutenant started toward him. "Is that—?"

"Reef your sails, Lieutenant," Fletcher snapped, holding up his hand. "It's unstable as blazes here. Whatever I find, I'll bring to you."

Mayhew snapped his mouth closed and seemed to vibrate in place. But he stayed where he was as Fletcher crouched down and tore at the scrub covering the metal.

Bits of shrubbery came up, and when that was cleared, he scraped away the dirt. As he did, he uncovered a flat metal surface. His heart began to pound. Was this really it? The odds were against them, but maybe, with everything else going to hell, there could be some bright spot.

He dug at the dried, brittle earth. At last, he exposed a twelve-inch long metal panel. Shoving his fingers into the soil, he felt more edges, like the shape of a box.

Ruddy hell. This had to be it.

He tugged, more gently than if he'd used his full measure of strength to keep the cliff from breaking apart. Another tug, and then the buried object broke free. Fletcher held it up. The strongbox, complete with a lock on the front.

Kali let out a little cheer. Mayhew, however, said nothing. Despite Fletcher's warnings, the lieutenant bounded forward, his eyes round and frenzied. Mayhew snatched the box from Fletcher's hands, then stroked his own hands over it lovingly.

"I can break it open," Fletcher offered.

But Mayhew tugged on a chain around his neck, at the

end of which dangled a key. He quickly opened the strong-box. The lid blocked Fletcher's view of the contents, but the moment the container was opened, something changed.

There was a new energy in the air, unseen, but crackling like electricity. Mayhew himself seemed to shift, as though his exterior was a mirage. A sudden power emanated from him. His mouth curved in a cruel grin. He reached into the strongbox and pulled out an object, then threw the strong-box aside. What he held wasn't a photograph, or a stack of letters, or even a little trinket. No, what he held up was an intricate mechanical device, roughly the size of a man's fist. Or a human heart.

"The hell?" Fletcher growled, a sentiment Kali echoed in different words from her place atop the hill.

Mayhew tore his gaze from the device and stared at Fletcher. *Jesus.* The lieutenant's eyes burned with sudden madness.

"Always thought you were better than us normal men," Mayhew spat, "didn't you? Stronger, faster. Worth a hell of a lot more to the navy than us regular blokes. What did we matter? We cost them nothing. But *you.* You bloody Man O' Wars. The prize of Her Majesty's Aerial Navy," he sneered. "There wouldn't even *be* a damned aerial navy without you. Britain's protectors. Heroes of the realm."

"What in God's blue sky are you ranting about?" Fletcher demanded.

"This, *Captain.*" With one hand, Mayhew tore at his clothes, ripping open his coat, waistcoat, and shirt. Revealing his bare chest.

Good fucking Christ.

A web of metallic fibers covered the lieutenant's skin, the wires embedded into his flesh. Fletcher's implants throbbed, and he realized that the wires dug crudely into Mayhew were telumium. A metal plate with what appeared to be a port was grafted in the center of the lieutenant's chest. Fletcher saw that on the back of the mechanized heart in Mayhew's hand was a piece that seemed to fit into the port.

"Dalet," Mayhew snapped. "That was my *aurora vires* ranking. Couldn't even edge into Gimmel. They turned me away with a bloody pat on the shoulder and *Too bad, old chap*, when all I ever wanted was to be one of you."

Fletcher shook his head in sad understanding. Wretched damned Mayhew. Denied the chance to become a Man O' War.

"It's not all glory and heroism, Lieutenant," he said gently. "We give up so much. Can't be away from our ships for too long. Most people treat us like monsters. I know from personal experience. And there's no possibility of having children. No chance at a normal life."

Instead of soothing Mayhew, Fletcher's words only seemed to inflame him more. "I didn't want *normal*, curse it! I was already normal, but I knew I could be so much more. I could captain an airship and tear our enemies from the skies. I'd beat them back to their miserable homes and annihilate every last one of them. All the Huns, all the Russians. Dead and cold, with Britain reigning over everything." He panted with rage and hatred—exactly the feelings a captain couldn't have when going into battle.

"But no," Mayhew continued, choking, "they turned me away. Denied me my chance at triumph and fame."

"Triumph and fame?" Fletcher snorted. "Mayhew, Man O' Wars are just weapons. Hell—there probably wouldn't even be a war if we didn't exist."

"But they *do* exist," the lieutenant fired back. "And they *are* the pride of every nation that creates them. That's what I've wanted. What I've always wanted."

"So you mutilated yourself?" Fletcher demanded, staring at the grisly network of telumium covering Mayhew's skin. Whatever procedures the lieutenant had performed, they hadn't been done by a skilled surgeon. The flesh around the wires was angry and torn, red. Scar tissue crisscrossed his torso.

"Perfected, not mutilated," Mayhew corrected. "I studied Dr. Rossini's old notes. Used them as a blueprint to create this." He waved at his chest. "Implanted all these pieces myself. Just like the telumium inside you. It's taken me years to become what you are. I was weeks away from finishing the last of it when Liverpool happened."

No wonder the lieutenant had to be dragged, screaming, to evacuate without the final piece to his mad puzzle. Which he currently held.

A realization hit Fletcher. "That telumium you've dug into your body, the parts for that thing you're holding—you took all of it from the *Persephone*."

"Piece by piece. Little bits here, there. No one ever noticed." Mayhew smirked at his own cleverness.

Fury threatened to choke Fletcher. "Thief," he snarled. The bastard had stolen from him, from the ship that had given him a home, protection.

"Not a thief," the lieutenant retorted. "Not if this should've been mine."

"A goddamn scavenging thief," Fletcher growled. "Stealing to make your own Man O' War's heart."

Mayhew glanced at the heart. "I wanted to be a better man. Now I can. Your heart concentrates all your power. This'll do the same for me. Complete my transformation. I'll be one of the elite."

"The navy won't take you," Fletcher said. "Doubt any civilized nation would."

"Navies are for fools who like dancing on the end of an Admiralty's chain," Mayhew answered. "Plenty of your kind have left their navies and gone rogue." He smirked. "I'm cutting out the middle man. And then ... oh, I've such glorious plans." His smile widened. "World's first assassin of Man O' Wars. It takes a Man O' War to kill a Man O' War." He chuckled at his own wit.

Much as Fletcher questioned the purpose and existence of Man O' Wars, he couldn't stomach the idea of someone deliberately murdering them.

He had his ether pistol out and pointed at Mayhew's head in an instant. "Drop the device."

But Mayhew didn't blink. He smiled blandly. "I think it'd be better if you drop your weapon." He glanced up the hill, and Fletcher followed his gaze.

His blood rusted to a stop.

Mayhew's men had Kali. One of them had grabbed her and pinned her arms to her sides, his hand clapped over her mouth. The other had a knife to her throat.

Pure fury blazed in her eyes, matching the rage surging through Fletcher. Rage—and terror.

He could move quickly, but there was still too great a

chance she'd be hurt. All it would take was one fast cut of the henchman's blade, and her blood would spill. He'd seen men take wounds to the neck. It was ugly—a spray of red and hands clutching uselessly to stem the flow.

Kali wouldn't see that fate.

He set his ether pistol on the ground.

"A dozen steps back, if you please," Mayhew commanded.

Fletcher had no choice. He took the dozen steps backward, hatred making every movement stiff and ungainly. The cliff was narrow, and it continued to shudder beneath him.

Ship captains needed to keep their heads level to emerge victorious in battle, but seeing that knife against Kali's flesh stole all rational thought. All he knew was that he had to cooperate. Just until he had a chance to beat to death those bastards who held her.

Satisfied that Fletcher wasn't going anywhere, Mayhew stared excitedly at the mechanized heart. His hand shook as he brought it closer to the port embedded into his chest. He pressed the device into position, and it clicked as it locked in place.

Nothing happened.

Mayhew cursed as he glared at the mechanical heart. Despair shattered his expression—an almost pitiful sight, if one didn't think about what the lieutenant had been trying to do.

But then, the heart glowed. It shook, sending a shudder through Mayhew, and a thin, high drone pierced the air. The telumium in Fletcher's body pulsed, sensing the surge of fresh energy.

Mayhew gasped, the sorrow in his face turning to pain. He tore off his shirt and coat, then held out his hands as he stared at his arms. The telumium wires covering the lieutenant began to glow, brighter and brighter, as if growing superheated. His veins bulged. Mayhew screamed and dropped to his knees.

From her vantage atop the hill, Kali had watched in horrified fascination as the mad lieutenant secured the heart device. Any other time, she would have loved to study the mechanism. But now she only feared it, and wanted it gone. And she prayed for Fletcher's safety, trapped as he was with that lunatic on a fragile cliff.

It didn't help that she was stuck on this hilltop, one thug holding her like a vise, his filthy hand covering her mouth, the brute called Robbins pressing a knife to her throat.

Mayhew's scream echoed up the hill. The device was doing something to his body, transforming him. He was on his knees. Vulnerable.

The edge of the blade against her skin lightened in pressure. And the other man—Grady, the lieutenant called him—loosened his hold. Just a little. Both of them were watching the scene playing out below, distracted.

Now.

Using her prosthetic leg, Kali slammed her calf against the side of Grady's knee. With a pained grunt, the man stumbled, pulling her away from Robbins's knife. His hold slackened even more, enough to gain her arms room to move. She rammed her elbow into his stomach. As he bent over, gagging, she spun around, driving the knee of her artificial leg up to meet his chin. The man's head snapped back, and he toppled to the ground. Conscious, but dazed and hurting.

She sent out a silent prayer of thanks to her father, for insisting that she learn not only the basics of firearms, but simple hand to hand combat, as well. A thorough man, her father.

Kali whirled back to face Robbins. He looked briefly stunned that she would even fight back at all, let alone take down Grady. But he recovered quickly, thrusting with his knife. She'd no weapon of her own. All she could do was dodge his attacks, ducking and weaving, trying to find an opening for a well-placed kick or hit from her knee or elbow.

Robbins swooped forward. She bobbed to one side. As she bent low, she scooped up a bit of dirt and rocks. She tossed the grit into his eyes. He cursed and fell back. When Robbins attacked again, she countered with a kick to his upper thigh, using her metal shin. Grunting, he stumbled away from her.

Thank Hephaestus and Agni and all the gods of the forge that I've got a metal foot. Causes some fine damage.

She glanced down the hill, and met Fletcher's furious glare. But his fury was for her attackers. Snarling, he started up the hill.

She pointed at Mayhew, still in the agonized throes of his transformation. "Stop him!"

But she'd spoken too late. Mayhew lunged for Fletcher. Pulled him down to the cliff.

Kali moved to help, then something smashed into her. She slammed into the ground. Her thoughts of Fletcher and Mayhew fled as she found herself on her back, Robbins pinning her to the earth with his thighs, his blade poised above her heart.

Damn it. She didn't have room to use her legs. And his

knife headed straight for her chest. Kali threw up her hands and gripped his wrist, trying to push him back. But Robbins was bloody strong. Determined. Angry that she'd even put up a fight. She shoved as hard as she could against his wrist, but she didn't know how long her strength would last.

The knife crept forward.

CHAPTER FIFTEEN

Fletcher and Mayhew tumbled down the incline toward the cliff's edge. Throwing out a leg, Fletcher stopped his roll before he fell over the edge of the precipice. He leapt up. Instantly, Mayhew attacked.

As they struggled, Fletcher felt the change in the lieutenant's body. Already, Mayhew was growing bigger, the way Fletcher and others had when they underwent the transformation from man to Man O' War. But Fletcher's change had happened over the course of weeks, not minutes, the agony diffused—though he'd spent too many damn nights clenching his jaw to hold back his groans of pain.

They broke apart. Fletcher dove for the ether pistol. But the lieutenant kicked the gun over the edge of the cliff.

Fletcher rammed his fist into Mayhew's face. The lieutenant took the blow, but there was no crunch of bone. No spray of blood. A punch from a Man O' War would make a normal man's face cave in, but Mayhew had changed enough that the hit only made his head snap to one side.

"See?" the lieutenant crowed, though he grimaced in pain. "Already I'm as good as you."

Fletcher didn't bother rising to the bait. He only cared about prying that mechanized heart off Mayhew's chest. If he could reach that, maybe he could stop the transformation. His muscles coiled, and he leapt, tackling the lieutenant.

Hell. Mayhew was hot as an iron straight from the forge, and Fletcher could actually feel the lieutenant's skin stretching to accommodate his growth. Energy surged and pulsed in invisible, palpable waves.

He and Mayhew rolled across the ground, trading punches. Beneath them, the cliff shuddered, and chucks of earth broke off, plunging down into the sea. Fletcher scrabbled at the heart, but Mayhew managed to hold him off, knocking his hands aside.

Fletcher jammed his forearm against Mayhew's windpipe, but as he did, the lieutenant rammed his knee up. Twisting to avoid the blow, Fletcher caught the hit in his ribs. Breath became scarce for both of them.

"You can't stop this from happening, *Captain*." Mayhew said through bared teeth. "Nothing. A waste of damn time— that's what you are. Who cares if you're alive or dead? Killing you is meaningless."

The cliff continued to shake and crumble as Fletcher and Mayhew fought, more and more earth and rocks tumbling into the waves. Fletcher might be able to survive the fall, but so might Mayhew, and the lieutenant could make his escape once they both hit the water. And plummeting into the sea would take Fletcher too far from Kali, and her own fight.

He managed a glimpse up the hill, and for the second time

that day, terror for her nearly froze him. She was pinned beneath Robbins, struggling to keep the thug's knife at a distance.

"I've got other targets in my sites," the lieutenant continued to taunt. "Targets that will make the world take notice."

"Don't give a fucking damn," Fletcher snarled.

All that mattered was reaching Kali. Protecting her.

With a roar, Fletcher pushed Mayhew away. The ground collapsed beneath them both.

Kali couldn't hold Robbins back forever. But she'd never be able to get the knife out of his hand, either. There had to be another way to break free of him.

She brought her legs up, planting her feet on the ground. Then thrust up with her hips, her prosthetic leg giving her extra leverage. The movement threw Robbins off balance. He fell forward. His free hand shot out to keep him from completely splaying on top of Kali.

With his equilibrium thrown, Kali twisted, and she rolled them both until she was on top, and Robbins beneath her. One hand she used to keep hold of his wrist, making sure he couldn't cut her with his knife. But her other hand had a different purpose. She reared back enough to give herself room. Then punched Robbins right in the groin. Several times.

Not standard military combat training—but as her father had reminded her, *This world's cruel to lasses. Only right that the lasses are cruel right back.*

Robbins turned red, then purple, as he screamed. Leaping up, Kali kicked the knife out of his hand. She took several steps back, putting distance between herself and the thug, but her legs were unsteady. One step, another, and then suddenly, the world spun as she tumbled down the hill. Right toward the cliff—the cliff that was, at that very moment, collapsing into the sea. With Fletcher on it.

The precipice broke apart under him and Mayhew, huge chunks of rocks and dirt plunging to the water. His blood chilled when he noticed at the same time that Kali was rolling down the hillside. Without the cliff to stop her fall, she'd plummet down, four hundred feet—right to her death.

Reflex took over. As the cliff disintegrated beneath him, he launched himself toward the hill, a diagonal jump that placed him directly in Kali's path. From the corner of his eye, he saw Mayhew also leap to the hill.

But Fletcher didn't care if Mayhew made it. His focus was only on Kali. She rolled toward him, trying to stop her fall with her hands. He threw himself over her, acting like a cage and pinning her down. She wasn't going anywhere.

They lay like that for a moment, both gasping. She had her back to his front, so he couldn't see her face, but he felt her shuddering breath through his own body. Proof that she'd not only fought, but survived. Relief poured through him like ether, making his head light.

"All right?" he managed to rasp.

"I'm a little dizzy . . . but tolerably well." Her voice was a balm to his thudding heart. She managed to turn her head a little so he could see her dirt-streaked face. "You?"

"Shipshape."

An unsteady smile curved her lips. "And heavy."

He snorted, but pushed himself up onto his forearms, taking his weight off her. "Ready to sit up?"

She nodded, and slowly, carefully, he rolled off of her. They both sat upright, bracing themselves to keep from sliding down the slope of the mountain. Damn everything—there'd been too many close shaves this morning. He'd been in countless battles, but nothing had rattled him like seeing Kali at the end of Robbins's knife, or tumbling down the hill, the dark blue of her dress like the sky itself falling.

But she was alive. He didn't have to see her lovely throat torn open and her blood upon the ground. He didn't need to pull her limp, battered body from the water.

They both looked down at where the cliff had once been. Nothing was left—not a single pebble or shrub. She let out a soft, quivering curse and her cheeks went pale.

"I'd have survived the fall," he said.

"That doesn't mean I want you taking that plunge."

He cursed when he saw that Mayhew was gone, along with his thugs. The need for revenge was a hard beat beneath his pulse. He leapt to his feet. "I'm going after him."

"*We* are." Kali also stood. Or tried to. Her legs wobbled beneath her, and he was at her side instantly, supporting her. Jesus, it felt good to have her safe in his arms.

He could go faster on his own, but he wouldn't leave her here. Not with her legs still unstable and the sea so far below. So he did exactly as she suggested, picking her up and swinging her onto his back. She made a slight burden. Even so, when they reached the top of the hill and were far enough away from the edge, he set her down.

"Stay here," he commanded. "Do not move a sodding inch."

Her lips pressed into a tight line, but she nodded.

He took off down the mountain at a dead run. Here was some benefit to his months on this island, hunting to feed himself: he could read tracks in the earth. Not so difficult when three large men had dashed down a mountain and over moorland within the past fifteen minutes.

They'd a goodly head start. Though they left him a decent trail, he couldn't see the men—or whatever Mayhew was now—ahead. He tore across the heath. Until he reached the northern shore. There wasn't a beach here, just a five-foot plunge from the land into the water.

No Mayhew, either. His boat was a heaving speck on the water, growing smaller by the second, the trail of tetrol smoke from the engine a dark stain against the sky.

Could Fletcher catch up to him? He could swim far, and fast, but fast enough? The sea rose up in angry, white-topped peaks. It'd be a rough swim.

Man O' War he might be, but even he had his limitations. The fight with Mayhew, his terror at seeing Kali in danger, the sprint across the island—if he swam after the lieutenant and managed to catch up with him, he'd arrive at his boat so spent he'd put up a piss poor fight. Accomplishing nothing.

He bellowed a curse. But there was nothing to be done. Furious with Mayhew and himself, he turned back and headed toward where Kali waited.

It stunned him that she stood precisely where he'd left her. Though she didn't look pleased about it. And she let out a string of oaths in Hindi when she saw that he was alone.

But he knew that her anger wasn't for him and his inability to catch Mayhew. No—he knew her well enough to understand she raged against the lieutenant's escape.

"Damn it," she fumed as she marched toward him, "what a bloody psychopath. To encourage our trust like that. We sodding *helped* him find that strongbox. And what it contained," she added darkly. "You two served together—you were his commanding officer—and *this* is the fruit of his so-called loyalty."

Fletcher shook his head as they made their way down the hill. Everything within him had coalesced into a knot he couldn't possibly untie. He took Kali's hand in his because he needed it, needed her touch.

"A mild one, Mayhew. Never gave a sign. Not a look, not a word about how he felt about Man O' Wars or wanting to be one. All that tinkering, but I never knew what it was he worked on."

"He was mutilating himself," she muttered. "Readying himself for . . . gods, I don't even know what."

"Vengeance." The word tasted oily and sour.

"He was on the *Persephone*, butchering his own body, and quietly, privately despising you." She looked appalled.

Fletcher could picture it: Mayhew in his cabin, shoving stolen telumium wires into his body without benefit of anesthetic, taking his anger and pain and transforming it into hate. Hate for him.

They'd reached the base of the hill, and she stopped walking, facing him. She placed one hand on his chest and looked up at him, her expression fierce. A woman who'd battled and would gladly fight again.

"They *looked* for you, Fletcher," she said, her voice hard.

"I'd wager my soldering iron he fed the navy bad information so they'd search the wrong areas for you."

He had to admit it made sense. Mayhew wouldn't want the navy finding him and recovering not just the ship, but everything that had been on it. Including Mayhew's strongbox, and the means of his transformation.

"The navy wanted their weapon back—me."

"Damn it, Fletcher." Her fingers closed around the fabric of his shirt, gripping him tighter. "You're so much more than that. Not just to the navy, but to me." Still fierce as a tigress, she held his gaze, while his heart set up a tattoo in his chest. "If he'd hurt you, killed you . . ." Her throat worked and her voice turned to rough, raw silk. "I'd have hunted him down. Made him suffer before pulling that false heart off of him, and sending him to Hell."

Vicious, bloodthirsty words from a woman who'd seen too much of violence, who lived to build and create, not destroy. Yet she would. Because of him.

He wouldn't tell her that, even if she'd removed Mayhew's mechanized heart, the man had been too altered to be killed by a normal human. Hers would've been a suicide mission. Either she had no idea, or knew and didn't care.

He kissed her. Gripped her head gently and took her mouth with his, greedy for the taste of her. Her hand on his shirt tightened even more, digging her nails into his flesh, as she kissed him back. She was flame, and he was fire, and together, they were an inferno.

But the kiss couldn't last. They broke apart, and silently continued back toward the *Persephone*, which sat broken and useless on the moor.

"He didn't kill you, though," Kali said in that tone that he knew meant she was puzzling something through. "Didn't hang about to continue your fight. Just ran off . . . as if he had somewhere to be." She looked up at him. "There was a reason he didn't try to finish the job. If the navy already thinks you're dead—"

"Then who'd care if he killed me?" Fletcher concluded. "He became a Man O' War to kill Man O' Wars. Nobody would notice my death."

"But he'd want the navy—the world—to take note of him. The way he always wanted."

Fletcher's mind furiously churned. "He's got a target in mind."

"A British Man O' War," Kali deduced. "The perfect payback to the system that destroyed his dream. How many Man O' Wars are there in the navy?"

"Fifty," he answered. "They wanted a hundred, but we're expensive to make and there aren't many naval men who meet the requirements. Airships cost a mountain of coin, too. Can't have one without the other."

She growled, "There's got to be a way to narrow down a list of fifty to one possible target."

They reached the *Persephone*, and climbed back aboard. Sunlight broke through the haze, casting shifting shadows upon the deck, almost as if the airship was back in the sky, where she belonged.

"Mayhew wants to exact revenge on the navy." Fletcher stared up at the clouds, squinting from the sun's glare.

"Then he'd want to assassinate the navy's top Man O' War," Kali concluded.

He knew she had to be exhausted from everything that had happened, but she didn't sit down on the crate he offered. Instead, she crossed her arms over her chest and leaned against the support beam that had once held the main ether tanks. The tanks themselves had rolled aft, and now rested against the rails. "Send them, and everyone else, a message," she reasoned.

He rubbed the back of his neck. Thinking of the navy, of the other Man O' Wars, felt like wearing a different uniform. It was tight, awkward. But there was no avoiding it. A man's life was at risk, possibly many lives.

"Redmond," he said suddenly. At Kali's questioning frown, he explained, "Captain Christopher Redmond. He's the jewel in the navy's crown."

She pushed away from the support beam. "I remember him. He went behind enemy lines and destroyed a key munitions plant. It was in all the papers."

"Redmond's always been a valuable asset," Fletcher murmured. "But after the destruction of the plant, he became matchless. Victory after victory against the enemy." He didn't add that Redmond's success was partly due to the presence of the captain's wife, Louisa, aboard his airship. It was a rare arrangement, but the former Miss Shaw was one of the navy's finest intelligence agents, and a crucial reason why Redmond knew exactly where to be and when. Of course, it was Redmond's skill as a captain that ensured his victories, but between him and his wife, they were nigh unstoppable.

Few outside of the highest levels in the navy knew about Louisa Redmond's contributions. Intelligence agents had to have their identities and work protected at all times. Mayhew wouldn't know anything about her.

"If Mayhew kills Captain Redmond," Kali said, "Her Majesty's Aerial Navy not only loses its best man, but loses face, as well."

"And Mayhew's reputation is set up. Everything he wants." Fletcher curled his hands into fists. "Wish I'd killed that lunatic bastard." He replayed his fight with the lieutenant in his mind, trying to figure out where he'd missed an opportunity, but nothing revealed itself.

Kali was suddenly standing before him, her gaze bright with urgency. "Captain Redmond has to be warned about Mayhew. The navy must know, too."

"Aye." But as he said it, he realized that if he did alert the navy, he'd no longer be dead. A possibility that had come to him that morning, when Mayhew had first arrived, yet it struck him anew. His haven was being torn away. He'd be forced back into a role he no longer wanted to play. But was that role truly what defined him?

Kali's gentled voice pierced his thoughts. "I can build a boat. Using wood from the *Persephone*. And building an engine wouldn't take more than a few hours. If I work all day and night, I could set out for South Uist tomorrow morning. By myself."

He stared at her. Here was her gift, her offering. No one ever needed to know about him. Mayhew certainly wouldn't tell anyone that Fletcher still lived. And Kali would keep his confidence. He could go on as he had these past months—dead.

And alone.

He'd lose her to the world. To duty and responsibility. To the pain and suffering and wonder that was life beyond Eilean Comhachag.

His lips were dry, his voice cracked, as he asked, "What would you tell them?"

"That I'd come to this island and found a crashed airship. No survivors. Then Mayhew showed up, got his strongbox, and all the rest. I witnessed it all without being seen, and heard him swear vengeance on the navy."

"They'd never believe a tale like that."

She shrugged, though there was nothing careless about the movement. "It's all I can do."

He turned away, dragging his hands through his hair. Paced the length of the deck and back.

"I'm coming with you," he said.

Her eyes widened. "You don't—"

"I do. I'm the one who's got to tell them about Mayhew. Otherwise, they'd shrug off your claims as the ravings of a woman scarred by her experience at Liverpool."

If his bluntness offended her, she made no sign. She only looked at him with those impossibly dark, beautiful eyes of hers, those eyes that saw too much, that revealed a mind of fathomless complexity.

"You won't be dead any longer," she said quietly.

"I haven't been," he answered. "You resurrected me, disinterred me from the grave I'd dug." He stepped closer, and she held her ground, so hardly any distance separated them. His voice rough, he continued, "Your breath became my breath. The beat of your heart pumps blood through my veins."

He could see her pulse now, fast and hard in the delicate

skin of her throat. Bringing his hand up, he cupped the side of her face. "Any thoughts that I can exist without you died today on that cliff."

"I have to go," she whispered.

"I'm coming with you," he said.

She swallowed hard. "Are you ready?"

"Aye." He realized as he said it that it was true. "I've been thinking. About what you've said to me. That a Man O' War brings safety, not just death."

"You've saved so many lives," she murmured. "Including mine."

"It's time to face the world again. And if I've got you beside me"—he brushed back a strand of her hair—"I'm ready for anything."

She looped her hands around his neck. But instead of kissing him, she pulled him down so his forehead touched hers. Her eyes remained open, too, their gazes holding. He felt himself falling, falling, from a height greater than anything he'd known aboard an airship. But there was nothing frightening about this fall. There would be no crash, no slam into the unyielding earth. It would go on forever, all rushing air and dizziness, and he welcomed it.

She must have known. Seen inside his mind. Because she murmured, "Together, we're going to fly."

Chapter Sixteen

He discovered that she wasn't just speaking metaphorically. Kali was intent on making the *Persephone* fly again. She reasoned it would take as much time to get the airship skyworthy as it would for her to build a seafaring vessel—and it'd move faster, too.

"And Mayhew's got to get himself an airship, too," she reasoned. "Unlikely that he's got one lined up already."

"They're not exactly easy or cheap to come by," Fletcher agreed. Any airships that weren't part of a country's aerial navy belonged to Man O' Wars who had gone rogue, their ships stolen from the nations they once served. Even Captain Mikhail Denisov, the rogue turned protector of those caught in war-torn regions, had taken his ship from the Russian Imperial Aerial Navy.

"We'll have enough time to get our downed lady up in the sky," Kali said eagerly, hauling her tools from her makeshift workshop to the turbines.

As they gathered everything to begin repairs, the thought of being back amongst the clouds made it feel as though he were the one filled with ether, not the tanks he helped Kali remount onto their supports. Anticipation and unease mixed within him, like a scientist's experiment combining emotions instead of chemicals. He assisted Kali throughout the day and into the night—lifting and carrying metal and wood and bundles of heavy pipes, handing her tools while getting an education as to what those tools were and what they did— and as he did, he kept peering out portholes at the sky above the horizon, or looking up if they were topside.

He studied the sky, watching the clouds and how the wind moved them. Once, he'd read the sky as often as some men read their newspapers—maybe more. He'd be a captain again soon. A true captain, back in the sky, in command of a ship. He'd need his sky literacy once again.

It had been his home for so long. He hadn't realized how much he missed the sensations, the freedom, until the prospect dangled before him.

It wouldn't be easy, returning to combat. But he had to. This was his purpose. To defend his country. If he'd helped in some way to save Kali's life, and the people of Liverpool, then perhaps being a Man O' War had more uses than for destruction. From the sky, he could protect the land and the people.

There was only one reason why he could even consider flying again: Kali. He wouldn't have believed the *Persephone* could be capable of flight, yet Kali never doubted herself or her ability. She worked without slowing, stopping just long enough to eat the food he forced on her. And she directed him with complete confidence when she gave him a hammer and nails, telling him to patch up the lower decks that hadn't been crushed.

He wanted her to stay behind, where it was safe. But an airship couldn't run with just one crewman. He could fly it, yes, but if anything went wrong with the ship, he'd need an engineer. And, damn it, he knew of only one engineer.

When she thought he wasn't looking, shadows of wariness flickered across her face. This would be her return to the world, too. Sooner than she'd planned, that much he knew. But whatever fear hounded her, she didn't allow it to stop her work. Or her determination.

Four scampered from chamber to chamber, both afraid of and intrigued by all the activity. Eventually, the rat became acclimated to the pounding of nails and hiss of the welding torch, and perched on Fletcher's shoulder as he labored on filling spare tanks with ether. The main tanks loaded quickly—as if the ship were a starving creature finally given sustenance.

He stroked the rat's furry head as another tank topped up. As the ship awakened, it fed from him more, drawing on his energy. But it gave back to him, too. The currents of power moving through the *Persephone* resonated in his own body. He felt like a lit fuse.

Never more so than when they could work no longer, and he and Kali retired to bed. It was there that he showed her, in ways words couldn't, what she'd come to mean to him. That he couldn't understand how he'd managed any kind of existence without her. That the feel of her skin was his oxygen. And her breathless words of encouragement and cries of pleasure gave him more strength than any telumium implanted in his body.

He kept a lantern burning as they made love. He could

see well enough in the dark, but he wanted her to be witness to what they gave each other, how their entwined bodies—scarred, marked—were beautiful and exactly right.

"Will this all change?" she asked, as they lay, sweat slick and tangled. Her head rested upon his chest, and her fingers traced all over his body—implants, flesh, tattoos—as if committing him to memory. "When we go back, will it all go away?"

He pulled her even closer, needing the press of her body to his. "I don't know," he said, though it killed him to say so. Beyond the possibility of flight, the future was unseen, hidden behind banks of dark thunderheads. Would he be called upon to return to duty? Would he ever see Kali again?

And Mayhew lurked out in the shadows, a madman with a thirst for Man O' War blood. It was certain the lieutenant would kill civilians in his quest for vengeance. Could he be stopped?

So much unknown. Like one of those old maps with monsters drawn in the areas where the cartographer's knowledge failed. Monsters did lurk, but whether they could be defeated, that wasn't certain.

"We'll find our course as we go," Fletcher said, stroking his hand down her arm.

She lifted her head to gaze at him. "You don't strike me as the sort of man who travels without a clear direction."

"I wasn't . . . once."

"Something's changed."

He allowed himself a smile, and despite everything—all the uncertainty, all the looming danger—the smile felt real. "When a ferryman brought a wary, clever woman to this heap of rock, everything changed."

In the morning, Kali immersed herself in running a litany of tests on the *Persephone*. Easier to focus on all the technical elements that needed attention than to think of what lay ahead. As she checked the airship's turbines, their roar drowned out the voices of doubt crowding inside her mind. Yes, Eilean Comhachag was never meant to be her permanent home, but she felt like a bird shoved from the nest before she was certain she could fly.

She wanted more time to put to rest memories of that day in Liverpool. More time to build strength—any kind of strength. More time alone with Fletcher.

She'd get none of this. They would have to leave the island. Today.

The turbines worked just as they should, and she moved on to the ether tanks to ensure that they had no cracks and could be called upon to vent as necessary. Venting ether, Fletcher told her, enabled the airship to move at heightened speeds. But it only lasted a brief while, and meant that the ship would drop precipitously. Yet it made for an effective tool in battle when one needed swiftness.

Surely, though, they wouldn't need to vent the tanks. Not for their brief trip to the nearest telegraph station to alert the navy, and then flying the ship to the dockyards in Greenwich for greater repairs. And then . . . she didn't know what then. Neither did Fletcher. A vast unknown. For herself, for him. For them.

They'd want him back on duty. A Man O' War couldn't be away from his ship for long, and he was too valuable in the ongoing war.

If they saw each other at all when they returned, it could only be for brief periods of time. Which would be worse? Having him for only a handful of days after months apart, or not having him at all? Both options would hurt—they hurt *now*, just thinking of them.

She glanced over to where he was finishing hammering the bow of the ship into a semblance of order. It had splintered apart in the crash, and needed to be as aerodynamic as possible for the upcoming flight.

Her eyes weren't on the repairs, but on Fletcher. He'd shed his coat, and worked in his shirtsleeves, muscles straining against the thin fabric, his braces framing the wide architecture of his back. She knew him well enough to know that he had to hold himself back and not use the full measure of his strength when working on fixing the ship, otherwise one hit of the hammer would cause the entire bow of the ship to break off.

And yet this was the same man who'd made love to her last night with such tenderness and reverence, she'd nearly wept. Her body heated as she remembered that last night hadn't been only soft caresses and whispered endearments. No, he'd shown her the full measure of his desire, the wildness he tried so hard to contain. And it had been ... The erotic poems of her homeland could never equal what she and Fletcher had shared last night. She'd felt like the incarnation of Rati, the goddess of passion.

There'd been more than lust and desire last night. In his touch, in hers. An aching yearning for something that might never be. Back in the world, they might spend months, years apart. If he returned at all.

Even now, as they both readied the airship for its first flight since the crash, Kali wanted to cross the deck and press herself against Fletcher, feel the movement of his body, the steady rhythm of his heart.

Instead, she continued with the rest of her tests. Each minute they spent on the island meant Mayhew was closer to obtaining his own airship. A minute closer to unleashing his madness on an unsuspecting world.

She'd lived through death and devastation before. There wasn't a chance in Hell or Naraka that she'd knowingly let that kind of destruction happen and not try to stop it. At least with the war, there was a terrible sort of sense to it. But Mayhew would bring only meaningless chaos. It wouldn't be a far leap for him to go from killing Man O' Wars to leveling towns and cities, simply because he could.

After Kali finished the last of her checks, she approached Fletcher, standing in the rebuilt forecastle. His arms were crossed over his chest, and he stared out at the moor rolling around the ship, and the tall hills to the southwest.

She knew he heard her coming, but he didn't turn when she approached. Instead, she stood beside him, taking in the land, the place that had been her home these past months.

"Everything's tested well," she said. "We can leave at your discretion."

"A minute more," he answered, voice distant. They both seemed to understand that there'd be no return to Eilean Comhachag once the *Persephone* took to the air.

This place had been theirs, but no longer. Her chest ached, and she had the absurd impulse to run and hide somewhere. The marshland that lay between her cottage and the ship might do—but he'd find her, and the time for hiding was over, anyway.

For a brief while longer, they had each other. But only fleetingly.

"It's time," she said.

He did turn to her then, one dark brow raised sharply. "Eager to put this place behind you?" *And me?* was the unspoken addition.

"He's out there," she replied. "There's no luxury of self-indulgence. And . . ." She made herself gaze directly into the unforgiving blue of his eyes. "I can't draw this out longer."

The anger cooled in his eyes. Something that looked suspiciously like heartache took its place. He unfolded his arms and wrapped them around her. His hand stroked down her hair, and he ran his mouth back and forth over the crown of her head. She let herself be held, her own hands pressed tight between the hard jut of his shoulder blades.

There might not be another chance. It wasn't wrong to need him like this—there would be plenty of time later to be on her own, independent. Even if they continued their relationship once they returned home, they'd never have this kind of time again. But for this small moment, she could have this. Have him all to herself.

And then it was over. By a silent, mutual agreement, they separated, then walked without touching to the pilot house.

Below deck, she had reexamined the fruits of their combined labors. She'd learned volumes about the design and functioning of an airship these past weeks, but it'd been fortunate that most of the controls within the pilot house hadn't needed too much repair. Just a matter of making certain the connections to the different parts of the ship still worked.

Now in the pilot house, she noted again how one panel controlled the ether tanks—the main tanks on the support beam, as well as the auxiliary ones below decks in the aft of the ship. There was a dial that controlled the levels of the buoyant gas in all of the tanks, and separate dials to adjust the levels in each one, giving the ship its lift and balance. Gauges atop the panel showed the level of ether in each container.

The other main control for the ship was the steering—a wheel mounted atop a column that moved back and forth in its yoke. The wheel controlled the louvers of the engines—louvers she and Fletcher had had to rebuild using pieces of bulkheads from inside the ship. Beside the wheel was the throttle, which regulated how much power went into the turbines.

And all of it was fueled by Fletcher. The batteries absorbed energy from him, and those batteries powered the turbines. The process even created the ether that enabled the airship to fly.

"The more I worked on this," she murmured, "the more I realized Dr. Rossini's genius."

"Genius that drove her mad," he noted.

"Everything has its cost." She knew that now, more than ever.

They were silent for a moment, each absorbing her words. Then, "Ready?" he asked.

"Yes—wait!"

His hand paused above the lever that activated the ether tanks.

"What about Four?"

"What of him?"

The rat himself was snug below decks, in a bed of rags in a corner of the galley. She'd fed him that morning and he'd fallen promptly asleep, utterly uninterested in the concerns of man.

"Perhaps Four needs to stay," she said. "The island's been his home his whole life. He might not want to leave."

But Fletcher's mouth curved into a brief smile. "He's protected, fed, and warm on the *Persephone*. And we've fattened him up nicely. An owl would take one look at him and see a banquet." He shook his head. "The rat stays with me. For his own safety."

"His safety. Of course."

Fletcher scowled at her. Then, drawing a deep breath, he pulled the ether tank activation lever.

For a moment, everything was still and silent. Kali's frustration surged. She'd been so certain that she'd done all the repairs, and her skills were up to the task of bringing *Persephone* back to life.

Her mind raced. There might still be time to build a boat, but she'd already cost them valuable time by attempting to fix the airship. Had she been too ambitious? Too full of hubris?

"Wait." Fletcher reached out and took her hand in his. As if he knew the twists and configurations of her mind and thoughts.

"But—"

An almighty groan sounded, shaking Kali all the way to her marrow. She braced herself in the doorway of the pilot house. The ship juddered, complaining loudly. It was if some massive creature was trying to crawl its way up from the depths of the earth.

And then—she felt the lift from the activated tanks. The ground moved away as the *Persephone* pulled herself into the air. It wasn't an easy rise upward. The ship had dug herself in deep when she'd crashed. Rocks and scrub held tight, then fell away as the airship went higher. Three feet. Ten. Twenty. Higher still. Until they were over one hundred feet above the ground.

Kali's heart leapt. They'd done it. After months buried in the earth, the *Persephone* flew again.

But she wouldn't allow herself any real celebration. Not until the ship did more than hover.

Fletcher's own expression was unreadable as a mountain. He seemed satisfied with the height of the ascent, but now was the crucial moment: could the *Persephone* move?

He pulled the lever that completed the circuit that activated the batteries, and powered the turbines. Again, everything was silent. The ship hung suspended in the air. Then a low hum began, deep in the hull. The same hum she'd heard faintly her first night on the island. Now the sound from the batteries was much louder, growing in volume. Suddenly she felt it—the turbines spinning to life.

Still, she kept her hands tight on the pilot house door frame, her excitement fiercely tamped down. But when Fletcher put his hands on the wheel and piloted the ship forward, and the vessel actually *responded*, the ground below sliding away, she let out a small yelp of exultation.

Fletcher kept silent, and stayed that way as he steered the ship up and around in gentle circles over the island. Kali released her grip on the door frame and edged cautiously across the deck toward the rail. There, below her, was Eilean Comhachag. Fletcher took them higher than they'd gone in the barrel, and she could see everything now. It stunned her how small the island appeared—just a collection of rocks and greenery clustered together in the middle of an iron gray sea. A deep wound marked the earth where the *Persephone* had lain.

Such a little place, hardly anything at all. But it had altered her. Brought her and Fletcher together, transforming them both.

Such huge metamorphoses seemed to demand someplace larger—a landscape as vast and remarkable as the Thar Desert or the Himalayas. But no, the island was a tiny, humble speck of land.

A great change can happen in the smallest of spaces. Even somewhere as modest as the human heart.

And what of her birthright? She could see the cottage, still in shambles, only a pile of pebbles from this height. Another MacNeil might come along in the future to repair it, though it wouldn't be her.

Before they'd gone, she'd insisted on leaving Campbell a note, telling the ferryman that, after her cottage had collapsed, she managed to get a ride back to the mainland from a passing fisherman. Hopefully, he'd find the note and believe her story.

"Careful." Fletcher's voice was sharp. "You're not used to being on an airship. Can't have you tumbling over the rail."

She wouldn't argue. Her head spinning from the height, she wobbled back to the pilot house. Fletcher continued to navigate the ship above the island, practicing, she supposed. It had been a long while since he'd been at the wheel of an airship. And he likely needed to test whether or not her repairs would hold. Staying close to the island would give them someplace to land if they needed to do so in a hurry.

He glanced over at her. "All right?"

She offered him a smile, thin though it was. "Sound as a bell."

"You'll get your airlegs."

"I never get seasick," she muttered.

"Not the same as flying. But I know you'll adapt. You always do."

His words helped steady her, even as he took the *Persephone* through her paces. As he piloted the ship, she studied him, watching how he seemed to grow even bigger, taller. His back was straight, his legs braced wide, and his hands were steady on the wheel. If he had any trepidation about flying again, he didn't show it. In truth, she'd never seen him so at ease. Confidence radiated from him as he steered the airship. He took expansive breaths, and his eyes gleamed with satisfaction.

This was his home. He might not have been born a Man O' War, but she saw now that it had always been his kismat. He'd moved with steadiness and purpose on land. But here . . . here nothing held him back.

Her eyes grew damp and hot, and she dug the heels of her hands into her eyes to keep her cheeks dry.

"Damn, I forgot." He shook his head at himself. "Spare goggles. Even in the pilot house the wind can get you."

She nodded. He didn't need to know the reason for her tears.

"You'll want your cloak, too," he added. "When we pick up speed, it gets bloody cold topside. That's what the crew told me. Never felt the chill, myself."

"No, you wouldn't." She knew from experience how warm he ran. Heat rolled off of him now, the scent of warm metal enveloping her, as his implants fed the airship with his energy.

A few more passes over the island, then, "We're ready. And losing time."

This was it. Though they flew above the island, they were still close. The open sky beckoned. Once Fletcher took the *Persephone* out there, neither of them would come back. She might return. Perhaps. But if she did, she'd be alone.

"All right," she answered tightly.

Fletcher pushed on the throttle, and the airship flew onward. They were headed south, to the closest telegraph station.

Don't look back. Nothing good ever came from looking back.

But she did, poking her head out from the pilot house and peering past the turbines to watch Eilean Comhachag grow smaller and smaller, until it disappeared like a dream upon waking.

She pulled her head back into the pilot house and kept her gaze fixed on the horizon.

"Kali," he said, as quietly as he could above the drone of the engines.

She looked at him. "I'll get my airlegs, like you said. No worry needed."

"I'm not worried." He kept his hands on the wheel, his gaze forward. "Only . . . I wanted to say . . ." He seemed to struggle with his words. "... Thank you. For giving this back to me." He waved at the pearl-colored sky, expansive as thought itself. "I'd forgotten what it meant to fly, how I ... loved it. Never thought I'd know it again."

His gaze turned to her, and his eyes shone, almost as if tears gathered there. "Yet you gave me this ... this gift. *Thank you* is such a puny thing to say for something so big. But those are the only words I know."

"*Dhanyavad*," she said. "That's how it's said back home. Only for the most significant occasions, though."

"*Dhanyavad*," he repeated. It sounded clumsy on his tongue, but no one had ever thanked her with such truth or sincerity.

"*Main tumse pyaar karthi hu*," she said.

"Is that *You're welcome?*"

"Yes," she answered. It meant, in truth, *I love you*.

CHAPTER SEVENTEEN

Kali stood at the rail—having gained her airlegs just as Fletcher had promised—and watched the shadow of the *Persephone* pass over the town of Lochboisdale. While it was a thriving port on South Uist, airships didn't likely make appearances here. As Fletcher brought the ship lower, she could see people hurrying out of their homes and businesses, staring and pointing up at the sky.

Even if the people of Lochboisdale were familiar with airships, no one here, nor anywhere else, had seen one like the *Persephone*. Missing half of her lower decks, she was flat-bottomed, not curved, and with all the other makeshift parts, she was a rare creature. But Kali took pride in it. She'd made the airship fly again. Otherwise it would've remained permanently berthed in the middle of a moor.

And Fletcher would have stayed with the ship. Both of them dug into the earth, lost.

"Where are you going to land?" she called over her shoulder. Neither had spoken since their exchange in the pilot house, a fine tension was growing tighter and tighter between them the closer they came to civilization and the outside world.

"There's a field north of the town," he answered, then smiled a little. "Advantage of having a flat-bottomed ship—I can set her down on land."

Most airships used jolly boats and other small ether-lifted vessels for transporting crew and cargo. Since they had neither, it would have to be an actual landing.

Her stomach tightened as they glided lower and closer to the town. Seven weeks, it had been, maybe more—she couldn't remember—since she'd last been around so many people. It was a small place, really, but compared to what she'd been used to, Lochboisdale seemed a bustling metropolis. After the heath and hills of Eilean Comhachag, these buildings jarred her eye, sharp and man-made. They clustered around the bay in little groups. Some boats bobbed in the harbor, fishing vessels and a ferry, and crewmen gathered on their decks to watch the *Persephone*.

Fletcher passed the *Persephone* over the town and brought the airship down in a field, just as he'd said. Kali braced herself as the ship bumped and shuddered with the landing.

"Not used to actually taking her down like this," he said as he strode from the pilot house.

"You'll get the way of it," she answered, but as soon as she said it, she realized that he likely wouldn't. As soon as the navy learned he was alive, he'd return to Admiralty headquarters at Greenwich and be assigned a new airship. One that didn't have a flat, patched-together keel or Kali's improvised repairs. The *Persephone* would probably be disassembled and her parts used for other airships. There'd be no record of Kali and Fletcher, of what they'd built together.

He seemed to grasp this, too, because his mouth flattened into a tight line. "Wait here." Then he disappeared down the companionway.

She tugged off her goggles, which she'd salvaged from a cabin, and watched as curious townsfolk gathered at the edge of the field. None of them approached the ship, held back by an invisible wall of trepidation. But she could hear the murmur of their joined voices, the fragments of their uncertainty.

"Is it the Huns?" "Never seen an airship like it." "You've never seen any airship." "Are we under attack?" "Pretty sorry specimen if we are."

An odd bubble of anger rose in her chest. Did these people know what the *Persephone* had endured? How hard Kali and Fletcher had worked to get her back into the sky? What did any of them know? The *Persephone* persevered and lived, and Kali would punch anyone who'd say an unkind word about the airship.

Survival left scars. And those scars needed to be celebrated.

Moments later, Fletcher returned topside. He carried a brass and wood device that resembled a cross between a telegraph and one of those new typing machines, though instead of letters, odd symbols covered the keys, and ports for connecting to electrical wires were fitted into its side.

"Can you operate that?" she asked, eyeing the device.

"Usually, an airship's got a crewman in charge of communications, but we're all trained to send and receive messages, in the event that crewman's hurt or killed." He raised a brow. "The bigger concern is whether you can make it work with the town's telegraph lines."

She patted the pouches on her belt, fully stocked with tools. "You fly the ship, I make mechanical apparatuses work."

She clung to his brief smile, flashing white in his dark beard. "A crew of two," he murmured. "That suits me." Then he studied the crowd gathered at the edge of the field. A shadow passed across his face—he must feel as she did about being amongst people again, or perhaps he felt it even more strongly, having been on his own for so much longer.

But the shadow vanished beneath the dispassionate look she now knew so well. He'd worn that same distant expression those first times they'd met, as if impassivity formed a protective barrier that couldn't be breached.

She wanted to tell him that she was afraid, too. Words felt hollow, so she pressed her hand to his chest.

He glanced at her hand, inhaled long and slow, then finally said, "Let's go."

They climbed down the ladder. A gust of wind coming off the bay lifted her skirts slightly, but she didn't care if any of the townsfolk caught a glimpse of her prosthetic leg. It was part of her, more evidence that she'd endured.

The curious citizens of Lochboisdale quieted as Kali and Fletcher approached. No one spoke at all. Even when Fletcher asked, "Telegraph office?" a man only pointed the way, his eyes round as sand dollars. The crowd parted to let them pass. Yet as she and Fletcher walked down the street, the people followed them—at a safe distance.

"An airship, a Man O' War, and an East Indian half-blood

with a mechanical leg," Kali murmured. "Likely the most excitement they've had in generations."

"They'll write songs about it," he answered, "and tell tales around the fire. *I remember it as if it were yesterday. Like gods, they were. Disheveled gods.*"

She fought a slightly hysterical giggle. Being in a town, even one as small as this, tightened all her nerves like wires around a battery terminal. They passed homes and shops— including a pastry shop, which nearly made her stop. The lure of fresh-cooked food, that she hadn't needed to skin or gut, made her stomach take notice.

Fletcher caught her longing glance at the pies and cakes displayed in the window. A similar look of hunger crossed his face. "After we've sent this message, I'll buy us so many pies they'll need a tetrol-powered wheelbarrow to roll us back to the ship."

"I'll hold you to that plan." She distracted herself from her tempest of thoughts by cataloguing all the different kinds of pastries she'd eat. Chicken and mushroom. Smoked trout. No steak and kidney, though—she kept her mother's belief, and ate no beef. And Kali wouldn't eat any rabbit or pheasant any time soon. She'd had enough of both.

Her thoughts kept her uneasiness at bay, until they reached the telegraph office. A man stood in front, his hands knotted together. The little cap he wore marked him as the telegraph operator. He looked both excited and terrified by Fletcher's appearance outside his workplace. She barely drew the man's notice.

"We need your telegraph wires," Fletcher said without preamble.

The operator coughed in surprise. "I assure you, ah, sir, that I can send any message you request."

"Can't use your machine," Fletcher answered.

"We've brought our own," Kali added.

"B-but . . ." the operator stammered.

"This concerns the safety of our nation." Fletcher sounded exactly like a captain in Her Majesty's Aerial Navy, a man who would brook no foolishness nor have his time wasted.

Without taking his eyes off of Fletcher, the telegraph operator pushed open the door to the office. As he took a step backward, inside, Fletcher said, "Absent yourself for the next half hour."

"They'll s-sack me if I leave my p-post," the man stuttered.

"The safety of our nation," Kali reminded him, and followed Fletcher inside. She shut the door and turned the key. As the operator and other townsfolk gathered on the sidewalk, staring in through the window, she drew the shades. The people outside cast shadows onto the fabric, like a puppet show.

She turned to find Fletcher waiting beside the telegraph with the typing device. "This won't take but moments," she said, stepping forward. Carefully, she began disconnecting the wires that led to the telegraph. Once the wires were disengaged, she motioned for Fletcher to put the typing machine on a table and drag it close enough for her to join the leads. The process of connecting these wires went a little slower, since she wasn't as familiar with the technology.

"Normally," she said, splicing wires, "an airship has a port attached to its hull, and this port connects to specially engineered telegraph poles situated around the globe, enabling the ship to communicate with the Admiralty. In code, of course," she added, glancing at the typing device.

Fletcher, watching her intently, nodded. "All airships are required to regularly dock at telegraph poles to send reports and receive orders." His lips quirked. "But the *Persephone*'s port was pulverized when we crashed. Bringing us to this fine town, and giving you yet another opportunity to dazzle me with your engineering skills."

She threw him a quick look. "Have I not dazzled you enough? There's an airship, not a mile from here, that's testament to my ability."

He held up his hands. "Consider me well and truly awed."

They volleyed light words in an attempt to lacquer over their apprehension. But within minutes, she had the coding device connected. She stepped back as Fletcher turned the mechanism's crank, creating a charge. The machine hummed to life.

Here it was. Their link back to the world.

He pulled a chair over to the table and sat, then drew a deep breath. The moment his fingers pressed the keys, he would be resurrected. For a second, he only rested his fingertips on the keys. She thought perhaps he might tremble slightly at the prospect of returning from the dead. But no. There was an enforced stillness in him, as if he were gathering himself.

Then he began to type. His fingers slipped a few times on the keys. "These damn things aren't meant for oversized Man O' War hands," he muttered. But he kept on typing, punching in a message as she looked on, trying to decipher the code.

"It's done." He sat back and folded his arms over his chest, the chair creaking beneath him. "Now we wait."

Minutes passed. She paced the length of the small office. There were advertisements pinned to a board—rooms to let, fishing nets repaired, an amateur theatrical performance—but none of these held her interest for long. She kept waiting for that moment, that one, fraught moment, when the answer would come, and everything changed. Not even a newspaper trumpeting the plans for rebuilding Liverpool could distract her.

She jumped when the machine clacked to life. A thin ribbon of paper spooled out of a slot in the side. Fletcher held the paper as it emerged, scanning it. She peered over his shoulder. The strange shapes punched into the ribbon made no sense to her.

But they did to Fletcher. He cursed as he continued to read the message.

Once the ribbon stopped moving, he sent another message. Fraught silence fell as he waited for a response, too strained for her to break it with questions. This went on for several more exchanges. Until the machine went silent, and he didn't reply.

Instead, he folded his arms across his chest, his brows lowered. She wouldn't have been surprised if the glass in the window at the back of the telegraph office shook from the force of his brooding.

"What?" she demanded. "What did they say?"

He glanced up from beneath his dark brows, as if he'd forgotten she was there. "A good deal of shock that I wasn't dead. Relief and gratification, too. They want me to report to headquarters as soon as possible."

She knew it was coming, but the inevitable loss hit her like a wrench to the stomach. Swallowing around her hurt, she pressed, "What of Mayhew and Redmond?"

"Redmond's in Greenland to investigate enemy incursions close to the Americas, including building supply stations. The Hapsburgs had been beaten in California by some audacious upstarts—local law and an Upland Ranger—and gone quiet." Judging by Fletcher's grim expression, the news wasn't comforting. "Intelligence thinks that might be the Huns gathering strength to try something new. So they sent Redmond to look into it. He has his wife on his ship—one of the best intelligence agents there is."

"If it's an espionage operation," Kali mused, "then Mayhew wouldn't know about Redmond's whereabouts."

"That's the goddamn twist," he growled. "Mayhew had been on leave, looking for us. Then he'd been reassigned to the *Circe*. Except he jumped ship two weeks ago. Just the same time that the *Circe* received a communication about Redmond's assignment."

She felt her own frown knot between her brows. "Mayhew must've seen the communiqué. He knew he had his target, and needed the mechanical heart to make the final transition. So he found us. And his damn strongbox." She paced in a small circle. "They'll warn Redmond, though, about Mayhew."

"No telegraph poles in Greenland to get the word out. And no goddamn ships close to his location."

She continued, striving for optimism, "Redmond will be able to defend himself, certainly."

Fletcher shoved back from the table, dark as a massing storm. "Mayhew will fight dirty. Maybe try to pass himself off as a sanctioned Man O' War and get close enough to strike a killing blow. No way to know."

She couldn't abandon hope. "The other British airships—"

"Won't arrive in time," he growled.

"There *has* to be a British Man O' War that's close enough to intercept Mayhew."

He held her gaze. "I am."

Kali looked at him as if he'd suggested taking on the Devil armed only with a rusty paring knife.

"No." She stepped close and grabbed handfuls of his coat. "He'll be further along in his transformation. He'll have an airship that isn't half-wrecked and armed with just one ether cannon and one Gatling gun. Plus he's mad as a bloody mortician."

"I won't sit here with my thumb up my damn arse and do nothing." He cupped her head. "You said that I don't just bring destruction—I bring safety, too. But if I don't go after Mayhew, the world becomes a hell of a lot less safe. It's down to me."

As he spoke, a sense of rightness filled him, like cold winter sun. It was time to fight again.

Her jaw hardened. "When will you leave?" she asked tightly.

"Soon as I get word of my plans to the Admiralty." Goodbye would come so fast. Too fast. But he had no choice. He could only hope to survive the battle, and maybe, just maybe, they'd see each other again.

She released her hold on his coat. Ran her hands over the fabric to smooth it. Then nodded.

"We're not leaving without buying some of those pies," she said.

"*We*," he said. "Damn it—no."

She only stared up at him, completely immune to the anger and authority in his voice. "This territory's already been gone over. You need an engineer. Someone to man those two guns."

He gripped her shoulders, holding her away from him. "That was just for the flight here. I'm not taking you into sodding battle. If you're hurt, or worse—there'd be no coming back for me."

"I'm not sending you after Mayhew on your own." Her eyes gleamed brightly. "This is *our* fight, Fletcher. Yours and mine. Together."

He felt certain that his heart would have burst from his chest, if the telumium plate hadn't held it in place.

"Battle is rough," he said, his voice a jagged rumble. "Bullets. Blood."

She raised a brow. "I've seen all of that. Lived through it."

"But," he asked gently, "can you face it again?" He hated to think of her fear. "All men going into battle are afraid, but I've seen crewmen freeze in the middle of a fight. Those are the men who don't survive."

Her face paled. But she lifted her chin. "I won't live my life afraid of my fear. And I won't let you face Mayhew alone."

"I'll have the local law throw you behind bars to keep you from coming with me."

She shook her head. "We're beyond that, you and I. We trust each other to make our own decisions. Honor my choice to fight beside you."

His throat felt raw, his eyes hot. He pulled her close and wrapped his arms around her. "Goddamn you. The minute I saw you on that island, I should've known."

Her own arms came up to hold him tightly. "Known what?"

"That I could live through an airship crash, but I'd have nothing to protect myself from you."

From his position in the pilot house, Fletcher kept one eye on the shrinking land beneath the airship, and the other on Kali, standing at the railing. She wore goggles and a cloak as protection again the wind. Her stance was looser than it had been when they'd first taken to the sky. She grew more comfortable with each minute they flew. Comfortable with flying, maybe, but she had her back straight as a level, a sign he'd come to recognize. She was afraid of what lay ahead.

Fear rimed his veins, too. Not for himself. Death was an old friend, one he'd met too many times to reckon. His body, too, thrummed in preparation for battle. As if he'd been waiting for a real fight. That's what he'd been built for—war.

No, not just war. Protection.

He couldn't fail. Mayhew was too dangerous, and Redmond too valuable.

And yet none of that meant anything compared to keeping Kali safe. If there had been any way to leave her behind, he'd have done so, and gladly. But he did need her for the upcoming clash with Mayhew. A fact that both tore him into scrap and gleamed through him like the biggest, brightest electrical lamp, rivaling the sun.

Once they'd put South Uist far behind them, Kali began examining their two weapons. The ether cannon was mounted portside, and they'd taken the Gatling gun from the bow and positioned it starboard. No side would go undefended. But if there was any ship-to-ship combat, Kali would be the one firing the weapons while he piloted the *Persephone*.

Before they'd departed South Uist, he'd shown her how to use both guns, and cautioned her about spending too much ammunition. Their supply was limited. Every shot had to count.

She'd been pale as ash as he'd instructed her on loading, aiming, and firing the weapons. Pale, but resolute.

Goddamn it if there wasn't a way to replicate himself, so she wouldn't be in the line of fire. There'd been wild rumors that a scientist in China had been experimenting with something called *bio-emulation*, creating perfect duplicates of living matter—plants, animals, even, possibly people. Why couldn't that sodding scientist have made good on his promises?

Fletcher leaned out of the pilot house. "Kali!"

She made her way back to him. As she crossed the deck, her cloak and skirts clung to her, revealing the curve of her waist, the line of her legs. A long while would pass before he'd get the chance to touch those curves once more. He might never again get the chance, in truth. The thought made his hands ache.

"It's about a thousand miles to the easternmost edge of Greenland," he said once she'd returned to the pilot house. "I'm going to push the *Persephone* to her limits so we can get there before Mayhew, or at least intercept him."

She nodded. "How long will it take us to get there?"

"At top speed, six and a half, seven hours."

Behind her goggles, her eyes widened. "The force of the wind topside . . ."

"A brutal place for anyone, even the strongest crewman. Only safe spot is the pilot house." He held her gaze. "You'll have to stay below."

"Or in the pilot house," she countered.

He made a show of looking around the small space. No place to sit, nowhere comfortable to rest. It was meant for one thing only: steering the ship. "Seven hours is the minimum," he said, turning back to her. "I checked the maps and charts before we shoved off. Most of the inhabited places in Greenland are on the coast—the middle's just a huge field of ice and glaciers."

"The enemy won't build their bases near habitations," she murmured.

"Inland won't work, either. Those bases, if they exist, would need to be resupplied, and they can't always use airships. Too noticeable. They'll use seafaring vessels."

She frowned. "So if there are enemy bases on Greenland, they'd be on the coast, too."

"Redmond's going to know that," Fletcher said. "He'll be covering the coastline, traveling counterclockwise since the east is closest to England. But he's been on this mission for at least a week—"

"So he'll probably have made it around the northernmost tip of the island," she deduced. "He could already be on the west coast by now."

"Mayhew's not stupid. He'll have figured this out, too. Either we stop him or we intercept and warn Redmond."

Fletcher clenched his jaw. "Either way, we'll get there faster if we cross the center of the island. That's hundreds more miles. At top speed."

She leaned against the back of the pilot house, eyeing him. "Seven more hours, then. A total of fourteen."

"Cold, long hours." He nodded toward the deck beneath his boots. "Stay below. Rest. Keep warm."

"And leave you alone up here?" She scowled.

"I've got food"—they'd purchased a mountain of pies and other provisions in Lochboisdale, and half of it was heaped in the pilot house—"I don't need much sleep, and the cold doesn't trouble me." When she opened her mouth to speak, he added, "Three months I was alone on that tiny island. Fourteen hours on my own is a speck of time."

For a while, she said nothing. Only stared out the glass, at the empty deck, and the sea and sky that surrounded them.

She spoke in a voice so low that a normal man wouldn't have heard her above the wind and drone of the turbines. "Perhaps I want to spend those specks of time with you."

Kali, with him as he flew. It filled him with a strange sense of being opened, as if some interior cabinet was thrown wide and sunlight poured in, illuminating all the places inside that had been dark and hidden.

"Stay, then," he answered. "But I'm sending you below the minute I see you start to nod off or shiver."

She gave him a clipped nod, and tucked her arms beneath her cloak.

"I'm giving her full throttle," he said. "Brace yourself."

She planted her feet. "Ready."

He pushed on the throttle, opening up the engines, urging

the airship as fast as she could go without venting the ether tanks. The *Persephone* shuddered, as if throwing off a long sleep. Then, she raced forward.

Kali caught her breath. Even he could feel it, that subtle, wondrous pressure against his body. The pilot house protected them, but didn't shield them from the sensation of racing like a levanter wind through the sky. He'd only undertaken this kind of speed in times of great emergency, the crew ordered to remain below until the ship had slowed. But it was a marvelous thing, letting his ship unleash the fullness of her power, him at the wheel.

He'd prefer knowing Kali was in their cabin, resting, or even tinkering in her makeshift workshop. But he also loved sharing this with her. Having her beside him. It was possible they wouldn't survive the coming fight. These hours together might be all they had left.

Chapter Eighteen

Fletcher had been right. The pilot house of a speeding airship wasn't a comfortable place. It hadn't been built with anything but utility in mind. She had nowhere to sit, and leaning provided little relief. There was always the option of sitting directly on the deck, but the floor was hard and chill and would leave her behind aching. She wore her warmest cloak and even wrapped a few spare blankets around her, yet despite this and the shelter of the pilot house, frigid air jabbed her like needles and worked its way into her bones.

Her body was miserable, but she ignored it. What she wouldn't, couldn't, ignore was this time with Fletcher. If they lived through the confrontation with Mayhew, Fletcher would likely be assigned to a new ship and sent on mission. Gone for who knew how long. So she had to clutch at whatever time she could spend with him now. She wouldn't toss these moments overboard like so much unwanted scrap.

So she stayed upright and forced herself not to shiver as they raced over the ocean. The water passed hundreds of feet beneath them in an unrelenting iron blue sweep. From this height, the rough waves appeared tiny, tipped with white. She'd no desire to get closer to them and see just how choppy those waters really were.

The sky fascinated her, because where the ocean seemed endless, the sky *was* without limit. It stretched up and up, boundless and blue. As blue, she realized, as Fletcher's eyes.

They passed the hours talking. More of their youth, and the years that led them to becoming their present selves. She spoke of Nagpur, and he told her of the many ports of call he'd seen—places she hadn't given much thought to, until she saw them through his eyes. She realized that anywhere could be fascinating with the right company.

"I'd be keen to go there with you," she murmured, when he talked of the mountains crowded around Hong Kong Bay, the countless junks in the water, and tetrol-powered gliders that wheeled across the bay, transporting passengers and cargo from one end to the other and trailing smoke like gray banners. Britain kept a supply of airships there, too, ready to protect their acquisition and keep enemy intrusions at a distance.

"You'd like it," he said, his grin white in his dark beard. "The street market in Sham Shui Po—you've never seen clockwork devices such as these. They would make British inventors throw away their tools and become crossing sweeps. Except you," he added. "The Chinese engineers would cry at their workbenches if they saw what you can build."

"I don't want to make anyone cry." She quirked a smile. "Maybe I can give them a small sense of inferiority. But tears—never."

"Crowds of inventors in Sham Shui Po. There'll be a

cloud of humility hovering over the district when you walk through. But I'll protect you if anyone gets drunk and rowdy on their shame."

"I'd say that I could protect myself," she answered, "but who'd refuse a Man O' War for a bodyguard? Or as a lover?"

His look grew heated. "There are hotels and pavilions along the bay. We could lie in bed and watch the lights and lanterns dance on the water, and make love while the street musicians play their *erhu* violins outside."

Her throat closed and behind her goggles, her eyes burned. It sounded wondrous. And something that would likely never happen. In wartime, a Man O' War didn't likely get leave long enough to take his lover on a trip to distant shores. If she and Fletcher had any time together at all, it would be in little fragments, grabbed here and there. It would be better than nothing, but far from perfect.

Eventually, the sky darkened as night fell. A rare privilege, seeing the sun slip beyond the horizon as the ship flew through the air. But with nightfall came a brittle wave of cold.

"You're going below," he commanded.

"I'm f-fine."

"And your lips are blue. Go now." He slowed the ship enough so that there was no possibility she'd be pushed overboard by the wind.

Arguing would be hopeless, and, she had to admit, her whole body ached with cold and weariness. She'd need to be in top form—or as good a form as she could manage—when they intercepted Mayhew. Before she left the pilot house, she raised up on the tips of her toes and brushed her mouth over Fletcher's, loving the feel of his beard against her skin and the warmth of his lips. They clung together like that, with him wrapping an arm around her waist, the other hand still on the wheel, until she shivered, and not from desire.

He sent her away, a gentle push on her lower back to urge her on. After one final look at him over her shoulder, she took a lantern and eased down the companionway. They hadn't turned on any of the lights topside or below decks, the better to hide their position. It felt eerie to move through the flying airship alone, but at least it was warmer. She gathered some food from the galley then took it to their quarters.

As she ate her dinner, she studied the charts that included Greenland. But they revealed nothing except a cartographer's skill—no prophecies of the future, only a sparsely populated coast and an interior filled with ice.

She awoke with a start and a stiff neck, still sitting at the table. Unrelenting night filled the windows. Fletcher was still up there, guiding the *Persephone*. The ship's internal audio communication devices had been damaged in the crash, and she hadn't possessed the time to restore them before they'd left the island. She had no way of speaking with him now. All she could hope was that he felt her thoughts of him.

Lonely and worried, she crawled into bed fully dressed, except for her boots. She kept her prosthetic leg on. If there was an emergency, it would take too long to put back on, and she needed to be ready in an instant.

She didn't think she'd be able to sleep. Too much weighed on her mind and heart. Yet as she lay in bed—their bed— she inhaled deeply, taking in his scent of flesh and metal. He might be several decks above her, but his presence enveloped her, and she slipped into a dreamless sleep.

Brilliant, unsparing white light filled the cabin. Kali blinked awake. Her movements roused Four, who'd burrowed beside her for warmth. He scurried beneath the blankets as she rose and walked to the windows.

Ice. Ice everywhere. She'd never seen such endless stretches of it. A few gray rocky peaks jutted up from the ice, but that constituted the whole of the landscape. Nothing could live down there. Nothing, it seemed, did. It was merciless, barren, beautiful.

She touched her fingertips to the glass, and immediately pulled them back. They burned with cold.

Checking her watch, she noted that they were nearing the time Fletcher had estimated. Not too long before they arrived close to Redmond's position on the west coast. She could feel the ship's slight deceleration as they neared their target. After bolting down some breakfast, she swaddled herself in her cloak and more blankets. Then hurried through the passageways of the ship, until she reached the companionway.

Wrapping a scarf around her lower face, hunching down to keep herself low and less likely to be blown off the ship, she raced up the companionway. The wind tried to claw her from the deck. But she ran the short distance to the pilot house.

Fletcher still stood at the wheel, guiding the ship over the ice. A bit of frost clung to the sleeves of his coat, glittering in the morning light, and his hair was windblown. Large, dark, and wild, he reminded her of one of the old Celtic gods from her father's tales. The kind of god that either brought the world into being, or destroyed it.

Her heart leapt to see him again. It was silly—less than

eight hours had passed since she'd gone belowdecks, and he'd been close the whole time—and yet it felt like a reunion after long, long years had passed.

He glanced at her, his gaze warm. "Sleep well?"

"It's hard to know."

He held out one arm, inviting her close. She wasted no time accepting the invitation, wrapping her arms around him while he held her. Coils and springs still wound within her, but their tension loosened at his touch.

"And you?" she asked. "Did you miss your bed?"

"Aye, but not for sleeping."

She warmed everywhere, the chill dispelling. And, in truth, he looked almost as fresh as when she'd left him, with only the slightest shadows beneath his eyes. He'd said that Man O' Wars didn't need much sleep—but when they'd shared a bed, he always stayed the whole night, even though he was likely awake for most of it. But he remained there because of her.

Now they stood together in the pilot house as a world of unending winter passed beneath them. Only a few moments passed before Fletcher pulled back on the throttle, slowing the airship.

"The coast's approaching," he said.

She couldn't see anything except ice and rocks, but then, within minutes, did: snow-topped mountains rose up sharply, then plunged down into the sea. As Fletcher brought the *Persephone* over the jagged coastline, Kali made out gentler slopes of stone, some even dusted with furze and gorse. Another time, she would've appreciated this rough, unsparing beauty. Yet it also revealed that, while the conditions wouldn't be easy, the enemy could certainly position a base here. Putting them within short distance of Canada, and then into the soya-rich fields of the United States.

"Any sign of Mayhew or Redmond?" she asked.

Fletcher peered into the distance. "None yet, but anything can change in an instant. You should go check to make sure the guns are warm enough to fire."

He'd slowed the ship and brought it low enough for Kali to comfortably walk on deck without fear of flying over the rails or suffering hypothermia. The air was clean and sharp as a surgical blade, and almost punishingly clear. She fumbled in her pockets and pulled out a second pair of goggles, ones with tinted lenses, and exchanged those for the others she wore. Much better. She didn't feel half-drunk on light, though any exposed skin felt the bite of the wind.

She tested both weapons, running them through their paces of loading and unloading, plus dry firing. If the metal was too cold, the superheating from shooting the gun could cause the whole thing to shatter. Not very desirable in a fight. She'd be as likely to be wounded or killed by her own weapon as the enemy's.

"Kali!" Fletcher called sharply from the pilot's house. Running back to him, her breath came fast and quick. The time had arrived.

"There." He pointed at a spot on the ground, about a mile ahead on one of the rocky inlets.

For a moment, she saw nothing. And then—something flashed on the ground. Again. And again. Forming a pattern.

"It looks like a mirror using sunlight to make a signal," she murmured.

"A distress signal," he said grimly. "In naval code."

"Mayhew?"

Fletcher gave a clipped nod. "He's laying a trap for Redmond. Whatever airship Mayhew procured, it won't be enough against the *Demeter*. So he'll bring Redmond down to him and attack him on the ground."

Kali shivered, but not from the cold. She squinted at the sky. "I don't see Redmond. No reinforcements, then."

"Going into this fight, I figured we'd be on our own." Fletcher's voice was stony. "Nothing's changed."

They talked quickly of their strategy. It wouldn't be long before Mayhew spotted them, if he hadn't already, and there wouldn't be time in the heat of the fight to discuss tactics.

With their plan settled, Fletcher hauled her against him and kissed her, hard and quick. She refused to cling when he broke the kiss, though part of her wanted to hold tight and not let go. Instead, she took a step back. And then another.

"Fletcher—" She could assemble the most complex clockwork device, but not the words she so desperately wanted to say. All she could manage was, "Fly well."

Inwardly, she winced. *Coward.* But she also knew that it would be disastrous to tell him how she felt in the moments leading up to battle. No use clouding their minds or hearts. Not with their lives—and the lives of Redmond and other Man O' Wars—at stake.

"Good shooting," he answered, but there was something in his voice, something raw that told her he understood, felt the same.

She spun away and ran for the ether cannon.

Fletcher's pulse hammered as he brought the ship closer to Mayhew's position. The blade-sharp calm he usually felt before a battle was nowhere to be found, and he knew exactly why: Kali. The welfare of his crew always concerned him—putting them in the line of fire wasn't an easy decision, but he'd done so when duty required it, and with the knowledge that his men fully expected to be in combat, and maybe even lose their lives in service to their country.

But he'd never loved any of his crew. The beat of his heart and the breath in his lungs didn't depend on them.

If anything happened to her . . .

He shoved the thought from his mind. Battles weren't won on fear. If that calm wouldn't come to him on its own, he'd force it on himself.

So he focused on the landscape. Mayhew had set his ship down between two peaks, giving him protection, but the pinnacles also offered a small vessel like the *Persephone* an excellent means of easing close without being seen. Fletcher brought his airship low and stole toward Mayhew's position. He skirted around the base of one crag, keeping the ship close to the mountain. From her position at the rail by the ether cannon, Kali could have reached out and brushed the tips of her fingers against the rocks. But she was wise and kept her hands safe.

There was a notch between the two peaks, just wide enough to accommodate the *Persephone*. Mayhew would be looking to the north, his attention fixed on the sky, giving Fletcher a small, brief advantage. He and Kali would have only a few moments of surprise before Mayhew turned his own weapons on them.

Fletcher slipped the *Persephone* through the narrow opening, his movements at the wheel precise. There, just ahead, was Mayhew's ship. It was the same one he'd used to reach Eilean Comhachag, but he'd modified it, transforming it from a seafaring vessel to an airship using scavenged and assembled parts to make ether tanks and turbines. Parts likely taken from naval ships.

Vessel and man, both altered. Fletcher almost admired Mayhew's ingenuity. Almost.

The distress signal continued to flash from the deck— one of Mayhew's henchmen was using a large mirror to transmit the false danger, clearly coached ahead of time by the lieutenant. The other thug, Robbins, stood ready beside an ether cannon. And lurking behind them was Mayhew. Fletcher only recognized the lieutenant by his hair color. But his size and form had changed, grown bulky and large.

There wasn't time to get a closer look at Mayhew's transformation. Instead, Fletcher brought the *Persephone* in at an angle, giving Kali a clear shot with the ether cannon.

She knew her cue. Without hesitating, Kali fired on Mayhew's ship. The ether-powered shot slammed into the deck, punching a massive hole in the planks. Grady, the thug holding the mirror, was flung to the side, the mirror he held shattering. Mayhew was also thrown back from the force of the blast, but he got right to his feet. The lieutenant ran to his own ether Gatling gun. He unloaded a barrage of fire. The high-powered bullets riddled the *Persephone*'s hull in fast succession.

Kali dove for cover, and Fletcher remembered to breathe only when she stood up, unhurt save for scratches.

Fletcher brought the airship around, making sure that Kali could keep up the cannon fire against Mayhew. But the *Persephone* quaked from the force of the enemy's ether cannon. Fletcher managed to steer the ship so she didn't take the full brunt of the shot, protecting the ether tanks and the turbines. But one of the lower decks suffered the blow, with a wound torn in the hull. He winced. Patched together as she was, the ship couldn't take many hits before turning to a rain of splinters and scrap.

Kali fired the ether cannon again. A huge explosion shook the air as her shot hit the enemy's cannon. The weapon erupted in a massive ball of flame, engulfing the thug manning it.

For a moment, Kali's hands fell away from the cannon. She stepped back. Fletcher couldn't see her face, but he knew the posture of a person in shock. He knew her thoughts: she'd never killed a man before. She was a builder, a creator. And she'd taken someone's life.

God, if only he could leave this bloody pilot's house and go to her. Comfort her.

Yet someone had to pilot the ship. Had to make sure they survived. And they needed someone manning the weapons. Otherwise, they had no defense against Mayhew.

Fletcher started to steer the *Persephone* into retreat. They'd have to find another way to fight Mayhew, or hope that Redmond would notice the battle and keep clear. But then there came the distinctive boom of an ether cannon. The *Persephone*'s ether cannon.

Kali was back at her post.

She wanted to vomit. Kali's hands shook—hell, everything in her body shook. She could hardly believe what she'd done.

With one pull of the rope attached to the cannon's firing lever, she'd erased one human's existence. After seeing thousands killed in Liverpool, now she was the killer.

But they had been civilians. Innocents. They'd posed no threat. The man she'd just killed had wanted her, and many more, dead. There had been no choice, only duty. This was a fight that had to be won.

And her responsibility wasn't over. She had to keep Redmond and the other Man O' Wars safe. More important, she had to protect Fletcher. If that meant exterminating a hired gun, then, by all the gods and goddesses, she'd do it.

So she took up her position again, despite the roiling in her belly and her nerves stretched tight enough to break. As more gunfire rang out, memories of Liverpool tried to flood her mind—the sounds of cannons, Gatling guns, rifles, the screams of the wounded and dying. She shook her head, driving the memories away. They were more dangerous than the guns shooting at her now.

Lining her eye with the sight of the ether cannon, she took a breath. Another. Then aimed and fired. More of Mayhew's ship blew apart, but the lieutenant and Grady continued to shoot back, riddling the *Persephone* with cannon and gunfire. Their little airship was turning to pulp.

She lined up Mayhew in the cannon's sight, but just as she fired, he leapt out of the way.

She ran to the pilot house. Before Fletcher could speak, she yelled above the din. "We're out of ammunition for the cannon. You'll have to bring us about so I can use the Gatling gun."

He shook his head. "Any more hits, and the *Persephone*'s destroyed. I'm taking her down."

"But . . . how will we fight him?"

He pressed an ether pistol into her grip. "With that." Then he briefly took his hands off the wheel and held them up. "And with these."

It wouldn't be an easy landing. There wasn't time.

"Brace yourself," Fletcher advised Kali. "Tight."

Heart thudding in her throat, she did as he suggested, wedging her shoulder tight into the front corner of the pilot house and gripping the rail that ran along the wall. But Fletcher stayed at the wheel. "What about you?"

His mouth hitched into a rueful half-smile. "Survived one airship crash. And I've got no objective to die in this one." He banked the ship sharply, taking her out over the water for his approach.

She ignored the pitching of her stomach. "You'd better not. I'm not keen to face Mayhew on my own." Better to hide behind bravado than face her real fear—losing Fletcher.

His smile faded, his gaze turning grave. "Not a possibility. Now get ready."

Glancing out the window of the pilot house, she saw the ground approaching at an alarming rate. It grew closer and closer, Fletcher pulling hard on the wheel to keep the airship level, and cutting power to the engines. She screwed her eyes shut. And then—

Her arms screamed with the effort to keep herself upright, her body banging hard into the wall, as the *Persephone* hit the ground. The ship slid for what felt like hundreds of yards over rocky terrain, bouncing as it skidded. She pried her eyes open to see Fletcher, his legs wide as he fought to stay upright, the muscles of his thighs straining from the effort. Teeth bared, he let out a groan as he battled to slow the ship. If the *Persephone* didn't stop soon, they'd plow right into the side of a mountain.

With a judder, the ship finally came to rest. Twenty feet away from the mountain.

Kali exhaled. It took several tries for her to release her death's grip on the railing.

Fletcher was instantly in front of her, hands on her shoulders. "All right?" he demanded.

"I'll have some pretty bruises tomorrow," she managed, "but nothing's broken. You?"

His mouth curled cruelly. "Ready to send Mayhew to hell."

She pulled the pistol from her belt. "Right behind you."

He wanted to order her to stay with the ship—she could see it in the set of his jaw—but said nothing. Only nodded, once. "Stay low, and don't take chances."

Now it was her time to smile. "My life is predicated on taking chances. There's no need to change that policy now."

He stared at her for a moment, his gaze fierce. "The hell with it," he muttered to himself. Then, louder, "Kali, I—"

Gunfire from an ether rifle pierced the back wall of the pilot house and shattered the window. Kali and Fletcher flung themselves to the floor as wood and broken glass rained down on them.

They shared a look, and then ran right into the teeth of battle.

CHAPTER NINETEEN

Bullets whined past Kali and Fletcher as they sped in a zigzag pattern toward Mayhew's ship. The ground exploded around them in a hail of rocks and hard-packed soil. She kept in a low crouch as she ran, grateful that she'd spent so much time on the island strengthening her legs and coordination—otherwise, she would've been a stumbling, panting disaster. A perfect target.

As she and Fletcher neared the ship, she saw that it didn't actually rest on the ground, as the *Persephone* could. The lieutenant's modified airship was originally a large fishing trawler. Its curved keel hovered inches above the ground. She also noted with satisfaction that a considerable portion of the ship's fifty-foot length had been heavily damaged by her ether cannon.

But there wasn't time to admire her handiwork. They reached the ship and pressed flat against its hull, positioning themselves so that Mayhew and Grady's gunfire couldn't reach them.

Fletcher eyed the rail above. It was a good twenty feet

from the ground to the edge of the ship, a distance they both knew proved little obstacle to him, but not to her.

"Give me a boost," she said. "Then you follow."

"Not sending you up there first," he growled.

"And I'm not staying down here."

He cursed. Finally, "There's a hawser by the starboard bow. I go up, then throw the line to you."

"I'll be waiting."

He gave her one last, searing look. Then turned, coiled his body, and leapt with the power and grace of a tiger. It didn't matter how many times she'd watched him do this, the sight always made her breath catch, even now was no exception. He disappeared over the rail, and from the shouts and swearing that greeted him, he made his landing easily. More shots rang out. Her heart stuttered. But the gunfire didn't stop, and neither did the sounds of heavy objects being broken. A battle.

That meant he was alive and fighting.

She ran around the perimeter of the ship, heading toward the starboard bow. The ground in front of her shattered from an ether-powered bullet. She threw her arm up to shield herself, but not before gravel scratched across her face. At least she still wore her goggles, protecting her eyes. But she felt the drip of blood down her cheek.

Fear rose up, and memories of Liverpool choked her.

Later. I'll let myself be afraid later. Now there was only the fight.

Reaching the starboard bow, she waited, huddling beneath the prow to protect herself from gunfire. She could hear more sounds of combat above. Maybe Fletcher wouldn't get the chance to throw her the line. Maybe he'd decide to leave her on the ground and take on Mayhew and the henchman on his own. She didn't like either option.

Suddenly, a thick rope dropped from the side of the bow.

She ran for it. Then stood gripping the hawser, looking up, and realized that she didn't know how to climb a rope.

Think, damn it. You've seen sailors climb.

It took an agonizing amount of time to picture it, but then the images came. She grabbed the rope with both hands above her head, then pulled down on it as she gave a small jump. She wrapped the rope around her artificial leg—no easy task with her skirts tangling about her—and pressed her feet together, securing herself. Like an inchworm, she crawled up the line, raising her arms, then bringing her legs up, and repeating the process in slow, burning increments. But the railing grew closer and closer.

She pressed against the hull as Grady shot at her. Using all her strength, she gripped the rope with one hand and pulled out her ether pistol with the other, then fired back. She missed, but it was enough to push Grady away from the rail. Giving her time to climb.

Finally, she reached the railing, and hauled herself over.

And froze at the sight of Fletcher locked in battle with a monster.

Fletcher hadn't been able to see the full effects of Mayhew's change, not until he'd leapt up onto the deck. The lieutenant had grown larger—he was now the same height as Fletcher, and nearly as broad with muscle—but that wasn't the extent of the transformation.

The madman was falling apart. Literally. Standing by
what remained of the portside, Mayhew wasn't wearing a
shirt, revealing that patches of his skin had turned black,
especially the areas around his implants and his glowing,
mechanized heart. Some flesh peeled away as if burnt off. The
experiment was a disaster.

"Jesus, Mayhew," Fletcher had sworn when he'd seen this.

The lieutenant had only sneered at him. "Only part of the
process. But the process doesn't include you." He'd taken aim
with an ether pistol.

Fletcher had grabbed a jagged piece of the exploded
cannon and thrown it at Mayhew's arm. It clipped him enough
to cause the shot to go wide. Before the lieutenant had time to
aim again, Fletcher had launched himself at Mayhew.

The lunatic might have been breaking apart, but he was
still strong as any Man O' War. He and Fletcher had grappled their way across the broken deck, trading blows. Each
strike from Mayhew sent Fletcher's bones rattling. He'd
never fought hand to hand with another Man O' War before.
Strikes that would've felled a normal man only made Mayhew
wince and stumble. But he stayed on his feet.

Fletcher had managed to break free from the fight long
enough to throw the hawser down to Kali. He didn't want
her in harm's way, but someone had to guard his back, and it
would be easier to keep watch over her on deck than on the
ground.

The moment he'd flung the line over the side, Mayhew attacked. He grabbed Fletcher around the middle, forming a
vise with his arms and squeezing so hard Fletcher felt a rib
crack. Fletcher slammed his heel down onto Mayhew's foot,

then kicked backward into the lieutenant's knee. Howling in pain, Mayhew loosened his grip. Fletcher pushed the lieutenant's arms up sharply and ducked out from beneath them.

Spinning around, he threw a punch right into Mayhew's face. The lieutenant staggered away, and Fletcher swallowed his bile when he saw a chunk of skin fly from Mayhew's jaw where Fletcher had hit him.

Fletcher advanced, pushing Mayhew back. Kali would be on deck soon, and he wanted the lieutenant as far from her as possible.

He managed to get the lieutenant to the main deck, away from the bow, before Mayhew took a stand. They threw punches and blocked hits, both of them grunting and swearing. But flecks of Mayhew's blackened skin kept breaking off.

"Falling apart, Mayhew," Fletcher growled between hits. "Your body can't take the strain. It's Gimmel or higher for a reason."

"The hell you know?" Mayhew lunged for him, but Fletcher sidestepped quickly and momentum carried the lieutenant forward until he sprawled on the deck.

Fletcher was on him in an instant. He pinned him to the ground, raining punches onto his face and anywhere exposed.

But when Kali finally climbed over the railing, Fletcher glanced up, making certain she was unhurt. Fury charred the edges of his vision when he saw the wounds on her face. And Grady was raising his ether pistol, pointing it at her head.

Then the world spun, and Mayhew flipped him onto his back. He gripped Fletcher's throat with hands as strong as death. Fletcher couldn't pry Mayhew's fingers off of him, and all the strikes he landed with his knees had no effect.

"Won't live long enough to murder any Man O' Wars," Fletcher gritted. "Your own body will destroy you first."

Rage and anguish darkened Mayhew's face, followed quickly by the fury of madness. He laughed riotously.

"I'll take as many of you with me as I can. We'll all go to hell together." Mayhew's hands tightened further.

Fletcher's sight dimmed. The sound of Mayhew's wild laughter began to fade.

Good God, he's killing me.

Kali took a step toward Fletcher battling Mayhew, but a bullet whizzed past her. She took cover behind a slab of metal torn from the vessel's hull by the ether cannon explosion. Peering around the edge of her shelter, she saw Grady crouched behind several metal drums, taking potshots at her.

She possessed a limited number of bullets. Three, in fact, after shooting at Grady when she'd hung on the rope. Each bullet now had to be used deliberately and with precision. If only she had Fletcher's eyesight, she could be sure none of her shots went wild. Pushing back her goggles, she pressed her back against the metal slab. She winced when one of Grady's bullets pierced the metal. A normal gunshot wouldn't have the same force. She could try to wait Grady out, but he probably had far more ammunition than she did.

Get rid of his gun. That was the only solution.

Cautiously, she sneaked a look around the side of her shelter, ether pistol ready. When Grady did the same, she shot. But her aim wasn't steady, and her fire went wide. He shot back, and she ducked. Once more, she waited, and once more, when she aimed, she'd only managed to nick the drum Grady hid behind.

One bullet left in her gun.

She breathed deep, forcing herself to calm. Told herself it didn't matter that this was her last bullet. Quieted the sounds of Fletcher and Mayhew struggling and her impulse to help—no one was more capable a fighter than Fletcher. He'd manage without her.

She'd survived the devastation of Liverpool, the loss of a limb, the despair that had followed. She'd get through this, too.

One more time, she glanced around the edge of her cover. Grady followed suit. She aimed. Fired.

And missed.

Instead of hitting Grady in his hand, she hit his gun. It shattered in his grip. He screamed as pieces of metal flew in every direction, including into his hand and face.

She wasted no time, sprinting across the deck. Reaching Grady, hunkered on the deck and clutching his blood-covered hand, she used her artificial leg to kick him in the jaw. He sprawled backward. For a moment, he struggled to get up, and she kicked him again. Blood spattered on her skirts as his head snapped back. He collapsed completely.

Carefully, she edged closer, then checked beneath his eyelids. He was alive, but quite, quite unconscious. From her tool belt, she pulled out a spool of wire, and wound it around his wrists, binding him. She grimaced at the sight of his hand. If he ever had use of it again, it would take an expert surgeon. Or gifted engineer. Of which she was one—but she wouldn't be the one to help this bastard.

She glanced up when she heard the sounds of a man choking. Terror ran cold down her spine when she saw Mayhew
atop Fletcher. Throttling him. Fletcher had his own hands
around Mayhew's wrists, squeezing tightly as if trying to snap
the bones. Somehow the lieutenant's insanity had given him
extraordinary power. Fletcher couldn't break his hold.

Her own strength would be laughable against Mayhew.
But she didn't need strength to combat him.

She pulled a long, thin screwdriver from her tool belt
and ran toward Mayhew. Focused on his task of strangling
Fletcher, Mayhew didn't turn. Didn't try to stop her.

But he screamed when she jammed the screwdriver into
his shoulder. Directly into a juncture of telumium wires that
led down into his right arm.

The arm dropped and hung useless at his side. Mayhew
stared at her in shocked disbelief.

"What in the bloody hell did you do?" he snarled.

"I jammed the circuits." She rifled through her tools for
another screwdriver, but suddenly she flew backward, feeling
as if she'd been hit by a tetrol-powered hammer. She slid along
the deck until she hit the railing. There she lay, gasping for
breath, her shoulder on fire from Mayhew's backhand strike.
She tried to sit up, but her head spun and pain wracked her.
All she could do was look up at the brilliant sky and pray her
help had been enough to save Fletcher.

Fletcher might have been on the edge of death moments
earlier, life slipping away like clouds racing across a wind-
swept sky.

But seeing Mayhew hit Kali, watching how she was flung backward and now lay upon the deck of the ship, alive but hurt, the darkness around his vision cleared instantly. He shoved back from the edge of nothingness, fueled by incandescent rage.

One of Mayhew's hands had fallen away from Fletcher's throat. The lieutenant's arm was useless. Fletcher grabbed that arm and used it to fling Mayhew off of him.

Instantly, Fletcher was on his feet. He advanced toward the lieutenant, yet even with the screwdriver still embedded in his shoulder, Mayhew leapt up.

They faced each other, circling. It was an agony not to go to Kali, and tend to her injuries, but Mayhew had to be dealt with. Now.

Both Fletcher and Mayhew spotted the unconscious Grady. Kali's work. Damn, he was proud of her. Yet seeing his thug sprawled upon the deck, Mayhew's face twisted with mad rage. He bellowed in frustration.

"Everything's been stolen," he shrieked. "My chance to become a Man O' War. My path to glory. I won't let myself be ordinary." He spat the word. "You can't take that from me."

"You're falling apart like a rusted hulk," Fletcher countered. "You won't even get a shot at Redmond."

Mayhew's wrath melted into hysterical giggles. "Contingency plans are always important. I've got a nice surprise in the hull of the ship. Even Grady and Robbins didn't know." More laughter. "There's enough TNT to send anyone within a mile radius right to the Devil's door. If the woman manning your ether cannon had been a better shot, she would've hit the TNT and ended the fight before it started. Now, I just wait until Redmond's ship is close enough . . . then . . ." He made a sound like an explosion, and cackled again.

Fuck. "What about the glory you craved? If you blow yourself up, there won't even be a body left to show the world what you've done."

A moment's confusion flickered across Mayhew's face. Clearly, he hadn't thought his plan through. And it made him all the more enraged. "Nothing matters! Death will take us all." He grimaced as he pulled Kali's screwdriver from his shoulder, and brandished it like a blade. "I'm nobody's dupe. No longer."

"Damn right, no longer," Fletcher snarled.

He charged, head down. Slammed into Mayhew. The screwdriver fell from Mayhew's hand as they grappled, each fighting for a hold on the other. Fletcher kicked at the back of Mayhew's leg, unbalancing him. With Mayhew destabilized, Fletcher shoved him until his back slammed into the enclosure surrounding the companionway. Fletcher pinned Mayhew's left wrist to the metal wall.

Mayhew struggled to dodge Fletcher's hail of punches. Still, the lieutenant managed to ram his head into the injured spot in Fletcher's side. A net of red pain spread through Fletcher.

"Maybe I won't wait for Redmond," Mayhew sneered. "Maybe I'll detonate the ship now, and you, me and your pretty brown friend will all die together."

He tried to twist out of Fletcher's grasp. But Fletcher held on. And when he grabbed onto Mayhew's mechanized heart with his other hand, the lieutenant's eyes widened. He thrashed and screamed, begged.

"Threatening her was your undoing," Fletcher said, grim and calm. Then he pulled on the heart.

It didn't break off cleanly from its port. The heart had connected with the telumium fibers implanted in Mayhew's body, and as Fletcher tore it off, wires ripped from Mayhew's skin, taking masses of flesh with it. Exposing muscle tissue and bone. Blood sprayed onto Fletcher, but he didn't stop. Not until he'd ripped the mechanized heart completely free.

Mayhew's shrieks echoed off the mountains.

The device in Fletcher's hand dimmed, the humming within it slowing, until it finally stopped. He threw it aside like the useless scrap it was. And he waited as Mayhew choked and shivered and bled, body shuddering. Then, like the mechanical heart, Mayhew simply . . . stopped. He slumped in Fletcher's grasp. When Fletcher released him, Mayhew slid to the deck, smearing blood on the companionway enclosure.

Fletcher gave him a kick. No movement. He checked Mayhew's pulse. Nothing. But then no one, not even a Man O' War, could survive having half his chest torn out.

Without sparing Mayhew another thought, Fletcher ran to Kali. She'd managed to lift herself up onto one elbow, and though she was pale, her gaze was clear, locking on to him as he neared.

He crouched beside Kali, carefully supporting her. It took all his willpower not to hold her close and tight. But she was hurt, so he had to resolve himself to gentleness. All he understood was his unruly joy at seeing her alive and holding her again.

Their voices overlapped. "Are you—" "Did he hurt—" And together, they said, "I'm all right" and "Nothing serious."

Her gaze strayed to Mayhew's body. She gave one shiver of disgust, but said, "Thank the gods and goddesses."

"He's rigged the ship with TNT," Fletcher said. "Didn't tell me where the detonator is."

She cursed at his news. Then, "I can disable it. Help me up."

"You certain you can stand?"

Her look said she wouldn't be argued with. So he carefully assisted her to her feet. And together, they went slowly down into the hold, where, true to Mayhew's word, crates and crates of TNT were stacked. Kali quickly found the wires that led to the detonator, and with a few snips of her pliers, disarmed the explosives.

Fletcher cocked his head, catching a sound. "The *Demeter* is almost here."

"We should greet her." Despite Kali's easy words, she still winced in pain as she moved. He scooped her up in his arms, and carried her topside.

They both watched the approach of the *Demeter*, a sleek form that glided trimly through the sky. As they did, she murmured, "I keep waiting for it, now that everything's over."

"Waiting for what?"

"The fear. The whole time I was terrified, but kept putting my fear in a little box, telling myself that I'd let myself feel it when the fight was done. I thought for certain I'd be a trembling, crying disaster by this point." She shook her head. "No shaking. No sobbing. I'm just . . ." She looked out at the mountains plunging into the water. "I'm relieved. And so bloody glad that we both survived." Her gaze turned back to him. "I didn't want to imagine life without you."

They'd come so far, the two of them. Changed so much from the two wounded, isolated creatures they had been.

"It wouldn't be a life if you weren't in it." He dragged in a breath, and took the biggest risk of his life. "I love you."

There was a moment. A long, terrifying moment. Where she said and did nothing.

And then—

Her answer was to pull his head down for a hungry kiss.

"I love you," she gasped when they finally broke apart. "So much that I think I might die of it."

"No, sweet." He brushed his lips back and forth across her forehead, marveling that such a woman—such a gift—could be his. "It's love that gives us life."

New Liverpool.

"The line for the ether tramway will run this way," Kali said, pointing to the plans on her desk. "From the outer suburbs to the main marketplace."

The young clerk standing beside her nodded. "Everyone can have access to fresh food and the goods right off the ships."

"You're a quick study, Miss Roth."

Despite her attempt to maintain a professional demeanor, the girl reddened. "It's not so difficult with the right teacher, Mrs. MacNeil-Adams."

Now it was Kali's turn to fight a blush. She ought to be more dignified, but she couldn't help the rush of gratification that came from helping other young women become better engineers. Her own engineering firm employed an even mix of men and women, and every day she received letters from people around the world, eager for work. And there was much work to do in the rebuilding of Liverpool.

Nine months into the job, and there was still so far to go.

"Now take our designs for the tram to the City Planning

office," she instructed Miss Roth. "We'll need them to sign off on the design before we can proceed with the construction."

"Of course they'll approve it. We're the best engineering firm in the city." The girl turned red again at her boldness, but instead of scolding her, Kali only smiled.

"From City Planning, you can head back to the main office," Kali said.

"Yes, ma'am." The clerk stopped on her way out to give Four a little pat. The rat gnawed gently on Miss Roth's finger, then went back to climbing up and down the series of tiny ladders mounted to the wall of Kali's field office. Miss Roth murmured a final goodbye before quitting the gently swaying room.

Kali looked out the window and waited until she saw the jolly boat glide away from the *Persephone II*, Miss Roth sitting on one of the small vessel's benches and holding tight to the portfolio of designs.

After the clerk had gone, Kali returned to examining her design for the electrical streetlamps, powered by efficient tetrol-fueled generators. Even the low-income districts would have enough light to keep their streets safe and bright. Herein lay one of the advantages of starting a city from scratch: the ability to create a place that benefited everyone.

She almost jumped from her chair when she felt a warm pair of lips against the back of her neck. Lips that were surrounded by a silky beard.

Spinning around, she looked up into the smiling face of her husband. "How do you always manage to sneak up on me?" she demanded playfully.

"Because when you're working, you wouldn't notice a steam-powered elephant trundling through here," Fletcher answered. "And you're always working."

She stood and smoothed her hands over the front of his uniform jacket. Every day she saw him in the crisp blue wool and brass buckles, and every day it made her pulse speed. Although, her heart wasn't steady when she saw him *out* of his uniform, either. "Not always," she murmured.

His gaze heated. "No spouse dare ask for more."

"While I have you here," she said, "how are those new crane mounts working out?"

"Top-notch," he answered. "But I'd expect nothing less from your designs."

While the *Persephone II* had been built new, she'd been modified from her original warship design to a vessel equipped for creation, not destruction. There were some weapons on the ship, but her decks were more likely to carry lumber and bricks than cannon shot and ether rifles. She was the only ship in the fleet with a flat hull. It helped in her service of rebuilding Liverpool. For Kali, it meant that the *Persephone* she and Fletcher had built lived on.

"I'm glad to see you," she said, "but aren't you supposed to be commanding your crew like the rest of the Engineering Corps captains?" She nodded toward her window, which showed a view of the rest of the sky, and the naval airships hovering over the city. The ships had been engaged in the rebuilding of the city, outfitted like the *Persephone II* with cranes and hoists so that they could perform construction tasks that other machines could not. When Kali wasn't in her field office on the ship and back on the ground at the main offices, she kept a telescope beside her other desk so she could watch her husband's work.

"We've got a skeleton crew. I decided to give my men the afternoon off." He slid his hands around her waist.

She checked to make sure the door was closed. "That's generous of you."

"Not especially. It was this morning that I realized something. A year ago today a boat sailed up to a tiny island. It left behind what I thought was going to be the ruination of my solitude."

She couldn't believe she'd forgotten the date. But he had remembered, and warmth cascaded through her. "It certainly was ruined."

"Ended, yes," he corrected. "Ruined, no."

Lacing her fingers behind his neck, she said, "We were refugees, from the rubble of our old selves. But we helped rebuild each other."

"I couldn't have asked for a better engineer," he murmured.

"Nor I a better captain. Because here we are, whole again."

"And home. You're my home, Kali. My home, and my heart."

"Fletcher?"

"Yes, love?"

"Is the door locked?"

He gave her one of his unhurried, smoldering smiles. "Locked it on my way in."

Perhaps it wasn't the most professional behavior to make love with one's husband in one's field office flying high above the city, but Kali didn't care. All that mattered was the man in her arms, the man who set her atop her desk and kissed her as if she was the source of all his happiness. She knew his touch, the feel of his skin. More than the physical aspect of him, she knew the rugged beauty of his soul. Just as he knew her.

Right before she closed her eyes and lost herself in his caresses, she saw the room fill with light. The sun broke through the clouds, turning everything to gold.

If you loved SKIES OF GOLD,
don't miss the rest of Zoë Archer
and Nico Rosso's smart, sexy
Ether Chronicles collaboration,
available now from Avon Impulse!

NIGHTS OF STEEL

By Nico Rosso

Bounty hunter Anna Blue always finds her fugitive. But her latest mission is filled with mystery—a high price for an eccentric inventor. A twisted trail. And a man tracking her every step. Her biggest competitor in the Western territories, Jack Hawkins, is also hunting the bounty. Two of the best at what they do, neither is willing to back off.

When a rogue Man O' War flies his airship out of the coastal fog, guns blazing, Anna and Jack are forced to team up, or die. But it isn't the danger that has them ready to flare like gunpowder. For years they'd circled around each other, but never said a word, thinking their interest was just rivalry. Deeper, though, a hot passion draws them together. Fighters and outsiders, they never thought they'd find a kindred soul. Can they survive this mission long enough to track the most elusive fugitive—their hearts?

SKIES OF STEEL
By Zoë Archer

The prim professor

Daphne Carlisle may be a scholar, but she's far more comfortable out in the field than lost in a stack of books. Still, when her parents are kidnapped by a notorious warlord, she knows she'll need more than her quick thinking if she is to reach them in time. Daphne's only hope to get across enemy territory is an airship powered and navigated by Mikhail Denisov, a rogue Man O' War who is as seductive as he is untrustworthy.

The jaded mercenary

Mikhail will do anything for the right price, and he's certain he has this mission and Daphne figured out: a simple job and a beautiful but sheltered Englishwoman. But as they traverse the skies above the Mediterranean and Arabia, Mikhail learns the fight ahead is anything but simple, and his lovely passenger is not entirely what she seems. The only thing Mikhail is certain of is their shared desire—both unexpected, and dangerous.

NIGHT OF FIRE

By Nico Rosso

Night of fire, night of passion

US Army Upland Ranger Tom Knox always knew going home wouldn't be easy. Three years ago, he skipped town leaving behind the one woman who ever mattered; now that he's seen the front lines of war, he's ready to do what he must to win her back.

Rosa Campos is long past wasting tears on Tom Knox, and now that she's sheriff of Thornville she has more than enough to do. Especially when a three-story rock-eating mining machine barrels toward the town she's sworn to protect.

Tom's the last person Rosa expects to see riding to her aid on his ether-borne mechanical horse. She may not be ready to forgive, but Rosa can't deny that having him at her side brings back blissful memories ... even as it reignites a flame more dangerous than the enemy threatening to destroy them both.

SKIES OF FIRE

By Zoë Archer

Man made of metal and flesh

Captain Christopher Redmond has just one weakness: the alluring spy who loved and left him years before . . . when he was still just a man. Now superhuman, a Man O' War, made as part of the British Navy's weapons program, his responsibility is to protect the skies of Europe. If only he could forget Louisa Shaw.

A most inconvenient desire

Louisa, a British Naval Intelligence Agent, has never left a job undone. But when her assignment is compromised, the one man who can help her complete her mission is also the only man ever to tempt her body and heart. As burning skies loom and passion ignites, Louisa and Christopher must slip behind enemy lines if they are to deliver a devastating strike against their foe . . . and still get out alive.

ABOUT THE AUTHOR

ZOË ARCHER is a RITA Award-nominated author who writes romance novels chock-full of adventure, sexy men, and women who make no apologies about kicking ass. Her books include The Hellraisers paranormal historical series and the acclaimed Blades of the Rose paranormal historical adventure series. She enjoys baking, tweeting about boots, and listening to music from the '80s. Zoë and her husband, fellow romance author Nico Rosso, live in Los Angeles.

Visit www.AuthorTracker.com for exclusive information on your favorite HarperCollins authors.

www.zoearcherbooks.com
www.avonimpulse.com
www.facebook.com/avonromance

Give in to your impulses . . .
Read on for a sneak peek at four brand-new
e-book original tales of romance
from Avon Books.
Available now wherever e-books are sold.

LESS THAN A GENTLEMAN
By Kerrelyn Sparks

WHEN I FIND YOU
A TRUST NO ONE NOVEL
By Dixie Lee Brown

PLAYING THE FIELD
A DIAMONDS AND DUGOUTS NOVEL
By Jennifer Seasons

HOW TO MARRY A HIGHLANDER
By Katharine Ashe

An Excerpt from

LESS THAN A GENTLEMAN

by Kerrelyn Sparks

New York Times bestselling author
Kerrelyn Sparks returns to romance during
the Revolutionary War with the sequel to her
debut historical novel, *The Forbidden Lady*.

Matthias gazed up the lattice to his balcony. As youngsters, he and his cousin had used the lattice to sneak out at night and go fishing. Of course the doors had not been bolted back then, but climbing down the lattice had seemed more exciting.

Matthias wasn't sure the lattice would hold his weight now, but with Dottie's restorative coursing through him, he felt eager to give it a jolly good try. Halfway up, a thin board cracked beneath his shoe. He shifted his weight and found another foothold. The last thing he wanted was to slip and tear Dottie's stitches from his shoulder.

He swung his legs over the balcony railing and landed with a soft thud. *How odd*. His door was open. *Of course*, he reminded himself. Dottie had gone there to fetch his clothes. She must have opened the door to air out the room.

He slipped inside. Moonlight filtered into the room, glimmering off the white mosquito netting. He strolled over to the secretaire, then kicked off his shoes and dropped his breeches. When he draped the breeches on the back of the chair, he noticed something was already there, something thick. He ran his fingers over the folds of cotton. The scent of roses drifted up to his nose. His mother's perfume. Why would she have left one of her gowns in his room?

Odd. He pulled off his stockings. He'd talk to his mother in the morning. For now, he simply wanted to sink into a mattress and forget about the war.

He unwrapped his neck cloth, then removed his shirt and undergarments. How could he forget the war when he had so much to do? Ferryboats to burn. Supplies to capture. He untied the bow from his hair and dropped the thin leather thong on the desk. And those two missing females. *Where the hell could they be?*

He strode to the bed and slipped under the netting. With a sigh of contentment, he stretched out between the clean cotton sheets.

The bed shifted.

He blinked, staring at the ghostly netting overhead. He hadn't budged an inch. There was only one explanation.

Slowly, he turned his head and peered into the darkness beside him. The counterpane appeared lumpy, as if— He listened carefully. Yes, soft breathing.

He sat up. A soft moan emanated from the form beside him. Female. His heart started to pound, his body reacting instinctively. Good God, it had been too long since he . . .

What the hell? He drew his racing libido to a screeching

halt. This had to be another one of his mother's plots to force him to marry! Even Dottie was in on it. She had insisted he bathe and go to the Great House. Then they had locked up the house, so he would be forced to climb the lattice to his bedchamber. Straight into their trap.

He scrambled out of bed, batting at the mosquito netting that still covered him.

The female gasped and sat up. "Who's there?"

"Bloody hell," he muttered. His mother's scheme had worked perfectly. He was alone and naked with whomever she had chosen for his bride.

Another gasp, and a rustling of sheets. The woman climbed out of bed. Damn! She would run straight to her witnesses to inform them that he'd bedded her.

"No!" He leapt across the bed and grabbed her. "You're not getting away." He hauled her squirming body back onto the bed. Her sudden intake of air warned him of her intent to scream.

He cupped a hand over her mouth. "Don't."

She clamped down with her teeth.

"Ow!" He ripped his hand from her mouth.

She slapped at his shoulders.

He winced as she pounded on his injury. "Enough." He seized her by the wrists and pinned her arms down. "No screaming. And no biting. Do you understand?"

Her breaths sounded quick and frightened.

He settled on top of her, applying just enough pressure to keep her from escaping. "I know what you're after. You think to trap me in wedlock so easily?"

"*What?*"

He could hardly see her pale face in the dark. His damp hair fell forward, further obstructing his view as he leaned closer. The scent of her soap surrounded him. Magnolia blossoms. His favorite, and Dottie knew it. This was a full-fledged conspiracy. "I assume you brought witnesses with you?"

"Witnesses?"

"Of course. Why would you want me in your bed if there were no one to see it?"

"My God, you're perverse."

"You're hoping I am, aren't you?" He stroked the inside of her wrist. "You're hoping I'll be tempted by your soft skin."

She shook her head and wiggled beneath him.

He gulped. She was definitely not wearing a corset beneath her shift. "You think I cannot resist a beautiful, womanly form?" Damn, but she *was* hard to resist.

"Get off of me," she hissed.

"I beg your pardon? That's hardly the language of a seductress. Didn't they coach you better than that?"

"Damn you, release me."

He chuckled. "You're supposed to coo in my ear, not curse me. Come now, let me hear your pretty little speech. Tell me how much you want me. Tell me how you're burning to make love to me."

"I'd rather burn in hell, you demented buffoon."

He paused, wondering for the first time whether he had misinterpreted the situation. "You're . . . not here to seduce me?"

"Of course not. Why would I have any interest in a demented buffoon?"

He gritted his teeth. "Then who are you and why are you in this bed?"

"I was in bed to sleep, which would be obvious if you weren't such a demented—"

"Enough! Who are you?"

She paused.

"Is the question too difficult?"

She huffed. "I . . . I'm Agatha Ludlow."

An Excerpt from

WHEN I FIND YOU
A TRUST NO ONE NOVEL
by *Dixie Lee Brown*

Dixie Lee Brown continues her
heart-racing *Trust No One* series with
a sexy veteran determined to protect
an innocent woman on the run.

"Okay—now that I've got your attention, let me tell you about my day." Walker resumed his pacing. "I've been up since four-thirty this morning. I've saved your neck three times so far today, and for my trouble I've been cracked on the skull, threatened by a bear, and nearly drowned. We're through doing it your way." He stopped and pinned her with a warning glance. "I realize you're confused and you've got no idea who I am, but there's only one thing you need to know. I'm taking you out of here with me, and I don't care if I have to throw you over my shoulder and carry you out. Are we clear?"

She watched him without saying a word, looking anything but resigned to her fate.

Walker stared back, daring her to defy him.

She never even flinched.

"If you were me, what would you do?" Her strong, clear voice challenged him, while her eyes flashed with fire.

"If I were you, I'd find someone I could trust and stick with him until this is over."

"And that's you, I suppose? How do I know I can trust you?"

He made a show of looking around. "You don't have a lot of options at the moment, but, in case you haven't noticed, I'm the one trying to keep you alive." He reached for her elbow and pulled her to her feet. The cool breeze through his wet clothes chilled him, and he worried about her. Even with her arms wrapped around herself, just beneath her breasts, she still shook. No sense putting this off. She wasn't magically going to start trusting him in the next few minutes, and they had to get moving.

He held up his jacket in front of her and took a deep breath. "Get out of those wet clothes and put this coat on."

Her eyes widened in alarm and she stared at him, resting her hands on her hips in a stance that would have made him smile if she hadn't been so serious. He held her gaze, expecting her to tell him to go to hell. He couldn't afford to give on this issue, so he kept talking. "We'll head back to higher ground, start a fire, and get our clothes dried out. I have to warm you up, and this is the only way I know to do it. We don't have time to argue about this."

"You can't seriously expect me to . . . you're wet and cold, too. Wear your own damn coat." She wrapped her arms around her waist again, as though she could stop her trembling.

The fear in her expression tugged at his conscience and sent him searching for the words to reassure her that he wasn't going to jump her as soon as she undressed. The suspicious glare she fixed him with succeeded in hardening his resolve, and he lowered the coat, raised an eyebrow, and swept his gaze over her. "Either you can get out of those clothes yourself, or I can help you."

"You wouldn't dare!"

"You'll find there's not too much I wouldn't do."

Darcy glowered at him a few more seconds, clearly wishing she had a tree branch in her hand. Then she sighed and dropped her gaze, blinking several times in quick succession, obviously determined that he wouldn't see her break down. So, the woman wasn't as tough as she wanted him to believe. Her vulnerability unleashed a wave of protectiveness that washed over him and left him feeling like an ass.

He frowned. "I'm not the enemy." He held the coat higher so it blocked his view of everything but her head and shoulders. "Hurry, we have to get moving." Trembling visibly, her lips still maintained a bluish tint. She wasn't out of danger yet.

An Excerpt from

PLAYING THE FIELD
A DIAMONDS AND DUGOUTS NOVEL

by Jennifer Seasons

The sexy baseball players of Jennifer Seasons'
Diamonds and Dugouts series are back
with the story of a single mom, a hot
rookie, and a second chance at love.

JP reached out an arm to snag her, but she slipped just out of reach—for the moment. Did she really think she could get away from him?

There was a reason he played shortstop in the major leagues. He was damn fast. And now that he'd decided to make Sonny his woman, she was about to find out just how quick he could be. All night he'd tossed and turned for her, his curiosity rampant. When he'd finally rolled out of bed, he'd had one clear goal: to see Sonny. Nothing had existed outside that.

Her leaving her cell phone at the restaurant last night had been the perfect excuse. All he'd had to do was run an internet search for her business to get her address. And now here he was, unexpectedly up close and personal with her. So close he could smell the scent of her shampoo, and it was doing funny things to him. Things like making him want to bury his nose in her hair and inhale.

No way was he going to miss this golden opportunity.

With a devil's grin, he moved and had her back against the aging barn wall before she'd finished gasping. "Look me in the eyes right now and tell me I don't affect you, that you're not interested." He traced a lazy path down the side of her neck with his fingertips and felt her shiver. "Because I don't believe that line for an instant, sunshine."

Close enough to feel the heat she was throwing from her deliciously curved body, JP laughed softly when she tried to sidestep and squeeze free. Her shyness was so damn cute. He raised an arm and blocked her in, his palm flush against the rough, splintering wood. Leaning in close, he grinned when she blushed and her gaze flickered to his lips. Her mouth opened on a soft rush of breath, and, for a suspended moment, something sparked and held between them.

But then Sonny shook back her rose-gold curls and tipped her chin with defiance. "Believe what you want, JP. I don't have to prove anything to you." Her denim blue eyes flashed with emotion. "This might come as a surprise, but I'm not interested in playing with a celebrity like you. I have a business to run and a son to raise. I don't need the headache."

There was an underlying nervousness to her tone that didn't quite jive with the tough-as-nails attitude she was trying to project. Either she was scared or he affected her more than she wanted to admit. She didn't look scared.

JP dropped his gaze to her mouth, wanting to kiss those juicy lips, and felt her body brush against his. He could feel her pulse, fast and frantic, under his fingertips.

It made his pulse kick up a notch in anticipation. "There's a surefire way to end this little disagreement right now, because I say you're lying. I say you *are* interested in a celebrity like me." He cupped her chin with his hand and watched her thick lashes flutter as she broke eye contact. But she didn't pull away. "In fact, I say you're interested in *me*."

JP knew he had her.

Her voice came, soft and a little shaky. "How do I prove I'm not?" The way she was staring at his mouth contradicted her words. So did the way her body was leaning into his.

Lowering his head until he was a whisper away, he issued the challenge, "Kiss me."

Her gaze flew to his, her eyes wide with shock. "You want me to do *what*?"

What he knew they both wanted.

"Kiss me. Prove to me you're not interested, and I'll leave here. You can go back to your business and your son and never see my celebrity ass again."

An Excerpt from

HOW TO MARRY
A HIGHLANDER

by Katharine Ashe

In this delightful novella from
award-winning author Katharine Ashe, a
young matchmaker may win the laird of her
dreams if she can manage to find husbands for
seven Scottish ladies—in just one month!

It would have been remarkable if Teresa had not been quivering in her prettiest slippers. Six pairs of eyes stared at her as though she wore horns atop her hat. She was astounded that she had not yet turned and run. Desperation and determination were all well and good when one was sitting in Mrs. Biddycock's parlor, traveling in one's best friend's commodious carriage, and living in one's best friend's comfortable town house. But standing in a strange flat in an alien part of town, anticipating meeting the man one had been dreaming about for eighteen months while being studied intensely by his female relatives, did give one pause.

Her cheeks felt like flame, which was dispiriting; when she blushed, her hair looked glaringly orange in contrast. And this was not the romantic setting in which she had long imagined they would again encounter each other—another ballroom glittering with candlelight, or a rose-trellised garden path in the moonlight, or even a field of waving heather aglow with sunshine. Instead she now stood in a dingy little flat three stories above what looked suspiciously like a gin house.

But desperate times called for desperate measures. She gripped the rim of her bonnet before her and tried to still her nerves.

The sister who had gone to fetch him reappeared in the doorway and smiled. "Here he is, then, miss."

A heavy tread sounded on the squeaking floorboards. Teresa's breath fled.

Then he was standing not two yards away, filling the doorway, and . . .

she . . .

was . . .

speechless.

Even if words had occurred to her, she could not have uttered a sound. Both her tongue and wits had gone on holiday to the colonies.

No wonder she had dreamed.

From his square jaw to the massive breadth of his shoulders to his dark hair tied in a queue, he was everything she had ever imagined a man should be. Aside from the neat whiskers skirting his mouth that looked positively barbaric and thrillingly virile, he was exactly as she remembered him. Indeed, seeing him now, she realized she had not forgotten a single detail of him from that night in the ballroom. She recognized him with the very fibers of her body, as though she already knew how it felt for him to take her hand. Just as on that night eighteen months before, an invisible wind pressed at her back, urging her to move toward him like a magnet drawn to a metal object. *As though they were meant to be touching.*

Despite the momentous tumult within her now, however, Teresa was able to see quite clearly in his intensely blue eyes a stark lack of any recognition whatsoever.

"Weel?" The single word was a booming accusation. "Who be ye, lass, and what do ye be wanting from me?"

It occurred to Teresa that either she could be thoroughly devastated by this unanticipated scenario and subsequently flee in utter shame, or she could continue as planned.

She gripped her bonnet tighter.

"How do you do, my lord? I am Teresa Finch-Freeworth of Brennon Manor at Harrows Court Crossing in Cheshire." She curtseyed upon wobbly legs.

His brow creased. "And?"

"And . . ." It was proving difficult to breathe. "I have come here to offer you my hand in marriage."